MW00477952

Steven Shepard

Inca Gold, Spanish Blood

Steven Shepard

Inca Gold, Spanish Blood

Steven Shepard

Copyright © 2019 by Steven Shepard

Published in January 2019 by Shepard
Communications Group, LLC

Front cover image of an ancient carving in the
Museo Arqueológico in Mexico City is from the
author's collection.

Shepard Communication Group, LLC

ISBN 9781795729413

This book is a work of fiction, but like most works
of fiction, it is based on some real events and
people. The names and details have been changed
to protect the privacy and reputation of those on
whom this work is based.

Shepard, Steven, 1954—

Inca Gold, Spanish Blood/

By Steven Shepard

ISBN 9781795729413

1. SCUBA diving-fiction. 2. Treasure. 3. Novel. 4.
History. 5. Latin America. 6. Inca. 7. Spain. 8.
California.

DEDICATION

For Bina. Thank you for being there for all my books—
and the adventures we've shared along the way.

ACKNOWLEDGMENTS

This is a work of fiction … sort of. With a few exceptions, everything described in this book happened to me, to friends of mine, or to customers who used the services of the dive shop I co-owned in the San Francisco Bay Area back in the late 70s, including the discovery of substantial amounts of gold on a previously undiscovered wreck. I simply built what I hope is an entertaining story from all of the adventures we collectively shared.

Many, many people contributed to this book, either by being participants in some of the adventures that form the basis for the story, by reminding me of things that happened that had faded from my memory but that would make the book better, and by serving as editors. Thank you all, so very much.

I have a few special people to thank that I can't overlook. My gratitude goes out to my professors in the Department of Spanish and Portuguese at the University of California, Berkeley. In 1972 I returned to the States for college after spending my teen years in Spain. At the time, I had no idea what an intense hold the Spanish culture had on me, and I remained ignorant of the fact until I enrolled at Berkeley (Go Bears) and decided to major in Spanish and Romance Philology, the field that examines the origins of Romance Languages. So: to Professors Jerry Craddock, Luis Murillo, Arthur Askins, and Charles Faulhaber, saludos y gracias por haberme regalado un sentido de agredicimiento para todo lo que representa la lengua, la filología, la cultura, la historia, y la literatura de España. Os mando todos un muy fuerte abrazo.

To all of the people whose spectacular adventures I drew from to create Inca Gold, Spanish Blood, thanks for the memories, and thank you for enlivening every day at the shop. I smile when I think of you.

In response to requests for anonymity (for certain obvious reasons), I've agreed to thank you by first names

i

only, but you know well who you are, so here goes: Bina P, Dennis M, Jack G, Pete M, Chris B, Pete S, Russ M, Mike M, Roland S, Lee F, Bob L, and Bruce L, thank you for the endless stories, and for making our shop the center of so many adventures. And to all of the countless students who granted me the honor to teach you and your trust in the water, thank you.

To my stable of long-suffering editors, who try, often in vain, to make sense of what I write, I thank you, even though I can never fully repay your efforts as my alternate sets of eyes. In no particular order I profusely thank Joe Candido, Jack Garrett, Dennis McCooey, Peter Mulvihill, Kenn Sato, my kids, Cristina, Mallory, Steve, and Joe, and my eternally patient, lovely wife Sabine, who for reasons I will never understand but for which I am eternally grateful, has put up with me for more than 40 years. I love you.

Thank you all for being a part of this adventure.

Steven Shepard

Williston, Vermont, January 2016

Inca Gold, Spanish Blood

PROLOGUE

November 1545, Northern California Coast

As his body shattered on the hidden reef, Francisco realized in his final moments of agony that his colleagues on shore weren't greeting him; they were warning him away. And now, it was too late.

He watched as death approached. The vessel rose impossibly high, its copper-clad hull ruptured by the unseen rocks. There, it paused for a moment before groaning downward. From the ragged gash in her hull, a king's fortune in Inca gold fell to the sea floor and embedded itself in the mud—seconds before the ship crushed the remaining life from Francisco de Orellana. As death approached, he thought of his wife, his home, and the terrible loss of gold and blood. And for what—a fool's errand?

The water closed over his head and he was carried below, embraced by the darkness that had taken his ship.

Trapped deep by the dying vessel, he drifted away forever.

Steven Shepard

424 Years Later: January 1969, Northern California Coast

It was a Japanese fishing net that fouled the tugboat's props.

First Mate Kenn Sato stood at the stern towing winch so that he could keep an eye on the barge behind him. He currently had 800-feet of two-and-a-half-inch braided steel cable running between the *Challenger* and the barge, but under tow, the cable had shrunk to about an inch in diameter, an indication of the immense tension that existed between the tug and the tow. Unbelievable. He'd heard stories of cables snapping at the tow end, whipping around and slicing off the top of the tug—or the top of a crewmember. He wasn't particularly interested in seeing either of those happen, which is why he was monitoring the tow so closely. The rough seas were putting a lot of variable strain on the cable, and even though the tow mechanism was designed to deal with that, it still made him nervous. The barge wasn't all that big, but it had a keel like a shoebox—which meant that towing it created immense drag.

The radio on his hip squawked to life. "Coming up on the Gate." It was the voice of Captain Andy Carson, calling down from the bridge. "There's no traffic at the moment so we'll line up for a straight-in approach." They had already reduced their speed as much as they possibly could for a safe entrance into the Bay; once they passed under the Golden Gate, the harbor tugs would meet them to help wrangle the barge into its slip in Alameda.

"Aye-Aye, Captain—tow looks good. I'll—"

From deep beneath him, Sato heard a horrifying squeal. The tugboat jerked violently to port, throwing him to the deck, the impact opening a two-inch gash across his forehead.

The radio crackled with emergency orders. "We've lost power! Total power loss! Cut the tow, I say again, cut the tow!"

Sato's head was pounding, but he didn't hesitate. Stumbling to the tow assembly, he lifted the protective cover and positioned his hand above the actuator. He had trained on this maneuver so many times that he could do it in his sleep. This scenario was a tug operator's worst nightmare. The tug and the tow were traveling at the same speed, which meant that if the tug lost power and didn't take evasive maneuvers immediately, it would be run over by the much larger barge, all in a matter of seconds.

Sato activated his radio. "Cutting the tow, Captain, in three, two, one, activate!" Wiping blood from his eyes, he slammed his fist down on the button, causing the hydraulics that powered the massive steel guillotine surrounding the tow cable to close. The instant he did so he ran forward—he didn't want to be anywhere near that thing when it let go.

It took the jaws about three seconds to cut through the cable. It snapped like a rifle shot and flew toward the towed barge, slamming into the hull with enough force to tear an eight-foot incision in the side of the vessel.

The tugboat pitched violently forward, burying the bow in the water, then settled back. Instantly, the Captain spun the wheel as far to starboard as he could in a desperate attempt to evade the oncoming tow. Sato watched, horrified, as the immense bow of the barge approached them, its shadow expanding over the starboard stern of the tugboat. *We aren't going to make it*, he thought, strangely calm.

What saved the *Challenger* was the momentum of eight hundred feet of two-and-a-half-inch tow cable. The combination of weight and velocity as it whipped back toward the barge was just enough to shift the juggernaut's course slightly to port. It missed the tug by fifty feet, but it didn't miss the rocks. The incoming tide drove the unpowered barge north and east, to a rough, rocky area on the north side of the Golden Gate called the Potato Patch.

Pounded by the relentless waves above and the rocks below, the barge clung to the rocks throughout the night, but inevitably, her hull breached and flooded. *The Challenger* stayed on station alongside the Coast Guard, but before a salvage operation could be mounted the following morning, the barge's back broke and she sank, scattering her guts in a wreckage field across the bottom. The bulk of the vessel eventually settled in the abyssal depths of the Golden Gate in more than 300 feet of water, where it posed no threat to shipping.

Steven Shepard

PART 1

CHAPTER 1

Present Day, the Potato Patch

The inflatable bounced on the chop as Michael McCain and Billy McAdams struggled into their drysuits, trying not to fall overboard. The water below them was only 18 feet deep, and with the current running the way it was, the little boat bounced around like a Ping-Pong ball.

"Great place to dive," Michael grumbled. "52-degree water and a six-and-a-half knot current that'll take us to the Farallons if we're not careful. Not to mention white sharks, shipping traffic, and rough water. I'm gonna feed the fish if we don't get in the water before long." He jerked on one of his neoprene booties, succeeding in poking a hole through the side of it with his thumb.

"Son of a bitch; that just figures, doesn't it?" Carefully pulling on the torn boot, he popped it into place and rolled it up and over the ankle seal of his drysuit. Looking west, he could just make out the Farallon Islands in the distance. The water around them was a known breeding ground for great white sharks, and the islands themselves were home to thousands of sea birds.

"Hey, at least you're not teaching," laughed Billy. He was sitting on the starboard tube of the inflatable, putting on his buoyancy compensator vest while attaching hoses from the regulator to the Velcro hold-downs that festooned the front of the BC. They were both certified master SCUBA instructors, but lately they had done less teaching and more pleasure diving, which suited them just fine. Teaching was a noble and rewarding profession, and they enjoyed it, but the emotional pressure of having ten or more neophytes in the water weighed heavily after a while. That aspect of the job they didn't miss when they didn't have to do it.

Billy looked like the Incredible Hulk's first cousin. Solid muscle, he weighed somewhere just south of 250 pounds. He and Michael had been diving together for 18 years; they had met at Berkeley in California, where Michael was studying Spanish while Billy studied engineering, although he ultimately left the field behind and became a chef. He liked to brag that he could engineer the finest meals in the northern hemisphere, and those who had been on the receiving end of some of his meals would confirm that he didn't have much in the way of competition.

"You look like the wall of the dive shop," laughed Billy, pointing at Michael. Michael was now fully dressed, and in addition to the standard dive gear—drysuit, BC, tank and regulator, weight belt, mask, fins and snorkel—he was encrusted with extra hoses attached to his regulator to provide air for power tools, a large mesh goodie bag filled with hand tools and lift bags, a slate and pencil, and a Ping-Pong paddle on a sling around his left wrist.

"You're not much better," Michael retorted. He was right; Billy was equally draped in paraphernalia, plus he was wearing twin 80s, two large tanks connected via a manifold to provide additional air for the power tools that they might need during the dive, assuming they found anything worth salvaging.

They were anchored at the Potato Patch because several weeks before, a fisherman had snagged his anchor on the bottom near where Michael and Billy were about to dive. When he finally freed the hook and pulled it aboard, he found that a corroded piece of brass pipe was caught between the stock and shank of the anchor. The fisherman, the father of a friend of theirs, mentioned the incident to Billy, who in turn told Michael. Intrigued, they decided to dive the site the following weekend, hoping that the piece of pipe was part of an as yet undiscovered wreck. Nothing in their research indicated that there was a significant vessel down there, although many had broken up on the Potato Patch because of the current and the area's extremely shallow water.

The two friends now sat on the inflatable's gunwales, facing each other. They had done this so many times before that they had little need to communicate vocally—they anticipated each other's thoughts and actions. Nodding, they put the second stages of their regulators in their mouths, placed one hand over their masks and regulators, the other over the buckle of their weight belts to prevent them from dislodging when they struck the water. Then, they rolled backward into the swells.

The first thing Michael felt when he struck the water was a slight sense of disorientation as he waited for the foam created by his entry to subside. He exhaled once and then carefully inhaled, making sure that the regulator was working properly and free of water. Looking around, he saw Billy's legs dangling below the other side of the boat. Raising the hose of his vest, he allowed air to escape until he sank below the surface, and then slowly swam below the Achilles inflatable. Billy did the same. They had learned that it paid to perform a complete equipment check before descending to the bottom. They had done their initial check of each other's gear before leaving the boat; now, they did it again, just to be safe. *Good decisions come from experience,* thought Michael, as he checked Billy's backpack, *and experience comes from a lot of bad decisions.* Wrecks are notorious collectors of fishing line, and since monofilament nylon is invisible in the water, a diver can become hopelessly tangled before realizing it has happened. The ability to reach a knife or other tool quickly could mean the difference between an emergency and a non-event.

Satisfied, they began their descent to the bottom.

Michael could feel the slow seep of cold water at the crotch and neck of his drysuit as he began to move about. *I don't know why they call them drysuits, he thought; they should be called dampsuits.* Why the hell they always leak at the crotch was a mystery to everyone who owned one.

Swimming to the anchor line, they began their slow descent to the bottom, equalizing the pressure in their ears as they descended. The water was extremely murky due to the powerful current that ran through the Golden Gate. Six feet below the surface, visibility dropped to a few inches and the light diminished to a dim, murky brown, forcing them to descend with one arm extended to prevent inadvertently running face-first into the muddy bottom.

As anticipated, the bottom loomed unexpectedly out of the murk, causing Michael to pull up short. He checked the inflatable's anchor; given the strength of the prevailing current, if it came loose while they were underwater, the boat would be halfway to Taiwan by the time they surfaced. Luckily, it was wedged tightly in the mud.

Michael tapped Billy on the shoulder, indicating he should take the lead. Moving ahead, Billy consulted the luminous compass on his left wrist and, with a backward nod to Michael, began to swim slowly in a northwesterly direction, picking his way across the silt-covered bottom. They were looking for anything that might indicate the presence of a wreck. It was slow going; if they strayed more than a foot or two from the bottom, it disappeared into the gloom; but if they swam too close, their fins raised great clouds of flour-like sediment that obscured whatever visibility they had. Most of what they did they did by feel: if they saw a likely anomaly on the bottom, a shape that might betray an artifact covered by mud, they used their Ping-Pong paddles to whisk away the overburden. Mostly, they uncovered rocks, beer bottles, tires, and fouled anchors, but it was far more effective than digging with their hands. And even though the majority of items they found didn't really count as artifacts—most of it was trash—there had been a few exceptions. Once, during a lake dive, Michael had pulled an old bottle out of the muck. There was nothing particularly special about the bottle except that it was clearly old; it had a smooth bore mouth, which meant that it predated screw-on lids. Embossed on its side were the words, "Skilton Pickles." The glass had a slightly purple tint; it was unusual, so Michael dropped it into his collecting bag. When he got home he cleaned it up and set it on the shelf. A month or so later, while working on an article, his eyes wandered across the bottle, and he decided to look up Skilton Pickles to see if the company still existed. It didn't, but what came up in the search was the Web site for Sotheby's Auction House and a photo of Michael's bottle, selling for a starting price of $800. That was the last time they discarded "trash" without looking at it first.

Billy swam a few feet off the bottom, concentrating on the sedimentary contour below him, when his neoprene-covered head bumped into an unseen object. Looking up, he saw the unmistakable curve of a section of steel protruding a few feet from the silt. Turning on his light, he saw that the artifact had rusted away unevenly so that it looked more like a natural formation of stone than something manufactured. He ran his gloved hand up it; it was extremely rough, and the brown and orange potato chip-like flakes of rusted iron would shred naked skin.

By now, Michael had arrived, and he busied himself attaching a yellow nylon line that was bright enough to be seen, even in dark water. Then, he and Billy swam away from the rib, leaving one end of the line firmly attached. Halfway out, Billy stopped, and grabbed the nylon with both hands. Michael continued out to the end of the unrolled section and did the same. They were far enough apart that they could still see each other, but just barely. When Michael was ready, he gave three jerks on the line, at which time he and Billy started swimming slowly. Because one end of the line was attached to the metal spar, they were forced to swim in a slow circle, which allowed them to conduct a thorough search of the area inside the circle.

In a matter of seconds, they found another rib, this one far more corroded than the first, and just beyond they could see the murky outline of a third. One artifact is a find; two is a coincidence; three is a holy shit moment. Clearly they had found the remains of some kind of vessel, although they didn't yet know what it was. The fact that it was on the Potato Patch meant that it was most likely already documented, which also meant that it had probably been picked clean by other divers.

They completed their search, and, finding nothing of interest, moved on. Untying the rope from the first rib, they moved to the second, tied the rope in place, and repeated the search process. Nothing. Moving to the third, they performed another circular pattern, and this time, they were rewarded. Approximately fifty seconds after starting the third search, they came upon a large, shapeless, metallic mass. Like the ribs, it was rusted beyond recognition; embedded in the rust, however, like raw opals in a quartz matrix, were telltale signs of verdigris, a byproduct of oxidizing copper, which indicated the presence of brass. Sure enough: when they looked closer, they found a complex valve assembly that had been partially eroded away.

Neither reached for the object. Michael bore a nasty scar on his right shoulder from an attempt to pry himself out of the tight confines of a collapsed passageway during a wreck dive in Mexico. The metal had ruptured from the pressure of his shoulders pushing against the bulkhead, and a razor-sharp piece of it had sliced through his wetsuit and deep into the muscle. Since then, they exercised more than conservative care when working in or near a wreck. They tended to be unforgiving.

Pulling a large chisel from the bag hanging at his waist, Billy began to pry and worry at the rusted steel surrounding the brass valve. It came away in great, scabby flakes; within a few minutes he freed the assembly from the surrounding mass of rust. Upon closer examination they realized that it wasn't a valve complex at all, but rather an oiler assembly. It looked like some sort of crazy flower bouquet, and would fetch a good price from collectors.

Swimming around the mass of metal, they found other pieces worth salvaging. They freed several, but were soon low enough on air that they had to call an end to the dive. They surfaced slowly, one arm extended above their heads. They listened carefully for propellers as they surfaced; hearing nothing nearby, they cautiously broke the surface and immediately looked in all directions. The Achilles inflatable was about 75 yards southeast of them, but thoughtfully they had thrown a knotted, 500-foot piece of yellow polypropylene line overboard before starting their dive. The current extended the floating line, and since they were down-current, they simply swam to the line and pulled themselves hand-over-hand back to the Achilles, eliminating the need to swim against the powerful current.

"That was great," smiled Michael, as he pulled on a sweatshirt. They sat with their one-piece drysuits pulled down to their waists. "We need to come back here as soon as we can. I think there's more down there; on the way up, I saw something off in the distance that looked like another big piece of metal. You available tomorrow?"

Billy nodded as he rummaged around in his gear bag. Pulling out a GPS, he turned it on and recorded a waypoint for their location. "I have to run an errand in the morning," said Billy, "but we can go after about 10:00. That work for you?"

Michael agreed. "That should work well with the tide, if I remember correctly; last thing I want to do is fight the tidal turn at the Gate."

With that, they started the outboard and motored back to the marina.

Steven Shepard

CHAPTER 2

Michael and Billy had known each other for what
seemed like forever. They met when they signed up for a
SCUBA diving course through the university, and were
paired as buddies by the instructor. They became instantly
entranced with the sport the first time they put their faces
in the water and breathed through a regulator. Since then
they had been inseparable, and had dived all over the
world. They had floated, mesmerized, with whales off
Nanakuli in Hawaii, and had found themselves engulfed by
huge schools of spotted eagle rays on French Bay Reef
near San Salvador in the Bahamas. At Cerralvo Island off
La Paz in the Sea of Cortez, they had floated motionless in
the water while a seemingly endless school of small
hammerheads swam past, oblivious to them. In Cozumel,
they had fed frozen corn to giant groupers, and while
there, rented a couple of Nikonos cameras to take pictures
in the warm, clear water. One morning in Palau, they had
drifted with the current through a reef passage with a
school of mantas, then swam with stingless jellyfish in the
afternoon wearing only their swim suits, a surreal
encounter given their experiences with the less-than-
friendly jellyfish population of Northern California.

They also dove close to home. They haunted the
California coast, from the crystalline coves of San Diego to
the rocky, starfish-covered tide pools near the Oregon
border. One sunny Saturday morning, not long after

completing the university program, they drove up the coast from San Francisco, passed Jenner-by-the-Sea at the mouth of the Russian River, and pulled into Salt Point State Park. Their plan was to dive for abalone, which, by California law, can only be taken while free diving. Abalone has become increasingly scarce, so to protect the fragile population, California Fish and Game imposed a no-SCUBA restriction years ago. The mollusks tend to live in fairly deep water, so Michael and Billy had to free dive to 30 feet or so to find them.

After several hours, they returned to shore, rested a bit, then put on tanks and picked their way down to the water. Careful to avoid the urchins that covered the rocks, they watched the waves, and when the timing was right, slipped in and kicked out beyond the surf zone. The water was uncommonly clear; the surface was fairly calm, but below, the sea was surging powerfully as the waves that crashed on the rocks rushed back down into the deep. The kelp forest swayed entrancingly like dancers in a water ballet. As Michael lay on the surface, catching his breath before giving the signal to Billy that he was ready to descend, his eye caught a greenish object in a crevice. It didn't belong there. Signaling to Billy, he placed his regulator in his mouth, released the air from his buoyancy compensator, and dropped below the surface, carefully slaloming between the giant kelp stalks that surrounded him. Swimming below the kelp canopy was like taking a hushed stroll through a giant cathedral.

Michael knew that if he took his eyes off the object, even for a second, he would never find it again; that was one of the immutable laws of diving. An object the size of a small car can disappear in seconds.

Keeping his eye on the crevice as he descended, he reached the rocky bottom. It didn't matter how many times he had done this; it always amazed him. Every square inch of the bottom was covered by a multicolored riot of life. The rocks were dressed in a green and purple salad of algae, which in turn was crawling with the snails, chitons, and nudibranchs that sought food and shelter among the plants. A decorator crab, its shell covered with a camouflage of seaweed that it had embedded in its own armor, reared back at him. He remembered the first time he dove in California: descending too rapidly because of inexperience with the buoyancy compensator, he had come close to panic as he realized that no matter where he touched down, he would land on something alive. That realization was renewed every time he dove. Holding on to a kelp stipe to keep himself stable in the swell, Michael pinched his nose through his mask and carefully equalized the pressure in his ears.

Swimming to where he had seen the object, he hovered above a rocky crevice that was decorated with slowly moving urchin spines. The object was wedged in the crevice. Reaching in, careful to avoid the spines, he grabbed the thing and tugged. It was stuck fast, and after wiggling it back and forth for about a minute, he succeeded in loosening it, although it was still trapped. While Michael rested for a moment, Billy pushed him gently out of the way, and with one enormous jerk, freed the thing from the rock.

Neither knew what it was; when they surfaced, they found that it was covered with the beautiful verdigris patina of oxidized copper, indicating that it was perhaps brass, if not bronze or pure copper. The body of the thing was barrel-shaped, about six inches tall, and had a long, thin shaft sticking out of its top like the handle of a milk churn. One side of the barrel was rusted away, revealing some sort of heavy spring mechanism inside. For a piece of sea junk, it was beautiful.

The following weekend, they took their find to the dive shop they frequented in Monterey and showed it to Vernon Fair, the shop's owner. He looked it over and pronounced it to be a valve of some sort, probably from a shipwreck.

"Where'd you find it?" he asked, looking closely at the base of the valve body.

"In a hole at Salt Point," said Michael. "We were

19

baloney diving off the north side of the cove, and ran across it just off the rocks. Any idea what it might be from?"

Vernon set the valve down on the desk and pulled a well-thumbed book off the shelf behind him. *California Shipwrecks* was the definitive guide to the known wrecks along the coast; it catalogued every known wreck—or remnant—that had been found to-date. Opening it, he ran his finger down the page, reading.

"I think I know exactly what it came from, but let me check here ... hmmm. Yep, that's what I thought." Picking up the valve and handing it to Billy, Vernon turned the book around and pointed to the page. "It's probably from the *Norlina*," he said. "Lumber ship. Lost power back in the 30s while cruising from Eureka down to Oakland loaded with logs, and broke up on the rocks before they could restore power. She's scattered all over the bottom out there, starting in about six feet of water. A real yard sale."

He led them over to a chart on the wall of the Northern California coastline, and pointed to the area where they had found the artifact. "If you go straight out from where you were to about 60 feet, you'll find her shaft and wheel. You can't miss either one; they're huge. Also, just over here"—pointing slightly north—"you'll find her boiler. People have been pulling stuff off the *Norlina* since she went down, but this is the first nice piece I've seen in a long time. Congratulations—that's a real keeper."

That had been the beginning of their professional relationship. Using nautical charts, Coast Guard publications on hazards to navigation, and early shipping manifests and logbooks preserved in the vaults of the Bancroft Archives on the Berkeley campus and the San Francisco Maritime Museum, they began a methodical study of as many wrecks as they could reach with SCUBA gear. Most of them were unrecognizable as vessels; over the years, the Pacific Ocean had reduced them to far-flung debris fields, now long overgrown with seaweed and calcified encrustations that often made them difficult to spot. Some, however, were intact, or nearly so.

From the debris fields of these wrecks, Michael and Billy had begun to harvest artifacts. They retrieved fittings, portholes, and valve assemblies; screws, eyes, and rigging stays; and in one case, near Point Arena on the Northern California coast, they found and recovered the propeller and a hatchway from an unknown wreck that had broken up north of the light. Some of the pieces they sold to collectors; most, however, went to the museums that helped them research their finds. The one piece they kept was the valve assembly they pried from the crevice near Salt Point.

* * *

Now, it seemed, they had found a new wreck—or at least, one they had not yet explored. They knew that the chances it would yield anything of interest were slim, but until they explored it they wouldn't know. There was all kinds of junk on the bottom at the Potato Patch and the deep channel that lay below the bridge, the accumulated detritus of careless (and often drunk) boaters who went up on the rocks and sank nearby, barges that came loose from their tows, and commercial vessels that lost power at the worst possible time, ending up scattered across the bottom. Most of them had already been picked clean by salvage divers, but there was always the chance that something good had been missed. They were hoping for the latter.

CHAPTER 3

The next morning, they loaded their gear in Billy's van, topped up the pressure in the inflatable, and headed over to Ocean Enterprises in Walnut Creek to fill their tanks and pick up a couple of spares. They had opened the dive shop together several years before, and since then had grown it into a successful, multi-armed dive operation. They employed a small but highly-skilled staff of sales people, instructors, and equipment technicians, and from day-one had operated the business the way they thought was best—as a business rather than as a hobby. It looked and felt like a professional enterprise.

The main door opened onto two areas. To the right, a door led to the retail area, which, unlike many dive shops, was kept spotlessly clean. There, customers could examine and buy equipment, ask about classes, and make their way to the classrooms upstairs. To the left were the equipment rental room, pool, dressing rooms, and the service and repair facility. The rental area housed a wide variety of sport and commercial diving equipment, while the repair facility and its cadre of technicians had the ability to repair everything from a shredded weight belt to the non-return valve on a Kirby-Morgan Band Mask or Mark-V hardhat. Most of the repair work they did was on sport diving equipment, but there were enough commercial divers in the area—themselves included—that the maintenance and repair business was kept busy year-round. They ran their

23

own small commercial operation out of the shop, a very lucrative enterprise in and of itself. They did hull inspections, minor repairs and a variety of other functions, often in very deep, zero-visibility water that was beyond the reach of sport divers.

On the other hand, they knew all too well that even shallow commercial work required specialized training. One afternoon a middle-aged man came into the shop and asked Billy if he could raise a boat that had sunk. The boat, he explained, a sailboat, had sunk in about ten feet of water in the Berkeley Marina, because someone had left a valve open somewhere—most likely in the head. Billy affirmed that he and Michael could easily raise the vessel, and that the cost would be in the neighborhood of $2,500. The man balked at the price and declined the offer.

Two days later, the man was back, asking if he could rent tanks. Michael was in the shop that day, so he didn't recognize the man; he explained that as long as the guy had a valid certification card, he could rent as many tanks as he wanted. He asked to rent ten, which seemed like a lot, but the guy presented a valid C-Card, so Michael tok his money and then helped him load the tanks into the back of a Lincoln SUV.

Later that day, Michael casually mentioned the odd customer who had rented ten tanks earlier in the day. Billy stopped what he was doing, asked what the guy looked like, and got a strange smile on his face. He then suggested that they take a field trip—on a hunch. Puzzled, Michael agreed. They drove over to Berkeley, got off at University Avenue, and meandered through the mud flats until they reached the marina. It took Billy less than ten minutes to spot the guy, standing on the dock in a swimsuit, next to an empty slip—empty, except for the mast that stuck out of the water, presumably attached to a sailboat that was *under* the water. Another fellow was handing him the tanks that he had rented from Michael earlier that day, which he was carefully lowering into the water. Michael and Billy could just make out the ghostly outline of a 27-foot sailboat, about eight feet down in the murk.

"Please tell me that he isn't going to do what I think he is…" Michael began.

Billy looked over at him, and then crossed his arms and called out to the guy in the water. "You do know that what I think you're planning to do won't work, right?"

The man in the water looked over and recognized Billy, then recognized Michael. "It'll work just fine, thanks," he said, lowering another tank into the water. "And it's a hell of a lot cheaper than you guys."

"But…" Michael began to argue, but Billy stopped him.

"OK, then," smiled Billy. "We'll be right over here in case you need some help." With that, Billy grabbed Michael by the arm and pulled him over to an equipment box on the dock. "Just sit down and enjoy the show," he told his friend, handing him a candy bar.

Once he had lowered all the tanks into the water, the man put on SCUBA gear, a mask and fins, and slipped below the surface. One by one he wrestled the tanks into the salon of the sailboat. Returning to the surface, he gave his friend a nod, then turned and gave Billy a quick thumbs-up. Billy gave it back. "This is going to be so much fun," he whispered to Michael.

A minute or so after he disappeared below the surface, air began to bubble up from the middle of the slip, and soon the slip turned into a bubbling cauldron, as the boat's owner opened the valves of the tanks, intent on floating his boat to the surface. Suddenly, the boat began to move. Ever so slowly, it shifted on the bottom, one end rising, then both, and then with a great gout of air, it rushed to the surface, the rails breaching the water's surface like a whale.

And then, just as quickly, the air inside the boat expanded just a little too much, and with a terrifying 'crack', the deck separated from the hull. Water rushed into the four-inch gap between the hull and the deck that wasn't there ten seconds before, and the boat sank unceremoniously to the bottom, belching out great masses of air.

Ambling over to the slip as the boat's owner came sputtering up from the depths, Billy said to him, "You see, sailboats have decks that are cleated down—they're not designed for upward pressure. We know that, and it takes special equipment to raise them, which is what you would have paid $2,500 for. Now you get to pay that, plus whatever it costs to put your boat back together. So have a nice day—and remember, rentals have to be returned by 3 PM to avoid an extra charge."

Walking away, Michael said to Billy, "You enjoyed that, didn't you?"

Billy just smiled. "Sometimes, Michael, you just have to throw a little chlorine in the old gene pool."

* * *

The pool in the shop was designed for teaching. It was indoors, and measured 20 by 25 yards. The shallow end was three feet deep, but the other end dropped off quickly to a very respectable 25 feet, perfect to give divers a sense of depth. On one side of the pool deck, a staircase led down into a pool-length well with seats for 15 students and windows that allowed them to observe divers working in the water. It was an ideal setup for learning diving skills and becoming comfortable with the underwater realm.

"Morning, guys," said a voice from the repair area, as they came in the door with their empty tanks.

"Morning, Jeff," they responded in unison. "Is the cascade topped off yet?" Michael asked, referring to the array of large air storage tanks in the tank fill area. The cascade was filled by the compressor every morning, and used throughout the day to fill SCUBA tanks, thus reducing the need to run the noisy compressor during the business day.

"Just finished," said Jeff. He was bent over a disassembled regulator on the workbench.

"You know what you're doing with that?" asked Billy.

No one—not even the most skilled technicians in the shop—knew as much about diving equipment as Billy did. He was a tinkerer, and could learn as much about a piece of equipment by taking it apart and putting it back together as most people could learn in a multi-week intensive training session.

"Yeah, it's just a regulator. No big deal. Besides, it's mine." Jeff was a wiry little guy, and they both remembered the day he had come into the shop two years before with a copy of *Soldier of Fortune Magazine* rolled up under his arm. "The journal of my profession," he had explained. It was quiet in the shop that day, so they had had time to get to know him.

Jeff Bryer was in the Marine Corps Reserves, a weekend warrior attached to the local Naval Weapons Station. In a brief period of time they learned that he had eaten monkeys and snake in Panama, tossed a red smoke grenade into the lowered Impala of an obnoxious lowrider in San Jose, and was preparing even now to board a raft with 50 other Marines for a leisurely cruise around South America, towed by a tugboat with no food and little water—or so he said. He was 5'4" tall, weighed 128 pounds on a good day, was infused with boundless energy, and could kill someone with his bare hands, a paper clip and really bad thoughts. Neither Michael nor Billy had ever encountered anyone like him.

The real fun had begun when Anne Royce, an instructor who worked in the shop, asked about the magazine under Jeff's arm. Unrolling it, he began to explain the contents and purpose of the "Journal of the Professional Soldier." Here were articles on surviving in the Congo, new and exciting ways to bare-handedly split an opponent's skull, and the latest in survival foods ("Packed with protein, and tasty, too!"). But the best part was the want-ads section in the back of the magazine. Over here, the for-hire stuff: mercenaries looking for work, governments (PO boxes) looking for professional soldiers to lead "exercises," mercenary groups looking for doctors to join an expedition. And over here, the mercenary stock in trade: throwing knives, flame throwers, and every conceivable pistol, rifle and assault weapon made; instruction books for making incendiary devices; and of course, hand-to-hand weapons for the purist. One particularly interesting ad was for something called "Godzilla's Dental Floss," which Jeff explained was a garrote. The ad described it as "an effective, soundless, low-cost anti-personnel device." Anne wasn't sure what a garrote was, so Jeff remedied her obvious lack of cultural exposure with relish, as he explained in technical terms the proper conditions under which such an instrument should be used. Following Jeff's description, which concluded with the victim's head sitting neatly atop his feet, Anne displayed appropriate levels of disgust, which Jeff countered with a promise to return that very afternoon with a working model so that he could properly demonstrate the panache with which a garrote should be employed.

By this time, they had decided that this was not a person who should be encouraged. After all, here was a guy they barely knew, who had promised to return to the shop to demonstrate garroting techniques. Who did he intend to demonstrate *on?*

Their curiosity got the best of them, though, and at the agreed-upon time, in he walked. He wore a yellow Marine Corps T-shirt, camouflaged pants and sneakers—off-duty attire, apparently. Carrying a paper bag, he mounted the steps to the classroom where they all waited for the next step in their worldly education.

From the bag, Jeff pulled his instrument of death. He had attached a guitar string to two spindly twigs, about the thickness of pencils. Not just any guitar string, mind you, but "High-E—because it penetrates flesh better than a thicker string," He explained with clinical detachment. Of course, they all nodded. Hey, they were worldly people. They knew that.

Next, the victim. "Anne, would you mind helping me?" Her eyes flew wide, and her hands instinctively went to her throat. From the bag, Jeff next withdrew the *real* victim, a gigantic, warty, phallic dill pickle, the kind you used to be able to buy from cloudy glass jars in movie theatres. Handing it to Anne, he instructed her to hold the six-inch pickle close to the base and away from her body, lest she be hurt by the diabolical device that was soon to be unleashed upon the hapless cuke—or, perhaps, by flying seeds.

The secret, Jeff explained, was to be smooth and quick. Taking one of the sticks in each hand, he crossed his wrists one over the other, forming a loop with the guitar string. The loop, he explained, is lowered over the victim's neck in a deft, practiced motion from behind. Once around the neck, the handles are jerked apart, "and if you're lucky, the head will pop right off. Clean."

At this point, Billy was working hard not to release an explosive laugh.

"...like this." Lowering the loop over the pickle in a deft, practiced motion, he jerked on the handles, prepared to decapitate the pickle. With a twang in the key of E, the string snapped, leaving the pickle hopelessly intact.

This was more than Billy could stand. Everyone, including Anne, completely lost it at that point. Everyone, that is, except Jeff. He just stood there, staring ruefully down at the now ruined implement of destruction in his hands. What a bummer. Not only was his garrote broken; now he couldn't even go home and strum melancholy chords about it on his guitar.

Jeff became a regular customer of the shop. They soon realized that he was harmless, and with his boundless energy he was a good assistant to instructors during the evening classes. He apparently had no other job (other than his commitment to the Marine Corps), because he began hanging around the shop from early morning until late evening, and before long, Billy offered him a part-time position. Billy had recently fired an employee for insubordination and for making inappropriate comments to female students (Billy's explanation was that he had actually fired the guy because he was a dickhead), so they were a little short-handed. Jeff filled tanks, took care of rental equipment, helped with sales, and assisted students during classes. He was a good employee, although his penchant for exaggeration inevitably made him the butt of more than a few jokes around the shop. He couldn't help himself; he would dig himself into a deep hole with some outlandish story that everyone knew to be pure fantasy, and every time, it came back to bite him. He just didn't learn. But he was a good-hearted kid, and capable in the water, so Billy and Michael put up with him.

Jeff took their tanks into the fill area, submerged them in the cooling tank, and connected them to the high-pressure manifold. Air rushed into them, squealing loudly. The cascade topped the tanks up to 3,000 PSI in less than 30 seconds. Closing the valves, he disconnected the tanks from the high-pressure hoses and put tape over the valves to indicate that they were full and to keep the O-ring seals from dislodging.

"You heading back out to the Patch again today?" Jeff asked, pulling the dripping tanks from the water. Why don't you let me come along? I can help out; I've had deep diving training in the Marines —"

Michael interrupted him. "Jeff, we've been over this already. There isn't enough room in the inflatable for a third diver with gear. Besides, you're scheduled to run the shop today, and it's supposed to be busy. Don't worry—you'll get your chance."

Billy and Michael knew that Jeff had had no such training in the Marine Corps; he knew nothing about commercial diving, and was under strict orders not to touch any of the regulators or other equipment that came into the shop for maintenance. If he wanted to work on his own regulator, he was welcome to do so; Billy had gotten into the habit of checking his work each time he did so to help him learn what he needed to know. Regulators were the one piece of equipment that required significant expertise. If they failed, air delivery failed, and at depth, that could ruin a diver's day.

As they left the shop, Michael called back over his shoulder. "We should be back before 7:00; if you close up before we get back, call me later this evening and let me know how the day went, OK?"

"No problem, Mike. I'll talk to you tonight." With that, they loaded their tanks in the van and pulled out of the parking lot.

CHAPTER 4

They drove to the Sausalito marina, where there was a public boat launch. There, they transferred their gear from the van to the inflatable, changed into their drysuits, and backed the boat into the water. As soon as it floated free of the trailer, Michael hopped in and started the outboard while Billy parked the van. Soon they were bouncing across the swells between the bridge and Angel Island, headed for the Golden Gate and the Potato Patch just beyond.

90 minutes later they were above the wreck, thanks to Billy's GPS waypoint. They anchored, dressed, raised the red-and-white Diver Down flag, and rolled overboard.

It took several minutes to orient themselves on the bottom; the GPS was accurate to within about ten feet or so, but without visual cues, that ten feet might as well have been ten miles. After several minutes of careful searching, however, they came upon the second rib sticking out of the mud, and shortly afterward, located the mass of metal from which they had pried the brass fitting the day before.

It was a very large piece of twisted metal, and was lying at a precarious angle as the sea bottom below the plate dropped off precipitously into deeper water. It was covered with barnacles and other marine growth. Judging from the rust and the size of the object, it was clearly from a relatively modern wreck—certainly no more than 30 years old or so, since so much of the metal remained intact.

Swimming alongside the plate, Michael turned on his old Tekna light; as he did, a four-foot cabezon, one of the Pacific's ugliest but most delicious fish, jetted without warning from beneath the metal. Pitching backward, Michael avoided the needle-sharp spines of the fish's dorsal fin, but in the process, pounded his left shoulder into the mud and raised an enormous cloud of silt that obscured what little visibility they had. The only thing to do was wait for the current to flush it away. It was running strongly, so the area would be clear within a matter of minutes.

While he waited, Michael settled belly-down on the bottom, put his facemask close to the mud, and examined the tiny shells and creatures that were mostly invisible to the average diver. He loved the smallest animals of the ocean, and when pleasure diving, often burned an entire tank of air lying on the bottom, watching the tiny parade go by. Billy liked to tell the story of the time he and Michael were diving at Otter Cove in Monterey Bay. They had entered the relatively shallow water and gone in different directions; an hour later, low on air, Billy had returned to the area where they had agreed to meet. Billy found Michael immediately; he was lying on the bottom, his chin on his hands, face down on the bottom, presumably watching the little critters he liked so much. But when Billy swam up and tapped him on the shoulder, Michael had startled. He was asleep.

As Michael lay on the bottom of the Potato Patch, the visibility gradually improved until he could make out some detail around him. With his light, he could see under the plate and could tell that it was half buried in the muddy bottom. Furthermore, it appeared to be attached to more metal below the surface. Suddenly, movement caught his eye; it was Billy's fin, just above him. Reaching out, Michael grabbed and tugged. Billy turned and joined him on the bottom. Signaling, Michael indicated that he wanted to lift the plate. Positioning themselves at each end of it, they planted their feet in the mud, once again raising an impenetrable cloud as the flourlike silt swirled around them. Pushing hard, they turned the plate over. Because a substantial amount of it was below the mud, the plate acted like a huge shovel, digging a divot in the bottom and further obscuring the area with silt. The metal fell over, revealing that it was indeed attached to some sort of mechanism. There was a central mass of corroded brass from which issued a tangle of pipes and fittings. Where the plate had been, there now lay a collection of metallic shapes that had been hidden below it. While Billy took his salvage tools to the mechanism attached to the plate, Michael grabbed the Ping-Pong paddle that hung on his right wrist and began to fan the overburden of mud away from the closest object. It was a large brass bolt of some kind; he fanned it further, and it proved to be one of several lying in a stack. Opening his goodie bag, he gathered the bolts and dropped them in.

Moving on to the next anomaly, Michael once again fanned away the silt, this time to reveal what looked like a crushed bucket. He pulled it from the sand, but the thing was iron, and it came apart. Carefully prying away the pieces, he revealed something in the mud below the iron. It was a brass rectangle, the top to something presumably, and like the bucket, had been crushed. It was about a foot long and perhaps six inches wide, and lay nearly two feet below the top of the mud. When Michael pulled on it, it erupted from the sand in pieces. In the hole lay the remnants of brass strapping that had once held together what was most likely a wooden box, now long decayed away. In the hole where the box had once been lay two irregularly shaped objects, which Michael took to be stone. Looking closely, he saw that they were thicker than his thumb and slightly more than six inches long. But they weren't stone: they were metallic, like brass. Upon closer examination, Michael saw that each one had a symbol stamped on its surface. And they weren't brass: they were carefully crafted gold.

Not believing what he had found, Michael pulled the dive knife from the scabbard on his inner left calf and banged loudly on the bottom of his tank to get Billy's attention. He could hear the steady swoosh of air escaping from Billy's pneumatic chisel as he worried the salvageable parts from the metal plate they had found. He hoped Billy would hear the banging.

He did. Because of the low visibility conditions they were working in, both wore small strobe lights on their mask straps to help them locate each other. In a matter of seconds, Billy swam out of the gloom with the pneumatic chisel in his hand. Motioning to him frantically, Michael guided Billy down to the hole in the sand where the gold lay. He looked at the bars for a long time, then looked at Michael. Slowly, he removed the regulator from his mouth, and flashed an enormous grin. Putting the regulator back in his mouth, he signaled to Michael to collect the bars and put them in a bag. Michael pulled a second heavy-canvas collecting bag from his BC pocket and carefully placed the gold in it before putting the cloth bag in the larger goodie bag. At that point, Billy tapped him on the shoulder, and showed him the slate upon which he had written a message:

> PROBABLY MORE AROUND.
> GOING TO MARK THIS SPOT
> WITH MY STROBE SO WE DON'T
> LOSE IT. YOU GO LEFT, I GO
> RIGHT, FIVE FEET. PADDLES
> ONLY. DIG A TRENCH. MEET
> BACK HERE IN 15.

Removing the flashing strobe from his mask, Billy attached its Velcro strap to the handle of his dive knife and jammed it firmly in the bottom next to the spot where Michael had found the gold bars. Then, with his paddle in hand, he began to fan the bottom vigorously, starting at the hole and working outward. Michael went the other direction, carefully pushing one hand through the mud ahead of the paddle to loosen the bottom, wary of sharp metal.

Almost immediately, Michael's light, held in the same hand with which he was digging, caught the telltale glimmer of gold. He stopped and waved the paddle over the spot where he had seen the metallic flash. After a minute or so of overburden removal, he saw gold again. Running his hand through the bottom mud, he came up with four more of the bars in his palm. They were identical to the ones he had found earlier. Breathing rapidly, he turned to get Billy's attention, when suddenly he heard the recognizable sound of something metallic banging frantically against a tank.

Because sound travels so much faster in water than it does in air, it is impossible to determine the direction of a sound underwater. However, Michael could see Billy's strobe through the gloom, so he swam toward it. There he found Billy. In his hands were a gold bar the size of a cigar, and an exquisitely crafted golden figurine about ten inches tall. Billy was smiling; Michael could tell, because whenever Billy smiled underwater, his mask leaked. Michael could see the top of a half-inch of water sloshing back and forth in the bottom of his mask. Signaling to Michael with his thumb that he wanted to surface, Billy disconnected his strobe from the knife. From his weight belt he unclipped a bright yellow float with fifty feet of line wrapped around it. He attached the end of the line to a large rock next to the excavation site, and released the float, letting it rocket to the surface.

After carefully placing the bars and the statuette in the cloth bag that Michael held open for him, Billy led the way to the surface, hand overhead. From below, Michael watched him disappear into the gloom.

We did it, he thought, as an overwhelming sense of elation filled him. We finally did it. All that hard work has finally paid off.

Rising slowly, he followed Billy to the surface.

They sat in the inflatable, looking down at the contents of the white cloth bag that lay open in the bottom of the boat. Gold doesn't tarnish after prolonged exposure to salt water like so many metals do. The bars were a deep, rich red, and because they were fairly thick, they were heavy. The statue was exotic, with a slightly Asian cast to its face. The figure was in a kneeling position, and held what looked like a basket or urn in its hands. The figure appeared to be dressed in exotic robes and draped with jewelry, clearly a representation of an important political or religious person.

For a long time, they just stared at the artifacts. Then, they looked up at each other, and broke into loud laughter and a huge bear hug.

"Man, I don't know what that is down there," laughed Billy, "but whatever it is, we have to find *all* of it."

"Hell yes!" said Michael. "Here we are diving on what we thought was a young wreck because of all that metal down there, but now we find that there's another wreck under it. Holy crap, Billy—this is gold! And there's gotta be more of it. These Ping-Pong paddles don't cut it. We have to build an airlift. Or do you still have the little one we built for the Feather River trip a few years ago?"

Billy shook his head. "I scrapped it a while ago; the pipe got crushed under something so I salvaged the parts and threw the rest away. But it's no big deal to build another one."

Michael nodded. The airlift was exactly what they needed for this job. It consisted of a five-foot section of four-inch diameter PVC pipe with a one-inch hole drilled in the side, a foot from the bottom of the pipe. Attached to the top of the rigid PVC was a flexible, corrugated hose some 25 feet long, the other end of which dumped into a large screen frame standing on the bottom somewhere down-current. A one-inch diameter iron pipe passed through the small hole near the bottom of the tube, extending upward in a U-shape inside the PVC pipe. The outside end of the U had a manual valve and was attached to an air supply at the surface, usually either an array of tanks or a low-pressure compressor.

Using the airlift was pretty straightforward, but it was a monotonous, mind-numbing task. It also required an inordinate amount of strength to control the thing. The rigid pipe is taken down to the area to be excavated and stuck into the sediment. When the air valve is opened, the air enters the pipe and expands rapidly as it rises, creating a vacuum. The vacuum sucks the sediment at the mouth of the pipe upward and carries it along the flexible hose to the screen, where it dumps out. Small particles such as sand and mud filter through; larger items are trapped in the screen for later examination. Any sediment that falls through the screen is carried away by the current.

Michael and Billy built their first airlift years before to dredge for gold in the rivers of Northern California. It was essentially the same process as gold panning, but on a larger scale; and because they were on SCUBA, they had access to deep crevices and holes that gold panners could not access from the surface. Their efforts were rewarded; over the course of several weekend trips to the gold rush country they had accumulated about $2,000 in gold dust and tiny nuggets. Since then, they had returned to the north fork of the Feather River with varying degrees of success, but the lure of gold—and the world's shipwrecks—beckoned to them. The airlift had been forgotten, until now.

"I can stop on the way home to buy the parts," said Billy. "It won't take more than an hour or so to put it together."

Michael nodded. "Let's head back to the marina, get this stuff put away, and find some food. I'm starving. Then we'll go back to the shop. This is going to require some planning."

Billy nodded. Tugging on the starter rope, he fired up the engine and pointed the inflatable toward Sausalito.

CHAPTER 5

The following day, they prepared for the large-scale salvage operation they now faced.

A number of things concerned them. Their long-term presence outside the Golden Gate would sooner or later be noticed, and they had no desire to attract other salvage divers to the site or bureaucrats who would bury them in an avalanche of salvage permits. They therefore decided to disguise what they were doing as much as they could. They would not use a compressor to run the airlift; instead, they decided to use large air storage tanks that would hang overboard on tethers. The tanks would connect to the airlift's hose, and could be changed underwater without being seen. Since the tanks would be suspended below the surface, they wouldn't attract attention. As a distraction, they also loaded the boat with spearfishing equipment.

To date, they had told no one about their find, and for the time being had no intention of doing so until they had a better idea of the magnitude of what they had discovered. While Billy constructed the new airlift, Michael built the screen array that the airlift would dump into, and performed an overall equipment check. He rebuilt their regulators, and modified the second stages with underwater communications devices that looked like a fighter pilot's facemask. Designed to form an airspace between the diver's face and the regulator, the masks allowed Billy and

Michael to communicate over distances up to 150 feet while submerged. They would be able to stay in constant contact as they moved about the excavation site.

Once they were satisfied that the equipment was in prime condition and that they had everything they needed for the task ahead and had arranged for coverage at the shop, they moved on to the next part of the exercise, which was dive site preparation. They returned to the wreck site and spent several days creating a map of the area to be excavated on a waterproof slate, by crisscrossing the bottom and recording large, obvious landmarks as they came across them. That gave them an idea of the size of the area that they would work. As it turned out, the debris field measured roughly 120 feet by 50 feet—not an overly large area, but one that would require careful management if they were to systematically excavate the entire field.

They returned to the shop and spent an evening drawing a scaled plan of the area on large graph paper, carefully noting the location of major debris, places that had already yielded artifacts, and obvious hazards and obstacles. Then, using standard archaeological techniques, they drew a grid over the map. Each square of the grid was five feet on a side, a reasonable area for a single diver to excavate. Based on the size of the debris field, they concluded that to physically build the excavation grid, they would need 240 five-foot tall stakes and about 1500 feet of nylon twine. The stakes had to be long so that they could be driven deep into the bottom sediment to firmly anchor them, yet still tall enough to provide clearance for a diver working under the grid of twine that they would ultimately support. They bought the twine at a local hardware store, as well as 24 ten-foot lengths of rebar that they cut into five-foot sections.

While Billy completed his check of the equipment and assembled the tools they would need, Michael began to research the identity of the statue and golden bars they had found in an attempt to determine their age, and hopefully to identify the ill-fated vessel that had transported them.

Early the next morning, he drove up and over Fish Ranch Road to UC Berkeley. He parked in the lot below the Student Union building and came up the stairs into Lower Sproul Plaza. The usual characters were in residence; they never seemed to change. In addition to the ever-present students that crisscrossed the plaza with their backpacks hanging from one shoulder, there was a recruitment table for the Peace Corps, a group of African-American students dancing and playing a collection of drums, and a strange-looking fellow walking in slow circles over by the bike shop. Michael smiled; he loved this place.

Passing under the iconic Sather Gate, he strolled across the campus, passing clusters of students and dogs wearing bandannas, the mark of a Berkeley canine. He paused for a moment at Dwinelle Hall, feeling a mild wash of familiarity as he regarded the labyrinthine building in which he had practically lived while an undergrad. His reverie broken by a Frisbee that flew through his field of vision, he continued past the sprawling mass of Wheeler Hall and headed for the far end of Doe Library. Turning left, he entered the Bancroft Archives.

The cool, dark, marble grotto of the library instantly felt familiar and comfortable. He had spent countless hours here, poring over early Spanish manuscripts and land grants. When he was 13, his family had been transferred to Spain because of his father's job. They had lived there for five years, during which time Michael became enchanted with the Spanish language and culture. At Berkeley he studied Spanish and Romance Philology, the field that attempts to uncover the origins of romance languages from their Latin, Greek, and Indo-European roots. His interest had grown into an all-consuming passion.

The Bancroft Archives had become his lair, for it was here that he found unimaginable riches as he explored the library's extraordinary holdings of rare books, incunabula, manuscripts, maps, and one-of-a-kind documents. The Archives had started in 1905 when the university acquired the private library of American historian and ethnologist Hubert Howe Bancroft. Since then, the collection had grown to over 44 million documents, ranging from 4,000 year-old papyrus scripts to modern political treatises. The Early California collection documented the colonization and exploration of western North America by European explorers, particularly the efforts of 16th century English and Spanish privateers who preyed on each other and sacked the riches of the indigenous populations of both North and South America. It was this collection that drew him to the Bancroft today.

After showing the guard his researcher's ID, stowing his belongings in a locker, and picking up a stack of notepaper and a handful of pencils from the box on the guard's desk—pens were strictly forbidden in the archives—he strolled over to the reference desk. Allen Shearer, a longtime Bancroft employee, was behind the desk. "Hey, Michael, this is a surprise!" he said, shaking Michael's hand in his huge paw. Shearer was well over six feet tall and was a bear of a man with unruly blond hair and a neatly trimmed beard. An expert in the cultures of the coastal Native American tribes of early California, he had helped Michael navigate his way around Bancroft when he had first begun his graduate research. Now they were good friends.

"Good to see you, too, Allen," said Michael. "How goes the book?"

Shearer beamed. His research was about as esoteric as it got, and he was pleased when anyone asked about it. He was writing about the social structures of the Costanoans, with particular attention paid to their relationships with neighboring groups.

"It's going well, Mike, thanks for asking. Another month or so and I'll be ready to have it looked at. You still willing?"

Michael nodded. He and Allen had long ago forged an agreement to critically review each other's work before publication, and both had come away the better for it.

"Just holler when you're ready, and I'll get out the

bucket of red ink and my paint roller," joked Michael. "Hey, is Lexie around?"

Allen nodded. "She's upstairs. I'm supposed to call her when you get here; I guess she's expecting you. So when's the wedding?"

Lexie was Alejandra Moliner, a fiery beauty who worked in the Bancroft Archives as a senior researcher. She was an expert in early California history, and had written extensively about the influence of the Spanish Conquistadores. She and Michael had met when he first began to spend time in the library, and their friendship had blossomed. They had been dating now for over a year, and were the talk of the bookish library staff.

Michael smiled. "You seem to think she'd have me, Allen. I'm just a smelly old diver. I've gotta have more to offer her than that, don't you think?"

"If you're just a smelly old diver, then I'm just a librarian," countered Shearer. "Deep down, you'll always be an academic; you just have fun wrapping it in water. Someday you'll hit the big time. You'll be the next Mel Fisher. I just hope you remember all of us little people when you're rich and famous."

Michael laughed. "Hey, no problem, Allen. I'll even publish those miserably boring books of yours for you. Now do me a favor and call Lexie before I have to climb over this desk and do it myself."

Minutes later, Lexie came down the stairs from the administrative offices above. Dressed in jeans, sneakers, and a loose-fitting white cotton blouse, she was a beauty. Blonde and curvaceous, she drew second looks from men everywhere she went. That always amused Michael; he often wondered how he had gotten so lucky. With a big grin, she grabbed him and wrapped him up in a big hug and planted a wet, noisy kiss on his lips. She loved to tease him like that; she knew that public affection embarrassed him and made him uncomfortable, a side of his personality that she had made it her mission to change. Looking over her shoulder, he saw the other two librarians behind the desk watching them; both were smiling, and Hannah Lawrence, the elderly woman who ran the place, winked at him.

"So, what's so important that it couldn't wait until tonight?" asked Lexie, taking his hand and walking him over to a vacant table in the Reading Room. "You haven't forgotten about dinner, have you?" It was still early in the day, and the room was deserted. Still, Michael didn't feel comfortable talking there.

"Nope, dinner's still on. You mind if we take a walk? I need to talk to you, but … not here."

Lexie raised one eyebrow and smiled at him. "Ooh, a mystery. I like that. As long as we end up somewhere that serves food, I don't care where we go. I haven't had breakfast yet."

They left the library and walked toward Hearst Avenue, crossed Strawberry Creek and into the stand of redwoods that graced the north side of the campus. They passed the Earth Sciences building and looped west toward Giannini Hall. Everything was still wet from the previous evening's rain, and the earth smelled richly of redwood humus and eucalyptus.

"So, what's so important?" she asked, wrapping her arm around his and hugging him close. This was one of the things he liked about her; she loved physical closeness. Pausing at a bench under a redwood tree, adjacent to the creek, he turned and sat down with her.

"I need your help, Lexie. Billy and I found a new wreck. We think it's a big one, and I really need your advice."

She was well aware of their interest in shipwrecks; more than once, she had accompanied them on dive trips and helped them research the provenance of their various finds. Her contacts at Bancroft and her access to restricted documents had been useful on more than one occasion.

Michael put his arm around her and pulled her closer to him, looking around to make sure no one else was within earshot. At the same time he put his other hand into the pocket of his light jacket. From it, he pulled a grey cloth jewelry bag. Looking around, once again ensuring that no one was within sight, he handed the bag over. Lexie took it, puzzled, and carefully pulled open the drawstring. Looking inside, her breath caught as she saw what the bag contained.

"You found this on a *wreck? Here?*" she asked incredulously. Reaching in, she carefully withdrew an ingot. It was heavy, rounded, and bore a distinct mintmark on one end. "Potosí," she whispered. She tried to reach the other bars in the bag with her fingers but couldn't. Impatiently, she shook them into her hand and looked at them carefully. "My God, they're from Potosí, Michael. Do you have any idea what this means? These things—this ingot—are nearly 500 years old. That means they must be from a Spanish ship that went down on its way back to Spain. That means … there are probably a lot more of these down there." She looked up at him slowly. "How many people know about this, Michael?" she whispered.

He kissed her gently on the forehead. "Besides Billy, you're it," he responded. "The last thing we want is a bunch of people diving on our wreck, or a bunch of bureaucrats coming down on us. And besides, Lexie—there's more. Billy found a solid gold statue not far from where I found these. It's in the safe at the shop." She carefully put the gold back in the bag and placed it in Michael's hand. She didn't release his hand, however.

"I could care less about the paperwork, Michael—I'm worried about you. Do you have any idea what you have here? This stuff, and whatever else is down there, is worth a fortune. I mean, the historical value alone is incalculable, but the gold…Michael, there are people who would do anything to get this. *Anything.*"

As she said this last, she was squeezing his hand painfully. "Sorry," she said, as he winced and pulled his hand away. He put the bag back in his jacket.

"Don't worry, Lexie. We know what we've got—I mean, we know what it may be worth. We've agreed not to tell anyone about this thing except you. We've already mapped the site and we're putting together everything we need to excavate it, but we need to know what we're looking for, and we're hoping you can help us. There are eight more bars like those in the safe at the shop, and we suspect that we'll find a lot more when we start digging." He explained their plan to grid the site and remove the overburden with the airlift, and how they intended to disguise what they were doing from prying eyes on the surface. She listened, nodding.

"OK, look. I need to get a closer look at those bars and the mint mark on them, because they might give me a clue about what else you should look for down there. I also have to see the statue; it'll help me nail down the period." She jumped up from the bench. "Michael, can we meet tonight at the shop after it closes? I have to go do some research on this. My God, Potosí. It could even be Sucre or Cochabamba. She looked at him, then enveloped him in a hug and kissed him gently on the lips. "I've got to get back to Bancroft. There are some books there that I need to look at. I'll see you tonight at nine." With that she ran down the path.

"Hey, what about breakfast?" he yelled after her. "And what about dinner?"

She waved back at him. "Pick me up at my place at seven." With that, she disappeared around a curve in the path.

Lexie was out of breath when she returned to the library. Rushing past the guard's desk, she flashed her ID at him and ran up the stairs to her office. She couldn't believe what Michael and Billy had found out there beyond the Gate. If it was what she suspected, then they were about to bring up a lot more than a few gold bars and a statue. And if they did, they'd have to be very, very careful.

CHAPTER 6

Michael left campus and headed back to the shop to meet Billy. He found him there, alone, having sent Jeff on an errand across town in exchange for some privacy, so that he could load equipment into the van. He had already cut the rebar into five-foot sections, and was now putting the finishing touches on the new airlift. It was a simple device, although larger than the last one they had constructed. The rigid body was a six-foot section of six-inch diameter PVC pipe. To prevent it from chipping and breaking when jammed into the bottom, Billy fashioned a sheet metal ring around the mouth of the pipe that would protect the plastic edges. One foot up from the bottom he drilled a ¾-inch diameter hole and glued the quick-release fitting and valve into place that would attach to the air source from above. Finally, he affixed metal handles on either side of the pipe, just above the air fitting, which would make it possible for them to maneuver the bulky device.

To ensure that the effluent would be carried away from the work area, he attached a 40-foot section of six-inch diameter hose to the top of the PVC pipe with a large hose clamp. The "exit" end of the hose would be suspended 15 feet above the bottom by a cable hung from the inflatable. The discharge end of the hose had to be higher than the suction end to ensure that the air flowing into the airlift would rise and expand, creating the vacuum that would pull the bottom sediment up behind it to the screen. The airlift was their only concern with regard to privacy: the air that came belching out of the hose after dropping its load of sediment in the screen assembly would rise to the surface and could potentially attract the attention of boaters. That was a chance they would have to take; they hoped that the surface chop would be enough to disguise the bubbles.

"So what did Lexie have to say?" asked Billy, as he carried the lift out the back door and loaded it in the van. Early that morning, before anyone else had arrived, he had filled the van with four 150-cubic foot air bottles, a collection of hand tools, their dive gear, the twine and rebar, a collection of inner tubes and lift bags, and an assortment of hoses and spare parts.

"Well, to say that she was excited is a bit of an understatement," replied Michael, as he helped Billy muscle the airlift's long grey hose into the van. "She looked at the mint marks on one of the bars, and thinks it's from Potosí. Right now, she's digging through her research stuff to nail down as much as she can about the gold. I'm taking her out to dinner tonight, and we're going to come here afterward so that she can explain to us what she found. Can you meet us around 10? I want to make sure that nobody else is around."

Billy nodded. "I gather we should keep this pretty quiet, right? I haven't told anybody, but I can imagine what would happen if word got out. So I've been thinking: we were going to fish while we were out there to disguise the real reason we're diving on the Patch. How about if we bag the fishing idea, since neither one of us likes to shoot fish, and just let anybody who asks believe that we're working a modern wreck? We do that all the time, and no one cares. If we come back with junk from one of our typical dives, no one will be curious. And if we *do* find more gold, we'll just keep it hidden."

Michael smiled. "There you go again, making sense. I absolutely agree: that's what we'll do."

Billy closed the rear door of the van just as the front door of the shop slammed shut. It was Jeff, returning from his errand.

"Here's that valve you wanted," said Jeff, handing a paper sack to Billy.

"Thanks, Jeff, you saved my butt. I had to get those Kirby-Morgans finished for Kevin this morning, and I wouldn't have been able to if I had to go get that too. I sure appreciate it."

Jeff beamed. He was an enthusiastic worker, loved his job, but was *so* energetic that he often made Michael and Billy tired just being around him. One evening he picked Lexie up in his arms and ran up and down the stairs with her, over and over, until she begged him to stop. He put her down, grinned, and disappeared into the back room. A minute later he emerged, still grinning, eating a tube of refrigerated cookie dough. The kid was a cyborg.

At 5:00, Michael left the shop for home, where he showered and changed. At 7:00, he picked up Lexie and drove down to Mabel's in Benicia for dinner. As usual, the food was unusual and delicious. They had ginger salmon, sage and onion rice, and stir-fried greens for dinner; they split a crème bruleé for dessert. Michael was dying to hear what Lexie had found in her research, but they refrained from talking about it in such a public place. Instead, they talked about the shop, their favorite students, and the things that had happened there. Lexie was as much a part of the shop as Billy, Jeff and Michael were; she was a skilled diver and often helped out in classes, occasionally accompanying them to Monterey when they took students out for their ocean dives. They laughed about the time Jeff had told them about the Marine Corps training he had received that taught him how to control wild animals with nothing more than the power of his voice. Always skeptical, Billy had raised one eyebrow, which was all it took to goad Jeff into yet another demonstration. That evening, he was given the opportunity to prove his ability.

One of the students in the class that evening was a construction foreman. He drove an old pickup truck, in the back of which always sat the meanest dog any of them had ever encountered. If anyone got too close to the truck, the dog would become a snarling maniac. Seeing this behavior, Jeff casually observed, "Thanks to my training, I can control that dog with the power of my voice alone"—at which point Billy dropped the gauntlet. "I'd really like to see that," he replied, and with that, the challenge was on. They agreed that after class they would gather in front of the shop, and when everyone had left, Jeff would demonstrate his remarkable animal control abilities.

At 11:00, after the students had returned from the pool and stowed their gear, they gathered around the truck. Paul, the dog's owner, dropped the tailgate. The dog stood at the back of the bed, shaking and wagging his tail while Paul stroked his head. Jeff, meanwhile, jogged to the top of a small grassy hill on the other side of the parking lot and stood there with his arms crossed, imperiously facing the dog.

"You ready?" called Paul.

Jeff nodded.

"You sure?"

Jeff nodded.

Paul looked over at Billy, shrugged his shoulders, whispered something into the dog's ear, and pointed to Jeff. Like a rocket, the dog shot out of the truck, careening toward Jeff.

"Do you remember that?" laughed Lexie. "He just stood there with that *beast* bearing down on him. And when the dog got about twenty feet away, he started to yell 'Heel! Heel!' but the dog wouldn't slow down. He looked like one of those cartoon dogs running so fast that his back legs were in front of his front legs."

Michael was now laughing as well. "All I remember is

Jeff disappearing over the top of that hill, shrieking 'Heel! Heel!' at the top of his lungs. We didn't see him for three days after that.'"

They left the restaurant and strolled up First Street, looking at the antiques and custom glass in the windows of the shops that catered to the many tourists who visited the state of California's first capital city. At 9:00, they got back in the car, drove over the Benicia Bridge, and returned to the shop. There was no pool class that night; the students were up in the classroom, learning about decompression tables and what happens to the human body if they are ignored. He could hear Rich Meyersonn's precise voice, explaining the intricacies of repetitive dives, saturation and off-gassing, and decompression stops. Rich was one of the shop's Assistant Instructors; like most AIs, he had taken a dive class a year before and had liked it so much, and was so good in the water, that he had begun to help out in classes in exchange for free rentals and equipment discounts. He had certified officially as an Assistant Instructor several months before, and was now teaching the classroom sessions for one of the current classes. Rich was a great resource; he was a dependable instructor, and was one of the more arcane individuals that Michael had ever met. He was an attorney who specialized in maritime law, and in his "spare" time studied Viking lore, collected full-size replicas of swords, wrote game software, played Dungeons and Dragons (which he had hooked Billy on and occasionally dragged Michael into), took part in Viking reenactments, and wove chain mail for the costumes he put together every year for the annual Renaissance Faire in Novato. Rich's wife and kids tolerated his interests and idiosyncrasies, and he was a good friend to the shop.

They found Billy in the repair shop, tinkering with the compressor.

"Rich's just about done; he should be out of here in a few minutes," said Billy, looking up. "How was dinner?" He had just checked the crankcase oil and was trying to insert the long, spindly dipstick back into its receptacle. "Let me guess—Mabel's. You guys are in a rut."

53

Lexie grinned, and threw her arms around Michael's neck. "Hey, when you find the best, you don't change, right?"

Michael kissed her on the cheek, and hugged her back. "I'll go along with that—and don't forget it."

They tinkered around the shop for a while, restocking shelves, checking the pool chemistry, and putting new inventory in the front windows for display. Michael brewed a pot of coffee while Billy completed the pool check; Lexie, meanwhile, went into the office.

Just before ten, Rich hollered down to Billy and Michael, asking if they would mind coming upstairs for a few minutes before he wrapped up his class. "The students were wondering if they could ask you some questions. They're headed out to Monterey this weekend for their first SCUBA dive, and a few of them are a little nervous about what they're going to see. Would you mind sharing some thoughts with them?"

They readily agreed, and headed upstairs. It was common for students to be nervous before their first experience with tanks in the ocean; After all, they'd heard all of the silly stories, seen *Jaws*, and been trained about the possible dangers that they might encounter.

Michael and Billy answered all of their questions and told them how exciting it would be for them to be in the ocean, and that they shouldn't be concerned. One of the students, a young woman in her late teens who was very good in the water and was in fact the best student in the class, asked if she could ask one more question before they left. "What's the scariest thing that's ever happened to you while diving?"

Michael looked over at Billy, who smiled knowingly. "The scariest thing that ever happened to us on a dive? That's an easy one." Billy looked down at the table he was sitting on, crossed his arms, and sighed.

Michael continued. "About three years ago Billy and I were doing some work for the City of San Francisco. They were planning a new sewage outfall, but the EPA got involved and wanted them to do a current flow study to make sure that whatever came out of the pipe wouldn't turn around and go back to the beaches. Bad for the tourists, you know." Everyone in the class laughed, each mentally picturing the results. "It was pretty simple work, really. The outfall was going to dump about ten miles out, so all we had to do was go out there and throw a couple of current meters overboard and pick them up later."

Current meters, they explained, are torpedo-shaped devices that collect data about ocean currents so that it can later be analyzed by oceanographers. "They're anchored to the bottom by a cable attached to a large concrete block on the bottom, and are supported in the water above the block by a large float. At the beginning of the study the entire assembly is thrown overboard, and that's exactly what we did – basically kicked them overboard, then went down to check them and make sure that they had landed right side up.

"When the time came to recover the meters," Michael continued, "we went back out in the work boat and located the marker buoys that showed us where they were. Billy and I had already decided that we would each recover one of them to save time. So, we geared up and jumped overboard."

Billy, at this point, was laughing softly. The others, bemused, looked at him expectantly. He shook his head and motioned extravagantly for Michael to continue.

"It wasn't that big a deal, except that the conditions could have been better," smiled Michael. "We were about halfway between the Farallons and San Francisco, a known breeding ground for great whites, so we were just a bit nervous."

"A bit," consented Billy. "Also, we were in about ninety feet of water and the bottom was flat sand, so we both knew that there would be nothing to hide behind if something *did* happen. At ninety feet, the visibility out there is nil—it's dark, cold, and frankly kind of freaky. So we didn't want to be down there any longer than we had to. All we wanted to do was release the meters and get out of the water."

"So," Michael continued, "we headed down to the bottom, and found the meters pretty quickly because they had these little xenon strobes on them that flashed every ten seconds or so. The job of releasing the meters was easy. We each had a come-along winch with us, and all we had to do was loosen the cable connecting the meter to the concrete block, remove a shackle, and the float would take the meters to the surface where the boat crew would pull them in.

"Well, I was down there cranking on that winch, looking around as much as I could, when suddenly, 'Wham,' something hit me *hard* from behind and slammed me ass over teakettle into the mud. I mean, my mask went one way, my regulator went another, and by the time I got myself put back together there wasn't anything around. So, not wanting to panic, I went back to work, this time cranking *just a little bit faster,* and *it happened again.* Only this time, I didn't lose my mask and was able to see a long, grey-white shape disappearing into the darkness. Screw panic, I thought, and I headed for Billy."

At this point, Michael looked out at the faces in the class, and saw that they were mesmerized by the story. Here comes the best part, he thought, suppressing a smile. "When I got to him, he had his back to me, so without thinking I tapped him on the shoulder to let him know I was there. Boy was that a mistake."

Billy was laughing loudly. "I almost clawed his face off."

Michael shook his head, half-smiling. "Billy's eyes looked like dinner plates, and I knew that whatever had hit me had also been by to visit him. I gave the thumbs-up signal meaning, 'Let's ascend,' and he didn't even hesitate. We headed for the surface, and when we got there we called the boat over and began to throw our fins and weight belts onto the dive platform, then we fought each other to get up the boarding ladder. We must have looked like the Three Stooges getting wedged in a doorway. As we were scrambling up the ladder like a couple of ferrets, one of the deckhands, himself a diver, nonchalantly leaned over the rail and asked, "Hey, did you guys see those two big Steller's sea lions down there? They've been playing with us all morning." Well, Billy and I looked at each other for a long time, and then Billy replied, 'Oh, yeah. Yeah, we saw 'em. We just came up to change tanks."

"And our pants," Billy added.

Everyone was laughing now, so Billy wrapped it up, saying, "You've got nothing to worry about out there. The biggest thing you're going to see in Monterey is a harbor seal or sea lion, and that's only if you're very, very lucky. They love to play with divers, and will hang around if they're feeling playful. You might see an otter, and you might see some reasonably big fish, but beyond that, don't worry. Just enjoy the experience—it's going to change you forever, I warn you right now."

The students drifted downstairs and hung around for a while, asking questions, buying a few things, and reserving equipment for the upcoming dive. Rich, Billy and Michael always took the students to Cannery Row and Otter Cove for their first dives, because they were relatively controlled environments, tended to have light to moderate surf, and offered a huge variety of things to see including kelp forests, wash rocks and plenty of life.

"How's the class doing, Rich—are they ready?" asked Michael. Rich was tall and thin, with a close-cut beard that looked like something a medieval warrior would sport. He was also one of the most fastidious people Michael had ever met. They joked about the fact that Rich was the only person they knew who stepped out of the shower and used a blow dryer on his hair just before he put on his wetsuit to go diving.

"Good group, Michael. They're ready to go. Lots of nerves, but that's pretty typical before the first dive. I know I was pretty nervous."

Michael nodded. "They looked pretty good in the pool the other day; I don't think we'll have any problems with any of them. One thing though: don't forget to ignore the "ten percent of your body weight plus six pounds" rule for weight belts on the first dive; give them two or three pounds more. First-time divers have a tendency to underestimate weight requirements, and then can't get below the surface. If you don't, you'll spend the first hour out beyond the surf line, bringing up rocks from the bottom to stick in people's BC pockets." Rich made a mental note, and wandered over to the rental desk to help the students fill out their reservation forms.

By 10:30 everyone was out of the shop. Michael locked the door, turned off the lights, and retreated into the office. Pouring himself a cup of coffee, he sat down next to Billy on the old green leather couch that occupied most of the room. Lexie was sitting at Michael's desk with a pile of notes, a sheaf of photographs, and a stack of ancient-looking books in front of her. She sat at the desk with her hands clasped, looking as if she were about to burst.

"It's about time," she said. "I was about to take my toys and go home."

Michael winked at her. "I'm the only toy you can take home," he replied.

"You wish," added Billy, and they all laughed.

"OK," Lexie began. Let me tell you what I've found out so far about your gold. It's definitely from Peru, and definitely 16th century, although I'm not sure anymore if it's from Potosí. I was mistaken about the mintmark; it isn't a royal stamp. It is, however, the mark of a nobleman. First, let me tell you a bit of history that will put this whole thing in perspective and might help explain why the wreck you found is where it is. Because truth be told, it shouldn't be. Michael, you're an expert on ancient Spanish and Spanish influence in Latin America, so keep me honest here. I may need you to translate some things." She gestured to the pile of books.

"So: In the early 1520s, Francisco Pizarro led an expedition from the Spanish base in western Panama all the way down the coast of what's now South America into Peru. They came back in 1528, and brought with them three llamas, two Indians, and a collection of gold and silver ornaments that they had collected along the way. That summer, he sailed back to Spain to show the king what he had found, but instead of being received as a hero, he was thrown in jail as a debtor who had fled to the new world without first paying off his debts. This is all in the historical record.

"After about a week, though, he was unexpectedly released from prison, because the king decided that there might be some merit to his story. After all, he did have gold, and besides, in those days, everyone was out looking for King Solomon's legendary golden kingdom of Ophir. So the king sent him back to continue his search."

Billy interrupted her. "What's Ophir?" he asked.

Michael got up to pour himself another cup of coffee, gesturing with the pot to see if anyone else wanted any. No one did.

"In the first book of Kings in the Bible," Lexie explained, "there's a story about a mythical land called Ophir, from which people brought gold and jewels to King Solomon as a tribute. No one ever knew where it was, although most historical scholars think it was probably in North Africa or along the Arabian peninsula somewhere— in fact, there's a town along the eastern side of the Red Sea that some believe is the original place. 16th century rulers didn't know its actual location, though; they just knew that somewhere out there was a source of unimaginable riches, and that the first country to find it would rule the world. So they sent all sorts of exploration parties out in search of the place. That's undoubtedly why the king freed Pizarro. He came home with gold, so maybe he was on to something."

She continued. "Anyway, he went back to Panama, and this time pulled together a pretty good-sized army—500 soldiers, according to the documents I could find, including 67 on horseback. They marched back into Peru, and somehow managed to capture Atahualpa, the ruler of the Incas at that time. According to legend"—she paused, and turned a copy of a 16th-century etching around so that they could see it—"the Spaniards held Atahualpa for ransom. They ordered the Incas to fill a room with gold in exchange for the life of their king. So the Incas filled the room, and in exchange, the Spaniards went back on their word and strangled Atahualpa." She gestured to the 1595 print by Theodor de Bry, which showed the hapless king being garroted.

"We should show this to Jeff," murmured Billy.

Lexie gestured to Michael for his coffee cup, and took a sip before continuing with her story. "This guy apparently had neither conscience nor scruples, because he immediately began to talk about Peru as if it were his personal property, declaring that any gold or riches he found there would be his, not the king's. Anyway, the next thing he did was to recruit his half-brother Gonzalo to help him out. He ordered Gonzalo to take an army and explore the land that lay to the east of where they were, probably part of what's now Bolivia. So Gonzalo took 350 Spaniards and 4,000 Indians, along with plenty of supplies and a herd of pigs, to look for more gold.

"Shortly after they left they came to a major river, and decided to split into two parties. The river was most likely a tributary of the Amazon. Gonzalo Pizarro would continue overland; Francisco de Orellana, another officer, would take a group and head off downstream to see what lay ahead. So Orellana chopped down trees to make boards, cut nails out of horseshoes, and built a boat. They caulked the wood with rubber tree sap, and when the boat was ready to go, he set sail with 50 men."

"I'm beginning to see the connection here," said Michael. "You said that the gold bars have the stamp of some Inca family on them. That means—"

Lexie shook her head. "Hang on, Michael. Let me

finish. Orellana sailed off down the river, stopping at villages along the way. Everywhere he stopped, according to the logs of the voyage kept by the expedition's priest, people told them about Curicuri, the village of gold that lay ahead. So he was pretty encouraged by all this. He sailed along for quite a few weeks—nobody really knows for sure how long—but never found more than a few tantalizing golden trinkets." She gestured to the stack of photographs. After some time, Orellana concluded that there was no way he could return to Pizarro because the boat couldn't sail upstream. Some of the men suggested an overland journey, but they collectively decided that the jungle was too thick. So they decided instead to continue their trek, seizing all the land they could in the name of the king.

"From that point on, everywhere they went they met Indians who told them that if they just continued downstream, they'd come to the "land of gold" that they were looking for. As they got farther and farther down the river, they started to hear about a village on the shore of a large lake where everything was made of gold—plates and bowls, tools, weapons, houses, even the paving blocks in the streets. So even though their food was running low and they were suffering from malnutrition, their lust for riches kept them going.

"The problem was that the farther into the jungle they went, the farther away the gold seemed to be. It was as if the Indians were all in collusion with each other, and knowing what we now know about their society, perhaps they were. They never did find the lake. Anyway, the Spaniards' tempers began to fray, and before long, they began to attack any Indians they came across. By now, they were desperate because they had managed to piss off most of the Indians in South America, and decided that the only thing they wanted was to return to the safety of their comrades. So as far as we know—and the record here is extremely vague—they trekked east through the jungle for many days, and eventually came to the mouth of the Amazon River. From there, they made their way 1,000 miles northwest to what is now Venezuela, where they encountered a detachment of Spanish soldiers with which they could share their story.

"Because Spain was accustomed to receiving regular shipments of gold from 'Nueva Andalucía,' they took Orellana seriously, and were apparently excited about what he and his men had found. So, Orellana and his men stayed there for a while until they had recovered from their trek through the jungle, managed to commandeer a ship in the name of the King, and sailed for Spain. They were never seen again. For years, stories emerged from the jungle about the fabulous riches that Orellana had found. None of them ever made it back to the Spanish crown, though, and the stories were eventually dismissed as legend. Orellana's priest kept records in his diary, including detailed descriptions of everything he found in the way of treasure, and these artifacts you've found are eerily similar to the things he describes—way too similar to be a coincidence. Of course, we have to find something conclusive that will serve as your provenance, but until you do, I'm pretty sure about this."

Michael and Billy sat quietly on the couch, listening to Lexie's story. "Are you saying that we've found something that this guy Orellana brought out of South America? That this is one of his ships?" Billy asked incredulously, shaking his head.

"Don't act so surprised, Billy," Michael responded. There are hundreds of wrecks along the coast that we know of, and probably a lot more that we *don't* know about. Besides, it isn't all that weird; think about how many Spanish ships sailed up and down this coast, looking for safe harbor."

Lexie nodded. "And don't forget how many of them broke up on the rocks during those searches. In fact, the wreck that you've found is right where I'd expect a wreck to be. Think about it, Michael: you took California History with Professor Bean at Cal the same time I did. If you were paying attention"—she grinned at him—"you'll recall that he told us that from the ocean side, the entrance to San

Francisco Bay is basically invisible without the Golden Gate Bridge there. The north and south sides of the bay entrance, combined with the locations of Angel Island and Alcatraz, make the actual bay almost impossible to see from outside. So by the time a ship sails in close enough to realize that there's an opening there, and if they've timed it badly, they're caught in the current and washed up on the rocks. That's why you've got two wrecks down there that appear to be on top of each other."

Billy shook his head emphatically. "You're forgetting one thing," he countered. "Our wreck is on the wrong side of the continent. Those guys were in the Caribbean; this is the Pacific. And I'm pretty sure the Panama Canal wasn't there yet."

Lexie smirked, then nodded in agreement. "What I think is that our friend Orellana somehow managed to make it back to the Pacific side," she explained. "There's evidence in the historical record that some of the gold—in fact, a statistically significant amount of it—that came out of Peru showed up in some odd places on the western Caribbean coast, gold that is common on the Pacific side—although Orellana would have called it the *Mar del Sur*, since it didn't become the Pacific Ocean until 1521 when Magellan renamed it. There's absolutely no reason why it would be there, except for the diary kept by Orellana's priest that documented their journey from Peru across what is basically Brazil. Keep in mind that there were quite a few Spanish settlements along the Pacific coast because of the riches that were being taken out of the region, and galleons sailed up and down the coast on a regular basis as both transport and protection.

"Orellana probably crossed the Isthmus of Panama, made it back to the Pacific, and somehow managed to sail north with the gold. My guess is that the ship didn't make it to wherever he was going—and you guys found it. I realize that this is pure conjecture on my part, and there are huge holes in my theory, but since Orellana disappeared and the gold was never recovered, it's as good a theory as any other. I can't explain why he headed back to the Pacific side of the continent, unless he just wanted to continue his search for gold, but if we can establish provenance between the historical record of the time and the artifacts you've uncovered, the story may prove to be more accurate than we think."

Michael and Billy were dumbstruck by the story that Lexie had spun. A Spanish treasure ship, on the wrong side of the continent, carrying gold, and all they were looking for was a few old portholes! This was the kind of thing people wrote novels about, only this was real.

"You want to hear the rest of the story?" asked Lexie. They looked at each other, then back at her. They nodded.

"OK. There's an old Inca legend that may be related to this. It seems that shortly after Pizarro killed Atahualpa, the Incas somehow gathered up most of the gold they had promised in ransom and took off with it. They headed southwest into the Andes, and led the Spaniards deep into the jungle. They climbed into the mountains, avoiding Vilcapampa, the royal city that the Incas established deep in a valley after the Spaniards sacked Cuzco. Apparently the Spaniards put into place a puppet ruler named Manco Capac who was led to believe that the Spaniards intended to restore Inca rule. When it became obvious that this was not the case, Manco Capac and a band of followers revolted in 1535, and after attacking Cuzco for nearly a year, they were finally forced to retreat.

They set up camp in two places, one of them Vilcapampa, where Manco Capac lived. They managed to keep its location secret, and when the last Inca ruler died in 1571, the place was inexplicably abandoned. According to local legend, the remaining Incas fled into the deep jungle, carrying their gold and silver with them. They passed Lake Titicaca, then disappeared into the Bolivian jungle beyond. Neither the Incas nor the gold were ever seen again. Some Spaniards made a half-hearted attempt to find them, but none of them ever came back. It's one of the world's great mysteries."

Billy stood and walked over to a bookshelf on the far

side of the room. Pulling down a world atlas, he opened it to a map of Peru. He laid it on the desk, and Lexie pointed to the region of the country where this had all taken place.

"This area is incredibly mountainous and rugged. In fact, a lot of it has never been explored."

Michael interjected. "I'd forgotten all about this, Lexie, but you're right. I remember one of my professors telling us that any number of expeditions has been mounted to explore that region, but most of them, even some of the more recent ones, have never returned. It's kind of spooky."

Lexie had risen while Michael was talking, and was opening the safe. She pulled open the door, and extracted the golden idol that lay there. Under the lights of the office, it gleamed dully. She turned it over in her hands, admiring the craftsmanship. It was exquisite, and smelled slightly of ocean. Sitting down, she laid it carefully on the desk.

"Look here," she said, pointing at the map. "Lake Titicaca is way up in the Andes, right on the Peru-Bolivia border, at about 13,000 feet. It has two basins, one called Uinamarca, the other Cuchuito. They're joined by the Strait of Tiquina. It's a big lake—about 3,200 square miles—and pretty deep. I think Uinamarca is about 600 feet at its deepest point. Anyway, there's an old legend that says that Uinamarca and Cuchuito are joined deep in the lake by a massive golden chain, placed there by the Inca gods."

"I remember this story," said Michael. "No one ever found the Incas, or the gold, or the silver, or the Spaniards that went looking for them. Some of the professors I worked with at Cal speculated that the gold may well be in the lake, thrown there as a tribute to the gods by the remaining Incas and as a way to keep it out of the hands of the Spaniards. And since gold had no meaning to them other than as a tribute to their religious figures—it had no monetary value—there was no compelling reason why they would hang on to it. There very well *may* be a fortune in that lake."

The room lapsed into silence, broken only by the quiet roar of the compressor downstairs, slowly filling the tank cascade. Lexie broke their reverie. "Look, that hasn't got much to do with what you guys have found, at least I don't think it does. I think you've stumbled onto a ship owned or maybe even piloted by Orellana that got lost and made it as far as San Francisco Bay before getting tossed on the rocks. And the only way we'll ever know is for you to get out there and start digging.

"This little statue may be enough to convey provenance, but if it doesn't, we'll need something else."

CHAPTER 7

They woke early and met at the shop, where they loaded the remaining equipment into the van. They were reasonably sure it would all fit in the inflatable; the boat was rated for a cargo capacity of well over 1,000 kilos, and they didn't expect to exceed that. But if they did, they would unload as much as they could, stow it on the bottom near the wreck site, and make a second trip to retrieve the rest.

Much to their pleasure, the morning dawned cool and foggy, a welcome contrast to the last few days. There was nothing worse than struggling into a quarter inch of neoprene under the hot California sun. Whenever they took groups of students to the ocean for their first dives, Michael and Billy waited until the students were fully dressed before beginning to get dressed themselves. They'd learned long ago that if they suited up at the same time as the students, they'd inevitably end up standing around in their wetsuits for a half hour, cooking in the sun while the group struggled with belts, straps and the nervousness that accompanies a first dive.

They left the shop at 5:30 in the morning and drove west toward the Berkeley Hills. As they approached the Caldecott Tunnel they could see the fog pouring over the tops of the hills like cotton batting. That was a good sign; it meant that the temperatures would remain cool for some of the day, anyway. Exiting the tunnel, they took the freeway to the Bay Bridge and then on to San Francisco. They passed through the city on their way to the Golden Gate; once across the Gate, they took the Sausalito exit and wound their way down into the town.

Michael and Billy had commercial maintenance contracts with a number of boat owners in the Sausalito marina, and therefore had boat launch privileges. Billy parked the van near the boat ramp and began the arduous task of transferring equipment from the van to the Achilles. It was hard work; not only did they have to transfer their personal diving gear, the four large air bottles that would power the airlift, the airlift itself, the floating screen assembly, a full set of tools, the rebar, and several sets of double 80s for themselves, they also had to ensure that the load was balanced in the inflatable and that the rebar was secured well enough to keep it from shifting and punching holes in the rubber boat. It took them the better part of an hour to load everything, but ultimately it all fit, even though they would have to sit on the inflatable's side tubes while they were underway. There was no way the boat would get up on a plane. That was OK, they decided; it was a short trip around the point to the Golden Gate, and from there, five minutes to the site. It would be a lumpy voyage, but thankfully, a short one.

They launched the Achilles, and after parking the van and trailer they motored slowly out of the marina. A few people recognized them and waved from the decks of their boats, but it was still early, and most of the marina's residents were not yet awake. Clearing the outer marker, Billy cranked the throttle, and the little boat tried in vain to get up on a plane, but just couldn't do it. He finally shrugged his shoulders, smiled, and proceeded to plow through the low swells. The flexible hull of the inflatable absorbed most of the bumpiness, and even though they were heavily loaded, the ride wasn't bad.

* * *

Alan Hackett watched from beneath a sailboat as Michael and Billy loaded the Achilles with salvage gear. Putting aside the wrench he was holding, he stood up and stretched, deforming the tattoos that stenciled his arms, neck and shoulders. He was a repair and maintenance worker at the marina, although he was also an experienced commercial diver and salvage operator.

As he worked to replace the broken cable that raised and lowered the sailboat's retractable keel, Alan seethed with contempt. Since getting out of prison he hadn't been able to find steady work, at least not doing what he was good at. He had had a great job as a commercial hardhat diver and welder on an offshore rig in the Gulf of Mexico, 100 miles off the coast of Texas. Three weeks on, one off, it was a great gig—made even greater when he was presented with an opportunity to nicely augment his income by doing a little courier work for a couple of yahoos he had met while on break in Panama City.

He and a few of the roughnecks from the rig had flown down for R&R; one night, in one of the innumerable local bars that were all over the town, they had gotten into a friendly conversation with two locals. A few beers later they were talking business. Just a little weed, they said; Alan Hackett reasoned that he and his friends came and went to Panama all the time and had never once been stopped or questioned by U.S. customs *or* the Federales. And since they were always carrying large, odd cases and duffels with them that contained not only their personal effects but work instruments and equipment as well, they weren't on the suspicion radar. Besides, an additional $5,000 every two weeks wasn't something to sneeze at.

So he had agreed, and two days later he returned to the rig via a commercial flight out of Panama City to Houston with five pounds of dope hidden in his dive bag. The weed was double-sealed in heavy-duty Ziploc bags, and the outer bag was heavily dusted with scented talcum powder. Throws off the sniffer dogs, they had told him.

Apparently it worked. He made it to Houston without incident, and then picked up the helicopter for the trip back to the rig. "Jackson"—clearly not his name--met him at the airport and relieved him of his cargo, swapping it for an envelope full of cash. Too easy, he thought.

Two weeks later he repeated the trip, again carrying sealed baggies. The third time he learned why it was so easy, when one of the men who had contacted him in Panama met him in Houston with a badge, a gun and a pair of handcuffs, and identified himself as a Federal Drug Enforcement Officer. He relieved Alan of the drugs and his freedom and tossed him into the backseat of a Crown Vic with Jackson, who sat without speaking, tears on his cheeks. "It isn't fair," he repeated, over and over.

Alan was processed in Houston, and after a quick trial was convicted of drug smuggling and sentenced to seven years in a Federal penitentiary, although his dumbass lawyer told him that he could probably get out in five. He was incarcerated in a shithole prison near San Angelo for a year before being transferred to Chowchilla. Five years and a day later he was paroled, and after living in a series of halfway houses for several months, he finally made his way to the San Francisco area. There, he answered an ad in the Contra Costa Times for a diving equipment technician at a shop in Walnut Creek—Ocean Adventures, it turned out, owned by Michael McCain and Billy McAdams. He worked on hard hats, regulators, and did tank inspections, all while ogling the little honeys who came in with their boyfriends to take dive classes—not to mention McCain's girlfriend. It was good work, and easy work, but it hadn't lasted long. Billy had caught him in the repair shop with his eye glued to the hole he had poked in the wall behind the compressor that divided the repair facility from the girls' dressing room, and that was the end of that. The asshole had fired him on the spot and threatened to call the cops if he didn't leave, and since a visit from the police would undoubtedly result in a parole violation, he had split—but not before hurling a few choice words into the dive shop.

That evening he called an old acquaintance—in fact, the only person who had bothered to stay in touch with him while he was inside—who ran a fly-by-night underwater construction company in Sausalito, north of San Francisco. Roland Wells did dam inspections, boat repair, and underwater welding, all of which were a piece of cake for Alan. Roland ran the business out of an old converted gas station in Sausalito, near the marina, and after agreeing to give Alan work (he conveniently neglected to mention what had happened in Walnut Creek), Roland let him live in a room behind the shop. Nothing fancy, but it had a bed and a sink, and he could shower at the marina across the street where Roland did boat repairs and salvage work.

Roland handed off as many of the jobs to Alan as he could afford. It wasn't ideal, but none of Alan's previous customers would touch him, which meant that if he wanted to stay in the diving business he had to work for somebody like Roland, doing menial chores for obnoxious customers who didn't give two shits that he was barely getting by.

The morning had started badly and gotten worse. His aging equipment always seemed to have something wrong with it, and if something broke, it was always at the most inopportune time. As he had prepared to start his first job of the day, cleaning the hull of a sailboat that was moored in a liveaboard slip, he mounted his regulator on the tank and turned on the tank valve, sending 3,000 pounds of air into the unit. Instantly, and without warning, the high-pressure hose on the pressure gauge ruptured, and the air jetting out of the hole in the end of the steel mesh-covered hose had caused it to whip around like a pissed-off cobra. By the time Alan finally managed to control it, the hose had whipped him across the face and cracked him across the top of his skull, opening a long cut in his scalp that still seeped blood. He needed stitches, for sure, assuming he bothered to go to the hospital. It was just his luck that the owner of the boat had come up from below decks just as he was getting lashed by the hose. He came stomping onto the deck of the boat, demanding that Alan stop that noise immediately because it would wake up his wife. Dickhead.

Once he'd replaced the hose, he'd finally gotten into the water to clean the hull, all the while being berated by the owner of the boat, standing up there with his wife in their ridiculous matching Greek fisherman's caps. The guy was pissed because Alan's late start was going to affect their oh-so-important sail. Whoopee fuckin'-do.

When he finally returned to the surface after replacing a zinc anode on the prop shaft, the cut on his head burning like a motherfucker, the guy yelled at him for dripping blood on the dock in front of his boat. That was the last straw. Alan lit into him, and in his anger had thrown a wooden scrub brush at the guy, narrowly missing his head. Luckily no one saw it, so it was his word against the old guy's. His buddy Roland was on good terms with the marina manager, so he wasn't too worried. But it would be just his luck to lose the job because of some asshole. That would be two in one month, he thought, sourly. First those assholes at the dive shop in Walnut Creek had booted him for trying to pick up the hot chick who was dating the owner, then for getting too chummy with their precious diving students. Jerkoffs. That had been a couple of weeks ago, but luckily this job with Roland had come through. He'd do it as long as he had to, then maybe pick up a welding job in Alaska. Anything was better than this—he was a glorified garbage man, for Christ's sake.

Now, here they were, the pricks from the dive shop, loading a whole bunch of shit in their rubber boat. I should go cut a hole in it, he thought, or slash two of their tires. As he watched Billy transfer the large storage cylinders into the inflatable, he grew curious. They're sure not putting those on their backs, he thought. Wonder what they're up to? Must be some kind of salvage job. Whatever: the sooner he got the cable replaced on the keel of this sailboat, the sooner he could knock off for the day and go back to his room and roll a fatty.

CHAPTER 8

The Golden Gate Bridge was already getting busy as they passed under the north anchorage. Above the bridge, Michael could make out the remnants of Fort Baker, and beyond, the ruins of Forts Barry and Cronkhite. Built during World War II, the structures were intended to protect the militarily critical port of San Francisco, but to his knowledge, none of the three forts had ever fired a shot in anger. Today, all that remained of the three was a warren of subterranean passages and ruined gun emplacements scattered along the western cliffs. He and Billy had exhaustively explored the ruins, but had turned up nothing of interest. Judging from the litter of matches, candle wax, and used condoms, they had concluded that any maneuvers taking place in the forts today were less than military in nature.

As they passed beneath the Gate and headed into the Pacific, the water got decidedly choppier. Reaching into his dive bag, Billy extracted the GPS, turned it on, selected the waypoint, and began to steer toward the marked wreck. Soon they were once again anchored above the dive site. Looking at each other, they grinned, realizing that they were about to begin a grand adventure.

"You ready for this?" asked Michael, punching his friend playfully in the shoulder.

"Ready as I'll ever be, I guess," smiled Billy. "If Lexie

is right, and that really is a Spanish wreck down there, maybe we can get something a little bigger to dive from— like maybe something that could *pull* this little pig." He slapped the side tube of the Achilles affectionately. They had purchased the inflatable together before they had much money, and it was one of the bonds that had sealed their friendship. It had been the host vessel for many, many diving adventures—but none as spectacular as this.

Michael remembered one in particular. He and Billy had just acquired their Achilles, and had decided to take it out for its maiden voyage to do a night dive in Monterey Harbor. The conditions were perfect: The bay was flat calm, the moon was full, and Michael was anxious to try out the brand new drysuit he had just acquired. It was a state-of-the-art suit with pressure seals at the wrists and neck, attached boots, and a newly designed zipper across the back. He climbed into it and Billy zipped it closed across his back, ensuring the seal was tight.

Loading up the inflatable, they motored across the bay from Cannery Row. At about 11 PM they arrived at the site they wanted to dive. They tied the boat to the kelp, put on their gear, and jumped in. They were in about 80 feet of water; both had cameras.

Once they reached the bottom, they checked each other's gear, then proceeded to search for subject matter. Spotting a large ling cod on the sandy bottom, Michael moved closer to photograph it, but the fish lifted off the sea floor, swam about five feet, and settled back down. Not wanting to spook the fish, Michael decided to shoot from where he was. The only problem was that there was a large piece of kelp between him and the fish, so he reached out to grab it and move it out of the frame. And that's when the defective zipper in his new drysuit decided to demonstrate the extent of its—defectiveness. When Michael extended his arm, the entire zipper popped open, from his left upper arm all the way to his right upper arm—and fifty-two degree water flooded the suit, prompting Michael to say several words that cannot be repeated. Billy swore that he heard him.

74

Within a minute or so, Michael's entire body was numb, and in water that cold, hypothermia would soon set in. So he and Billy headed for the surface, their dive cut short by the failure of the zipper.

Reaching the Achilles, they realized that they had a serious problem. In water, *water* weighs nothing. But once it enters the air, it weighs a lot—64 pounds per cubic foot in the case of seawater. And Michael's new suit, with the attached boots, was full of it. In fact, in his blue drysuit, he looked like Violet Beauregarde, the giant blueberry character from Willy Wonka. And given the size of the suit, the extent to which it was distended, and the fact that it had attached boots that prevented the water from leaving, Michael and his suit now weighed around 2,100 pounds, which meant that there was no way he was climbing back into the boat.

To remedy the problem, Billy ordered Michael to flip upside down with his feet sticking out of the water. Michael complied, and Billy attached a polypropylene line to his feet. Then, pulling with everything he had, he slowly pulled Michael up and over the gunwale of the inflatable, while the water exited through the broken zipper. It took about five minutes, but luckily Michael still had plenty of air in his tank. Once he was in the boat, Billy gunned it and thy made their way to shore. Michael was blue by the time they got back to the hotel, but a hot shower and a bottle of Talisker single malt brought him back to life. Needless to say, the manufacturer compensated Michael handsomely for the "difficulty" and replaced the suit overnight.

It was still cool, so they quickly climbed into their suits, put on their twin 80s and BC jackets, and gathered up all the tools they would need. As soon as he finished dressing, Billy tied a drop line to the heavy canvas bag that contained the rebar and twine, and carefully lowered it over the side to Michael, who was already in the water. Nodding to Billy, Michael grabbed the bag, put his regulator in his mouth, and after a quick thumbs-up to Billy, rode the bag slowly to the bottom as Billy played out the line. Once there, he untied the rope and ascended with the end of the yellow line. This time, Billy attached the airlift and the screen platform to the line along with an empty inner tube, and again, Michael rode it down, adding the additional gear to the growing pile.

After three more trips they had lowered the remaining tools and collection bags to the bottom, and were now ready to rig the air for the airlift. In the bottom of the inflatable were four large tanks, each five feet tall and weighing about 125 pounds. To two of them Billy attached deflated inner tubes. The inner tubes would be partially filled once underwater to make the tanks neutrally buoyant. After tying 15-foot ropes to the rigid rubber cleats on both sides of the inflatable, Billy tied the other end of each rope to a tank, and carefully lowered them over the side to Michael, who lowered the tanks until they were at the end of the ropes. Then he used the inflation hose on his regulator to squirt air into each inner tube until each tank was essentially weightless in the water, thus reducing the strain on the inflatable as it pitched and heaved on the surface swells. As the air in each tank was consumed, the tanks would get lighter, so they would have to occasionally burp air out of each inner tube to keep the tanks at the same depth.

With the supply tanks now secured and the equipment arranged on the bottom, Billy raised a red-and-white diver-down flag and a blue-and-white Alpha flag on the boat's five-foot mast, adjusted his equipment, and rolled overboard. As he adjusted his equipment, checked his buckles, and cleared the squirt of water that always entered his mask through the bottom seal over his moustache, he spoke into the microphone. "Michael, can you hear me?"

The response was immediate and welcome. "Gotcha, Billy, loud and clear." Billy was now close to the bottom, and in the low visibility water, he was on top of his friend before he knew it. Pulling up suddenly and pirouetting in the water, he narrowly avoided coming down on Michael's head.

Michael was already unloading the rebar from the gear

bag, laying them out in bundles on the bottom. They had rehearsed this exercise in the pool, so they knew exactly what they had to do to build the grid once they were on the bottom. Four of the rebar sections had twine already attached to them, carefully coiled and secured with a rubber band. These were to serve as the corner posts; they would be the first pieces Billy and Michael would drive into the bottom. One piece of twine on each post was white; the other was dark red. The white pieces were longer than the red ones, and would serve as the long sides of the grid perimeter; the shorter red segments would serve as the top and bottom of the grid array.

Michael and Billy each grabbed a set of the rebar sections with string attached, and positioned themselves at what they perceived to be the extreme southeastern end of the wreck's debris field. As near as they could tell, the wreck was positioned in a roughly northwest-southeast orientation, which was how they intended to construct the grid. Once they were in position, Billy swam away until he was hovering above an old tire that they had placed in position as the extreme southeast corner. There, he hammered one of the rebar sections into the bottom. Extending the red string, he swam back toward Michael until the string was fully extended. There, he hammered another piece of rebar into the bottom and tied the string to it. One side of the grid was now complete.

"You take the right side, I'll take the left," said Michael, swimming off into the gloom. When he reached the southwest stake near the tire, he uncoiled the white line attached to it and swam northwest until the line pulled tight, at which point he hammered another stake into the sandy bottom, startling a sculpin that had settled near him. Once it was anchored, he tied the string to the stake.

Billy, meanwhile, had done the same; Michael could hear the sound of his hammer as he drove the stake home.

"Coming your way," he said into the microphone. He untangled the bundle of red string that was attached to the stake, and swam toward Billy with it. He quickly came upon him, floating above the bottom near the fourth stake.

Now, they had to do some adjustment. One of their stakes was off, because the string, which should have been fully extended when Michael reached the final stake that Billy had planted, still had five feet to go, indicating that either Michael's stake needed to come closer to Billy's, or Billy's had to go farther away. They moved Billy's stake out until it was at the end of the string, and it quickly became obvious from the angle that Michael's needed to be moved farther away—they had staked out a parallelogram rather than a square. While Billy replanted his stake in its original position, Michael moved his back. The outer perimeter was now in position and for the most part, square. The corner posts supported the string about four feet above the bottom, which was plenty high for the work they would be doing.

The next step was to complete the grid itself. They had thought ahead and tied knots every five feet in the twine, so it was a simple matter to drive rebar into the bottom at each knot around the perimeter. They did that quickly, using nylon cable ties to anchor the string to the stakes. It was eerie to be in constant communication without being able to see each other. The phones were terrific tools, and they were once again grateful for the fact that they had purchased them the year before. At the time, they were really just cool toys, but they had proven to be valuable many times over.

The only remaining task was to run the actual grid strings. This took a while because it was difficult to tie knots while wearing neoprene rubber gloves, and the water was too cold to take them off for very long. If they'd thought it through, they would have tied loops in each string to make the fastening process easier.

By the time they finished, they had been underwater for nearly two hours, and their tanks were close to empty. They went to the anchor line and slowly ascended, stopping at ten feet to off-gas for ten minutes before surfacing. They were well within the limits of the U.S.

Navy Diving Tables, but they knew enough not to take chances, particularly since they would be doing repetitive dives all day. The last thing they needed was for one of them to get bent on this dive; wouldn't *that* attract the attention they didn't want. Nothing like a day in a decompression chamber to make your day special.

Once they had decompressed for ten minutes, they surfaced, inflated their BC vests, and squirmed out of them, anchoring them with a kelp anchor to the boat so that they wouldn't float away in the ever-present current. Climbing aboard, they dropped their weight belts on the floor of the Achilles, unzipped their drysuits, and peeled them down to their waists.

Pulling on a sweatshirt, Billy reached into the cooler and pulled out two cans of Coke. Handing one to Michael, he said, "I'm starving. It's only 10:30, but are you ready for lunch?"

Nodding appreciatively, Michael replied. "Oh, yeah, am I ever. Those donuts didn't go very far this morning. So what did you bring this time? Caviar heroes?" It had become a favorite joke between them: whenever they traveled, Billy always made gourmet-quality lunches, and always surprised Michael with the ingredients. The joke had started when the two had traveled to Yosemite together to camp in the park and photograph the valley. Because he was an accomplished cook, Billy's job had been to provide the food. To Michael, good camping food meant hot dogs, sometimes actually cooked. So on the first evening of the trip after he had gone off to call Lexie, Michael returned to the campsite to find Billy putting dinner on the table: grilled ribeyes, sautéed mushrooms in a rich Madeira sauce, French fries cooked in olive oil, and hot, fresh-baked camp bread. Dessert, he was informed, was still in the camp oven—a chocolate pie.

Billy smiled as he dug around in the cooler. "Actually, nothing special today—I didn't have time to make much. Prosciutto and cheddar on seven grain bread, brown mustard, sliced tomatoes and sprouts, and my famous caper mayonnaise. Oh, and dill potato salad, thanks to Lexie's recipe. For dessert—" he pulled out a small brown paper bag—"voila!" and produced two cherry pies. "I know you love these things. Here—one for each of us."

Michael slapped his friend on the back. "Thanks, man. You're amazing. Let's eat so that we can get back down there."

They sat on the boat's side tubes facing each other and munched their sandwiches, occasionally forking bites of potato salad from the container that sat between them. To the north, the Marin Headlands towered above, while the Golden Gate stood directly to their east. Overhead, cormorants and gulls wheeled and called, and the slightly iodine-scented smell of the ocean filled their noses and gave them enormous appetites. There was something about diving that made them ridiculously hungry: they still laughed about the time that they and their friend Russ had gone into Dairy Queen for lunch one day in Monterey after a full morning of diving. Russ had stepped up to the counter and ordered a dozen tacos; the woman behind the counter rang up the bill and walked away, thinking that the order was for all three of them. When she returned, Billy and Michael *also* ordered a dozen tacos. At first she thought it was a joke; it took them a while to convince her that they intended to eat all 36 tacos. They did. Throughout their meal, employees of the restaurant kept sticking their heads out to see if they really intended to eat all of the food.

After lunch they lay in the sun for about an hour, watching the birds, enjoying the motion of the inflatable as it rocked gently on the swells, and talking about the shop and their friends who worked there. They laughed about Jeff as they remembered his first "commercial diving" adventure. He had begged Billy to find him a commercial diving job somewhere, something that Billy was reluctant to do, since the full extent of Jeff's commercial training and experience consisted of keeping the pool at the shop clean and helping them scrub the occasional boat hull in the Berkeley Marina. Ultimately, Billy found him a job with a local construction company that was putting in a water intake for a local power plant, a position that required very shallow diving and skills that anyone with a snorkel and the ability to hold their breath for 30 seconds could accomplish. Jeff, for some reason wrapped up in the belief that commercial diving was a romantic profession, managed to expand the nature and danger of the assignment every time he told someone about it. Billy and Michael knew that commercial diving was dirty, boring, dangerous work, and that most commercial divers faced the same hazards that construction workers did, with the added complication of doing the job underwater. So the position that Billy found for him involved very little danger. The intake that was being constructed comprised twelve eight-foot long sections of six-foot diameter concrete pipe, bolted together and submerged in twelve feet of water in the Sacramento River near the town of Antioch. As each section of pipe was dropped into the water by a crane, mated to the in-place section and bolted into place by divers, Jeff's job was to swim into the new section afterward and ensure that it and the prior section were properly seated against each other and sealed.

Over the course of six weeks, Jeff's telling of the story became more and more lavish. The job went from being a one-minute long, twelve foot penetration of a six-foot diameter pipe in twelve feet of brown water to a 150-foot penetration of an eighteen-inch diameter pipe in 100 feet of shark-infested black water. By the time the job was about to end, Michael and Billy couldn't stay in the same room when Jeff told the latest version to whomever would listen. Jeff would stand there in the shop with a band mask under his arm, as if that was what he wore while performing his acts of derring-do. Meanwhile, Michael and Billy usually retreated to the office, where their laughter was masked by compressor noise.

On the last day of the job, Jeff asked—practically begged—Michael and Billy to come down to the worksite to watch him in action. Reluctantly, they agreed, leaving the shop in the hands of Rich Meyersonn while they ran down to the river.

When they arrived, Jeff was underwater, so they stood on the work barge, chatting with Kevin Kelly, the foreman, and waited for him to surface. They weren't sure exactly what it was Jeff wanted them to see, but if it made him happy, then they were willing to stand around for a while.

By now, the intake pipe extended 90 feet into the river, which meant that Jeff was working quite a ways offshore. "He should be up any minute now," said Kevin. "He's been down there for about ten minutes." He turned to Billy and smiled, raising one eyebrow. "That's a good worker you got me there, Billy, but he sure is impressed with himself. You'd think he was diving on the Titanic itself the way he talks about it."

Billy just smiled and nodded. Jeff was immature, but he was a hard worker, sincere, and the customers liked him. Consequently, they tolerated his eccentricities.

Offshore there was a commotion, as Jeff's head broke the surface about 100 feet out in the river. Looking over at the barge, he spotted Billy and Michael, tapped his head with his hand in the universal 'Hello—all good here' signal that divers use to avoid waving (which can look like a cry for help), and broke into a wide grin. In response, they touched the tops of their heads with one hand. As they stood there watching Jeff, Billy's attention was drawn to something floating upriver that was making its way toward Jeff, undulating in the slow current. Jeff obviously did not see it.

"What is that?" asked Billy, elbowing Michael and pointing to the object. It seemed to change shape and size as it made its way along, like a kelp mat.

"I can't tell," said Michael, shielding his eyes and squinting upriver. "If I didn't know better, I'd swear it looks like—like—no, never mind. It couldn't be."

Billy looked over at him, puzzled. "What?" They both looked back at the thing, which by now was about ten feet upriver from Jeff and approaching him steadily. They tried to draw his attention to it, but he just smiled idiotically and waved at them. Then, as if some inner sense told him to look to his left, he turned and gazed at the thing floating toward him. Like an obscene mink stole, it languidly wrapped itself around Jeff's shoulders. As realization dawned that the thing that was inexorably encasing him and getting hopelessly entangled in his gear—all the more so as he struggled—was the rotting carcass of a dead horse, he began to scream, "Get it off me! Get it off me!" The more he struggled, the more inextricably he wrapped himself in the thing.

Naturally, everyone on shore was immediately reduced to hysterical laughter. Michael, Billy and Kevin were doubled over, supporting each other as they tried to catch their breath. Jeff continued to scream invective at all of them, and eventually they recovered enough to start the engine on the little workboat and go to his aid. None of them wanted to touch the carcass, so after calming him down, they used the oars in the boat to extricate him from the smelly mass of bone, hide and sinew that had enveloped him—but not before Billy took fully a hundred pictures, capturing the moment for posterity.

They were in a storytelling mood, and one led to another. "Remember the time Bogosian had a class up at Salt Point the same weekend we did?" Billy asked, and again, they collapsed in hearty laughter. Paul Bogosian was a freelance instructor who at the time worked for another dive shop in the area. He was a competent instructor, good in the water and in front of the classroom, and he also happened to be an FBI agent, although he didn't tell that to his students. On the weekend in question, Michael and Billy had a group up at the state park for their first ocean experience, one in which they were taken into the water in full gear—everything, that is, except their weight belts. They wanted the students to get the feel of the surf without the risk of sinking. After a day of doing surf entries and exits, they could handle just about anything the ocean could throw at them.

That night, Billy, Michael, and Paul were standing

around the campfire, having a beer after a long day in the water. Paul's group had chosen the site adjacent to Michael and Billy's, which gave them the opportunity to catch up. Most of the students were asleep, although a few still lingered around the fire. One of Paul's students, who had the odd name of Thomas Thomas, joined them. As he listened to the conversation, he casually retrieved a baggie of weed from his shirt pocket along with a package of rolling papers, and proceeded to assemble a joint. Michael and Billy watched in confusion; obviously, Thomas had no clue about Paul's alter ego. Looking over at Paul, they were puzzled to see him standing there with an enormous grin on his face, his arms crossed. And then it happened.

"So Paul," Thomas asked, "What do you do when you're not teaching diving?" By this time he had the joint glowing cheerily, and as he put it in his mouth and took a deep breath, Paul responded, "Actually, I'm an FBI agent."

What happened next was one of the funniest things any of them had ever seen. Thomas stuffed the glowing joint in his mouth and swallowed it in one rapid motion, grimacing against the pain. "Really? That's interesting," he choked.

Paul exploded, and Billy and Michael followed suit. "You're cool, Thomas," croaked Paul, "but now that you know, I'd appreciate it if you did that somewhere else to avoid any—how shall I say this—*awkward* situations. That okay with you?"

Thomas nodded, mutely.

It took them a full half hour to recover, and Billy was pretty sure he wet himself just a little bit.

CHAPTER 9

At 1:00, they decided that it was time to get back in the water. The grid over the site was complete, so excavation could finally begin. On a large white slate they had labeled the five-foot sections on the short sides as one through six, while the long side sections were labeled alphabetically, A through P. That way they could quickly and easily find the location of any given five-foot square, and accurately record artifacts found at each location during the excavation. They were familiar with the widely accepted standards for archaeological excavations and intended to use them to the letter.

They had agreed that they would excavate on a square-by-square basis, beginning with the northwest five-foot quadrant (the upper left square of the grid, labeled A1), then move on to A2, A3, and so on, working one row at a time until they completed the excavation of the debris field at P6. They were hoping that they would be able to excavate one row per day, although they acknowledged that sixteen days to complete the entire debris field was highly optimistic. More likely, they would require two days or more per row, with more time required if a particular area proved to be fruitful or, for whatever reason, difficult.

Tied to the stern of the Achilles was an inflated inner tube covered by a red nylon net that was festooned with brass gear clips. Designed as a support float for spearfishing, in this case it would serve as the support for the sediment screen, which would hang ten feet below on nylon ropes. Billy attached a 20-foot nylon line to a clip on the inner tube and threw it overboard. They then suited up and changed the tanks in their backpacks, waving as they did so to a group of fishermen on their way out to the Farallon Islands. They hopped in the water and descended to the bottom, meeting at the pile of equipment. The communicators continued to work flawlessly.

"I'll go up and rig the screen if you'll hook the airlift hose to one of the cascade bottles," suggested Billy.

"No problem," Michael replied, and turned to grab the end of the 75-foot hose that lay coiled on the bottom. He swam up to the bottles that hung suspended from the inflatable, and quickly attached the screw yoke to the valve on one of the tanks.

Done," he said into his mask, looking down at the hose as it disappeared into the gloom.

"OK," replied Billy. "Come help me with this thing, then; it's turning out to be a pain. I'm about ten feet below you off to the north."

Michael consulted his compass, then looked in that general direction. He immediately saw Billy's xenon strobe flashing dimly in the distance. Swimming down, pausing momentarily to clear his ears, he grabbed one side of the unwieldy screen frame and held it while Billy ascended with a rope attached to one corner of the screen and secured it to a gear clip on the inner tube float. Once the first was secure, he attached the other three without incident, and the screen hung level, ready to receive its bounty.

The only thing left to do now was to rig the airlift itself. Descending once again to the sea floor, Michael uncoiled the 75-foot air hose that rose into the green gloom above while Billy dragged the airlift over. Working quickly and efficiently, they attached the hose to the lift with a large hose clamp, and checked to make sure that the valve was closed. Then, Michael swam up to the supply bottle and carefully turned on the valve that would allow air to flow to the lift.

"Any leaks?" he asked, knowing that Billy would be watching very carefully for any signs of problems. They had tested the apparatus in the pool without incident, but they knew all too well that things could go wrong at the most inconvenient times, and that you couldn't check equipment too many times.

"Looks good from here," came the reply. "Everything seems to be holding...let me give it a quick try to test the valve." Michael waited, and soon the hose convulsed three times in quick succession, indicating that Billy had opened the valve three times.

"Nope, no problems at all. Looks like it's going to work just fine," continued Billy.

"I'll bring up the drop hose; meet me over at the screen. You can help me attach it." Michael replied, and then swam over.

It took Billy a minute or so to wrestle the hose up to the screen assembly. Michael grabbed it and together they wrestled it into place and attached it to the screen frame so that the effluent would leave the hose and flush out against a cloth backsplash before dropping into the screen basin itself. Once that was done, the only thing left to do was to test the thing.

"You go down and give it a shot," directed Michael. "I'll holler if I see a problem."

Billy nodded his assent and swam down to where the rigid airlift lay on the bottom. Picking it up, he stuck its nose in the sediment and called out to Michael.

"Okay, turn on the air," Billy instructed. Far above, Michael slowly opened the tank valve, allowing air to fill the hose that snaked down to the airlift. Billy slowly opened the valve, and as air rushed into the body of the airlift, it expanded as it rose, creating suction that drew sediment up behind it. Billy knew enough to keep his hands clear of the mouth of the tube; the suction was powerful enough that it could pull his gloves right off his hands. Besides, he had to be vigilant, because fragile artifacts could easily be sucked into the hose and dashed against the rigid screen, possibly destroyed by the impact. They therefore secured the exit end of the hose so that it was close to the soft backsplash to minimize the impact objects would experience as they left the hose.

Billy called out to Michael. "How's it looking up there? You getting anything yet?"

The response was immediate. "I should hope so: I'm glad I have a good sense of orientation and something to hold onto, because I'm in the middle of a Texas-size dust cloud," replied Michael. "Lots of rocks, including a few about the size of golf balls. Looks like we've got plenty of suction, and the current is carrying most of it away. Let's get this show on the road."

CHAPTER 10

"OK, Billy, anytime you're ready. We've got 2500 PSI in the tank and you should have pressure. Start digging."

They started in sector A1 of their grid, in the extreme western corner of the array. While Billy dragged the airlift to the grid point, Michael ascended to the feeder tank and turned on the valve, checking it once again for leaks.

"Good to go," he told Billy, who was waiting for the all-clear. In response, Michael felt the hose convulse as Billy released a first tentative blast of air into the airlift.

When he was sure it was functioning properly, Michael swam over to the screen and checked the hose; it was secured tightly, but he re-aimed it slightly so that the effluent would strike the center of the backsplash before falling into the screen. They were now ready to begin the excavation.

"OK, my friend, here we go," came the response. "Let's get rich."

Moments later, the hose convulsed again and began to belch a steady flow of mud and rock that pinged and rattled against the backsplash before falling into the screen below. The smaller sediment passed through the quarter-inch screen; larger objects fell into the catch basin. In less than a minute, the basin was full, and Michael asked Billy to hold up a minute while he cleared it. In response, Billy pulled the airlift mouth away from the bottom, allowing air to rise up the hose, clearing the pipe. Once it was clear, he shut off the valve to conserve the compressed air.

As soon as the flow stopped, Michael dug carefully through the accumulated overburden, looking for anything unusual. In addition to rocks he found two fishing lures, a beer can, and a piece of glass from a beer bottle, all of which he dropped into a canvas collection bag. When he was sure there was nothing of value in the screen, he upended it, allowing the remaining rocks to fall to the bottom some 30 feet west of where Billy waited on the bottom.

"OK, go ahead. Nothing in this first batch."

The hose convulsed again, and soon began to spew mud into the screen array. Again, nothing of value emerged, although they recovered a few more things of interest: three more fishing lures, a plastic monofilament line spool, and a plastic doll's head which shocked Michael when it emerged. The eyes were covered with algae, and with the refraction from the water, the head looked larger than it actually was. It took him aback for a moment when it popped out of the hose into the screen.

By six o'clock in the evening the light was beginning to fade, so they decided to call it a day. They had changed their own tanks twice, emptied all but one of the airlift bottles, and excavated four of the five-foot grid squares down to hardpan, about 30 inches below the surface. They found nothing of particular interest. However, this was the first day, and they had a long way to go. They disconnected the airlift hoses and screen assembly and dropped them in a pile on the bottom. At the surface, they rolled out of their BCs and tanks, threw them aboard the inflatable, and climbed in after them. They then pulled in the storage bottles and the screen float, tied everything down with bungee cords, and opened a couple of water bottles.

Sitting back on the side tubes of the Achilles, they reflected on the day's activities and made preliminary plans for the next. Given that they had managed to excavate four squares in roughly half a day, they concluded that the complete excavation would take a little more than a month if they worked straight through. The weather was good, so they anticipated that they should be finished by mid-August, if all went well. They agreed that their schedule was aggressive, but they would certainly shoot to be done by September.

Starting the little motor on the Achilles, Billy looked around for other vessels, turned on his running lights, pulled down the dive flags, and, hugging the shore, motored into the fog that was now pushing its way through the Golden Gate, erasing the city.

CHAPTER 11

After a long day of bullshit work at the marina, Alan walked across the street to the shop and borrowed Roland's car. He needed to get away for a while to clear his head, smoke a little weed and think about things. He'd had another argument with a boat-owner; this time he had shoved the guy, and the bozo had almost fallen over the rail between the boat and the dock. The guy complained to the marina manager, but before the manager could catch up to him, Alan had left. He knew he'd hear more about it, but right now that was the last thing he needed.

He didn't have a destination; he just drove, and soon found himself on the winding road that led up to the overlook above the Golden Gate Bridge. Parking the car he got out and stepped over the guardrail, where a trail wound down to the edge of the cliff. There, he had a fine view of the city to his left, the bridge just in front of him, and the Point Bonita lighthouse far off to the right. Lighting a joint, he settled back to enjoy the view, the effect of the herb reminding him that one reason he'd been fired from the dive shop was because the students had reported him to the owner for burning a fat one before diving. Who gives a shit, he thought; but they had argued some bullshit about liability and brand damage and then canned his ass, even though he had more experience in the water than all of them put together. That, in fact, was why they had hired him in the first place. He was pretty sure the main reason they had fired him, though, was because he'd made a play for the owner's squeeze. Whatever.

Far below, just outside the Gate, he could see the choppy water that marked the Potato Patch, along with a couple of small fishing boats, and a large inflatable, flying a diver-down flag. Shitty place to dive, he mused; between the boat traffic going in and out of the bay and the rough water, you'd have to be crazy to dive there for fun. Must be a salvage job, he thought. Morons probably lost their outboard motor and are going after it. Good luck.

As he watched, a diver appeared alongside the inflatable and began to wrestle air bottles into the boat. It dawned on him that the guy must be Billy from the dive shop, whom he had seen at the Marina on and off for the last couple of weeks with the other guy, Michael, loading up a big Achilles. Right on cue, a second diver surfaced beside him and helped the first guy out of his tank—how sweet. He was almost positive that these were the assholes that had fired him. What the hell were they doing diving in that shithole?

He watched for a few more minutes, finished the joint, and headed back down the hill. He parked the car behind the shop, then walked around to the front door and let himself in. Roland was at one of the scarred worktables, replacing a shackle on an anchor line.

Roland was an old man who reeked of alcohol, was perpetually drunk, yet somehow was always fully functional.

"Heard about your dust up at the marina, Alan," he said, putting down the fid he was using to back-braid the rope on the shackle. "You can't be doing that shit, man. I've got a good thing going over there and I can't afford to fuck it up—and I can't afford to have YOU fuck it up. I know those people can be assholes sometimes but you've just gotta suck it up. One of the boat owners apparently yelled at the marina manager for 15 minutes because you tried to throw him overboard, and it took me a good half hour to calm him down and convince him that it wasn't you. But I know better, so please—cut that shit out, or I'll have to send you packing."

Alan mumbled his assent, gave Roland a half-assed apology and headed over to the ancient fridge to grab them both a beer, an act of kindness that assuaged Roland's anger. Drinking deeply from the bottle, Roland nodded his thanks.

"I'm going to be out of town for the next week or so," he said, "and I hope you can keep the place together while I'm gone. I've got a salvage job over in Emeryville that's gonna take the better part of a week, and I can't be here and there at the same time. We've got work lined up at the marina for the entire time I'll be gone; can you deal with it?"

Alan nodded. "Yeah, I've got it. I got nowhere else to be and its nothing complicated that requires more than one person. And yes, I'll keep my temper in check—you don't have to ask twice."

They chatted for a few minutes, and then Alan told Roland he was going out for a walk. He wanted to be at the marina's boat launch when Billy and Michael returned from their dive—assuming, of course, it was them that he had seen from the Marin Headlands overlook.

Walking across the street, Alan wound his way through the sailboats on their hard stands until he was close to the launch. He remained out of sight; the last thing he needed was to be seen by the marina manager. Moving carefully, he managed to get close enough to the boat launch that he could hear a conversation between two guys who were maneuvering a fishing boat onto its submerged trailer. Perfect.

Fifteen minutes after he took up position among the boats, he saw the heavily laden inflatable come around the point and enter the marina. He could now see that he was right; Billy was driving, and Michael was sitting on the bow tube with a line in his hand, ready to jump ashore. Billy waited until the fishing boat ahead of them was secured on its trailer and the two men drove away, then slowly pulled into the launch area. Michael jumped out, tied the Achilles up to a cleat and then trotted over to the van. He backed the trailer into the water, then untied the line and pulled the inflatable onto the trailer. Once it was secured, Michael put the van into gear and pulled away. He parked on the far side of the parking lot, close enough that Alan had a clear view of the trailer and its contents from his hiding place.

Michael opened the back of the van, then walked around to the side of the inflatable where Billy stood holding one of the large air tanks. Michael took it from him, laid it in the van, and came back for another. He loaded four of them in all. That was a lot of air; what the hell were they doing down there, he wondered?

They unloaded SCUBA tanks, drysuits, the usual masks, fins, and weight belts. After handing over a couple of ice chests that disappeared into the back of the van, they paused, talking so quietly that Alan couldn't make out what they were saying. Then, they walked to the front of the van, got in, and drove away. Weird: clearly they were salvaging something down there on the Potato Patch; there was no other reason to be diving there, especially with so much air.

Heading back to the shop, he let himself in, smoked a final doobie, and went to bed. As he fell asleep, he couldn't stop thinking about the dive shop guys. *What the hell were they looking for?* With Roland gone he'd be working his ass off all week, but at least he'd be able to keep an eye on them and their boat. If they found something good, maybe he'd be able to boost it out of the van. And maybe, just maybe, he'd make another play for Lexie. What were they going to do, fire him? Smiling, he drifted off, carried by the weed to a better place.

CHAPTER 12

On the 17th official day of the project, after taking a well-deserved three-day break from diving, Michael and Billy once again motored under the Golden Gate Bridge in the crepuscular light of dawn. The ocean air, foggy and cold, was like wet wool. By the time they had passed under the Gate and anchored, the bridge had disappeared in the fog. It was an eerie feeling; they had no visual points of reference other than the boat and each other, and wanted to get underwater quickly where the visibility was better—how ironic was that, they thought. Curiously, no one had expressed any particular interest in what they were doing; a few fishermen had waved at them, as well as the crews of a few sailboats. The interest, however, was casual, and no one came close. With any luck they'd complete the project before anyone developed more than a passing interest in what had kept them coming back, day after day.

They had found very little of value. The most significant item was the rusted hulk of an outboard motor, lying on its side about six inches below the surface in quadrant E3. It had obviously fallen off a small boat, and its reluctant owner had decided to leave it on the bottom—a donation to the Pacific Ocean's steadily growing collection of irretrievable gear. To their own collection they also added 31 fishing lures, enough beer cans to pay for a college education, two tires, a USCG-approved fire extinguisher, three license plates, the remains of an umbrella, and a folding chair. They weren't about to give up, though; they knew something was there, waiting for them to uncover it. They'd been skunked before, but this project had a different feel to it.

Alan, meanwhile, had made repeated trips to the overlook above their position, surreptitiously watching their activities from the cliff edge with a pair of binoculars he had boosted from an unattended powerboat. Every day, it seemed, Michael and Billy returned to the marina with the tanks, their gear, and, occasionally, objects wrapped in towels that they had apparently removed from a wreck. He wanted to get his hands on whatever they were finding. It had to be valuable; they wouldn't make this many trips to the site if it weren't. They owed him, big time; they'd never pay, of course, so he'd just wait until he got a chance and take whatever he wanted from the van. That, and the gear he had stolen from the shop while he worked there.

* * *

After rigging the airlift supply tanks, the screen float, their running lights, and setting a second anchor to safeguard the inflatable against a more-powerful-than-normal current, they raised diver's flags and attached a strobe to the mast to make the boat slightly more visible in the fog, although that was probably overkill since the area they were in was so hazardous to vessels. "Tell that to the guy who was driving our wreck," Billy muttered.

Next, they suited up and completed the preliminary tasks of attaching the screen to the float lines and the supply hoses to the airlift and screen. They had established a routine by now; While Billy swam down to the airlift at the dig site, Michael turned on the air at the first supply tank and took up his position at the screen. "Anytime you're ready," he called.

"OK," came the reply. "Here we go again." With that, the hose convulsed, and once again began to spew mud and rocks, just as it had done every day for the past several weeks. Every time they returned to the site they found that the current had moved enough silt to fill in the areas they had already excavated, but that was par for the course. For that reason they never left a quadrant incompletely excavated, lest they have to excavate it twice.

By mid-morning they were deep into the mud of quadrant F2; as Michael lapsed into the largely mindless routine of watching what came out of the hose and telling Billy when to stop dredging so that he could empty the screen, his mind wandered to other things. He thought about students, the shop, and his relationship with Billy. They were so different, yet Billy had become his best friend and capable partner in a very short period of time. The shop's success was due as much to Billy's profound technical skills as it was to Michael's sense of people and ability to get them excited about diving. Mostly, though, he thought about Lexie. She was the one who had made the real difference in his life, helping him focus on a career and feel as if he was doing something valuable. He knew that they were destined to be together; he just hoped that she felt the same way. He was pretty sure she did, but...

His reverie was interrupted by the sound of Billy's voice in the earphone. "Shit!" he yelled, and the airflow stopped abruptly.

"You okay down there?" Michael called, concerned. He knew that the airlift could be dangerous, and hoped that it hadn't bitten Billy.

"I'm fine," came the reply. "There's a big chunk of clay wedged up in the mouth of the lift, and I'm going to have to hack it out. Bear with me a minute; I'll be finished in a second."

Michael responded, relieved that it wasn't anything serious. "Tell me before you start dredging again; I'll go ahead and pick through the screen while you're doing that, since it's almost full. I'll let you know when I'm done."

"No problem," Came the quick reply.

Michael began to pick through the detritus in the screen, tossing the large rocks off the side and filtering the smaller pebbles through his fingers. He could hear Billy's labored breathing through his earphone, indicating that his "little problem" was bigger than he thought. A tiny decorator crab in the screen reared up and thrust its diminutive claws at him in defiance; he carefully picked up the little creature and let it drift to the bottom. Grabbing another handful of silt and stones, he let them filter through his fingers...and stopped. There in front of him floated a handful of what looked like wood fibers, although when he touched them, they dissolved into a jellylike cloud.

Picking through the remaining material in his hand, he carefully lifted out the rocks. Sure enough, there was more of the stuff. Turning on his light, he placed the faceplate of his mask very close to the remaining material in the screen, looking closely at the area where he had scooped up the last handful. Reaching down, he grabbed the Ping-Pong paddle that hung on a lanyard at his side and began to fan it carefully over the area. Reddish-brown sediment drifted up and away from the screen like smoke, leaving behind pebbles and other sediment too heavy to be moved by the fanning motion of the paddle. As the flourlike cloud cleared, he looked more carefully; moving aside a few rounded rocks and half of a beer bottle, he revealed what appeared to be a piece of wood about two inches square. It was clearly very old; when he touched it, it had the consistency of jelly.

Carefully removing the debris that surrounded the fragment, Michael was able to carefully slide his paddle under it and lift it free. Reaching into his BC pocket, he removed a Ziploc bag and carefully slid the artifact into it. He squeezed out some of the water, leaving enough to cushion and moisten the sample. When he had sealed the bag, he laid it carefully on the side of the screen assembly, far enough away from the edge that it wouldn't fall off. Then, he called to Billy.

"Hold off for a minute, Billy. I've got wood fragments up here that are pretty old. I think we may have found something."

The response was immediate. "No problem. I've moved over to the edge of the dig with this thing anyway; this chunk of clay is tougher to break up than I thought. Just let me know when you're ready to go."

Michael responded, then began to once again pick carefully through the material in the screen, using the paddle to lift and float away the silt and his fingers to remove more pebbles. The screen was full of the wood fragments, and one of them had a hole in it that showed clear signs of staining from metallic oxidation, probably copper. This piece he also placed carefully in a baggie before proceeding. There was no question that this was a very old wreck; perhaps Lexie would be able to tell them the age of the thing from the wood samples they had collected.

If he hadn't squeezed the tennis ball-sized nodule of clay that he lifted out of the screen, he would have missed it. Squeezing the lump absentmindedly, it broke apart. As he rubbed the pieces away he realized that there was something hard embedded in the clay that felt like a pencil, or perhaps a razor clam shell. Looking down, he pried open the mass and took a sharp, deep breath as he saw what lay inside. There, protruding from the clay, in a mold of its own making, lay an exquisite golden medallion with filigreed edges and an encrustation of tiny seed pearls. It bore the faintly raised outline of a religious symbol of some sort. The medallion was perhaps an inch across.

"Holy Mother of God," he said into the microphone. The response from below was curious, perhaps even cautious. "Michael?" asked Billy.

"Get up here, Billy," came Michael's reply. "Get up here right now. You need to see this before we go any farther. I think we found the mother lode." He turned the object over and over in his hand, noting faint scratch marks on the back. They looked like the letters 'LMO,' but he couldn't be sure.

Michael placed the medallion in a baggie with water, and waited for Billy to ascend to him. When he arrived, Michael signaled that they should surface. Doffing their weight belts and tanks, they climbed into the inflatable, at which point Michael showed the exquisite piece of jewelry to Billy. He was speechless. His lips moved, but no sounds emerged.

Ever so carefully, Michael wrapped the piece in a T-shirt before stowing it safely in an equipment case on the boat. They scarcely spoke as he did this; they were close, they realized, very close. After swapping the tanks in their backpacks for fresh ones, pausing for a drink, and moving the airlift supply hose to a new tank, they once again descended and took up their positions at the airlift and screen.

"Take your time, Billy, and keep an eye out," said Michael to his friend. "The stuff could be scattered all over the bottom. Watch for anything that looks out of place."

Billy laughed. "As far as I can tell, *everything* looks out of place down here, Mikey. But I'll be careful. Let's get on it."

Moments later, effluent was once again pouring out of the upper end of the airlift. Michael let the screen fill before asking Billy to hold off. He picked through the sediment, dropping handfuls of rock over the side, but other than more wood fragments, he found nothing of interest. The hour that followed proved to be fruitless; the screen filled four times, but nothing of value emerged. By now, Billy had moved into quadrant G4, and the end of the day was approaching. It was just after four o'clock, and Michael was feeling the exhaustion of a long dive. He was completely enveloped in a mud cloud from the airlift, and was took several seconds before he realized that the flow from the airlift had stopped.

"Billy? Everything OK down there?" he called. No response. "Billy? Talk to me. You okay?"

The response was not what he expected. Concerned, he

left the screen and headed for the bottom. As he descended to the dig site, the only sound in his ears was laughter. Then, Billy began to sing, "If I Were a Rich Man."

PART II

Steven Shepard

CHAPTER 13

April 4, 1545: Río Amazonas

"Damn this jungle, damn these flies, and damn Pizarro," muttered Francisco de Orellana. He and his men—what were left of them—had now been crossing the *Cuenca Amazonas*—the Amazon Basin—for more than four months. Under orders from Francisco Pizarro, they had trekked across the Andes from Peru into Bolivia, searching for Curicuri, the legendary province of gold. And gold they had found: they were heavily laden with ingots, goblets, figurines, and countless golden beads and teardrops. More correctly, the Indians they had pressed into service in Peru as they looted the villages and pillaged their stores were heavily laden. And while they were clearly in possession of a great fortune, Orellana and his men knew that they had left behind much more treasure, and it galled them that they had been forced to flee from an increasingly large and bellicose army of locals, many armed with traditional—and deadly—Inca weapons—the *estolica*, a spear-thrower that was particularly deadly in the jungle; the *huaraca*, a sling that powered stones with great accuracy; and the *macana*, a star-headed club that was particularly effective at breaking bones. Many of his men had succumbed to the primitive weapons before they realized just how ineffective their European weapons were in a skirmish in the jungle.

For the most part, the men in Orellana's party had

come to the New World from Extremadura, that aptly-named region of southwestern Spain—the name means, 'extremely hard'—that supported olive trees and little else. At best, it offered a hardscrabble life with little future, so when the opportunity to join an expedition that involved leaving Extremadura presented itself, many jumped at the opportunity. How much worse could an uncertain future in the new world be? These were tough men, hard men, but they dropped in numbers from the constant onslaught of disease and the incessant attacks from the small groups of native marauders who seemed to materialize from the wet jungle air. One minute there would be nothing but the sounds of the jungle; the next, two or three or four men would be found with their skulls split or their bellies hacked open, the insects feasting on their exposed entrails. Never, ever, did they see their attackers; the priest began to talk of *las fantasmas de la selva*—the ghosts of the jungle.

They had dropped off the spine of the Andes into the dense jungle on the eastern side of the mountains, and had wandered through the jungle for months, heading roughly northeast. Eventually, they split into two groups; Gonzalo Pizarro, it was decided, would continue along the foothills of the mountains, looking for further riches to carry back to Spain, while Orellana would take a complement of soldiers and find a waterway that would take him deeper into the jungle in search of Curicuri. Their plan was to meet again six months hence, on the coast where they had first made landfall. From there, they would sail north for a time, looking for a route back to Spain.

After several months, Orellana and his party came to a large river, swollen and green and flowing slowly. They named it La Madre de Diós. On its banks they built a camp, and after some discussion, decided to fell trees for the lumber they would need to build a boat. Enough of this jungle trekking: they would sail to the mouth of this river.

Some of the soldiers, trained as sawyers, used two-man saws to cut boards from the huge logs; others used hammers and axes to fashion crude nails from the horseshoes they had brought with them for the horses. As the vessel took shape, Orellana realized that it looked more like a keeled barge than it did a caravel; it would serve them well on the river, or in a calm bay, but would be less capable when they arrived at the mouth of the river and entered the open sea. That, he decided, was a concern for another day.

From the dense green of the jungle he and his men jumped as a strangled cry emanated from behind them. Another man down, he thought; Madre de Dios, will this madness ever end? He sent a party to recover what would surely be another body; for now, they had to get out of this accursed jungle before the locals killed them all.

For six weeks Orellana and his team of soldiers and local laborers toiled to build the crude little vessel that would see them downriver. It was hellishly hot in the jungle, and the humidity, coupled with scurvy, dysentery, and the incessant biting insects, drove more than one man screaming into the jungle or deep into the river, where the *pongos,* the inescapable whirlpools, drew them into the inescapable depths. Well over two-thirds of Orellana's men had succumbed to the horrors of the forest; a trail of Spanish corpses marked their route from Peru.

The few indigenous people they encountered during their trek through the jungle willing to speak with them talked about a massive river that lay far to the east, a river that would take them to the open sea for the long voyage home. They realized by now that they would probably not meet up again with Gonzalo Pizarro until they returned to Spain, but hopefully they would return with the riches they had amassed, and would reap the rewards that had been accorded to all explorers returning with gold: social prominence, wealth, perhaps even an appointment to the court of the King.

As the vessel neared completion, Orellana sent laborers into the jungle to slash rubber trees. The white, sticky sap was ideal for caulking the hull of the ship. They boiled it in copper kettles with the dense fiber from fig trees that were thick in the jungle, and crushed the mixture thickly into the cracks between the hull timbers. As it dried, it expanded, making a near-watertight seal.

When the broad, flat hull with its shallow keel was complete, they laid mahogany decking over the joists and hammered it into place. They stepped the mast, mounted its cross-members, and rigged the makeshift sail they had sewn from cloth collected during their journey. It would shred if subjected to much more than a gentle breeze, but for their journey downriver, it would do. If need be, they would replace it when they arrived at a settlement.

They launched their vessel early one morning, and watched as it rolled high and sat proudly on the water. Soon the word came from below decks: no leaks in the hull. They left her there, tied to the shore, for three days. When they were sure she was watertight, they began to load their bounty of gold and what was left of their supplies and men. The weight of the cargo settled the hull deeply into the water, but they had designed her well and she handled the added weight easily. That evening, they christened her with a splash of rum across her bow, and named her *Nuestra Señora de la Selva,* Our Lady of the Jungle. The next day, just before the sun rose above the dense tree line of the jungle, they cast off and set sail for the mouth of the Amazon.

CHAPTER 14

The *Nuestra Señora de la Selva* slowly made her way down the river. The crew stopped periodically to harvest fruit and hunt wild pigs and the occasional capybara, caught arapaima in the river on hand lines, and as they moved to lower elevations and ate more fresh food, their health improved. They knew nothing, of course, about the relationship between the scurvy that wracked their bodies and the vitamin C in the fruit that they ate, but soon they were feeling better than they had felt since they had left Extremadura. Occasionally, they encountered local tribes of indigenous people, most of them cautiously friendly and willing to trade for food. Some shared medical treatments with the Spaniards, botanical solutions that miraculously cured the skin lesions and other ailments that plagued them throughout the journey. It was clear that their understanding of what the jungle had to offer was profound. Nowhere, though, did they find evidence of Curicuri.

After weeks of travel, they came to a larger river that would later be named *Madeira* by Portuguese explorers. They followed it downstream, and soon it emptied into the *Río Amazonas,* which would eventually take them to the Caribbean. Compared to the rivers they had spent the last few months on, this one was immense. In some cases they could scarcely see through the riverine mists to the other side.

Once they reached the main channel of the massive river, the wind coming down-current picked up, and soon they were under full sail, heading for the delta and, they hoped, home.

CHAPTER 15

Days passed. The great river moved them inexorably
onward, but after more than a week, Orellana began to
wonder if they would ever again see anything but the
impenetrably dense walls of the jungle on either side. As
wide as the river was, it still caused claustrophobia among
the men, who were accustomed to sailing on the open sea.
They became restless, and minor squabbles became
fistfights as the frustrations built. Orellana knew that
something had to change, and soon. As the river widened,
their hopes narrowed.

The call from the lookout came just before dawn.

"Capitán, aquí hay barcos! Estamos en la boca del río!"
'Captain, there are boats here! We've arrived at the river's
mouth!'

Immediately, Orellana came running up from below
decks. At the forward rail, the sight of hundreds of reed
boats surrounding their vessel greeted him, their
passengers smiling and waving wildly. In the distance, to
the northeast, he could see the wide mouth of the river,
and the Caribbean beyond. They had made it. They were
out of the jungle, and would soon set sail for home.

As they neared the mouth of the river, they spotted a
settlement on a small island to the east. Cautiously guiding
the *Señora de la Selva* in that direction, they approached the

113

island's natural harbor, and were greeted by the smell of cooking fires and the unmistakable sound of their native Spanish. Calling out to soldiers on the shoreline, they were quickly greeted in kind, and directed to tie their tiny vessel to the floating dock that extended into the broad mouth of the river. Another vessel, a caravel, was already tied alongside. She was called *La Plata*.

Orellana cautioned his crew not to speak of the gold they had in the hold, and posted guards with explicit instructions to prohibit anyone aboard who was not a member of the vessel's crew. Then he took leave of the ship with his senior officers and paid a visit to the Alcalde of the village, which, he had learned, was called Afuá.

The Alcalde, Don José Jorge de Beas, was gracious and helpful, although somewhat suspicious of the rag-tag group of men that had come floating out of the jungle with their fantastic tale of a harrowing journey from the *Mar del Sur*. In spite of his doubts, he fed and clothed them, gave them temporary housing, and promised to provision them as best he could for their intended journey to Spain. Truth be told, however, he put very little faith in their ability to reach the Antilles, much less Spain; their flat-hulled vessel was barely capable of handling the light chop of the coastline; it wouldn't survive an hour on the open ocean. But that was their problem, not his.

That evening, he invited Orellana and his senior officers to dinner, during which he explained his reason for being posted to such a lonely outpost.

"We have been here now for more than two years," he said, pouring brandy. "We were sent as part of an expedition that followed the voyage of Magellan, and upon reaching the mouth of this river, we decided to establish a presence here. This river is the mouth of *América del Sur*, and is therefore important to us. After all, you managed to traverse the entire continent from the *Mar del Sur* to the heights of the Andes all the way to the Caribbean by traveling the rivers that feed *Amazonas*. We will, I suspect, be here for some time to come."

He took a long drink of his brandy, settled back in his chair, and eyed the snifter that he held.

"And you, my friend: tell me your fantastic story. I know that you came out of the jungle like a *fantasma,* but I still don't know why you were there in the first place. What insanity convinced you to undertake such a long and arduous journey through uncharted territory?"

Orellana looked over at his first officer, Antonio de la Cierva, before he spoke.

"We were part of an exploratory party led by Gonzalo Pizarro, under the command of Francisco Pizarro. Our assignment was to explore the lands that lie to the east of the Inca Empire. We divided into two parties; Don Gonzalo was to continue overland to the south, while I was to march directly east. That was nearly six months ago; after three months we came upon a great river that flowed to the east, so rather than continue overland, we determined to build a boat and follow the river downstream. That river led us to another river, which in turn poured into Amazonas, which brought us to you."

De Beas nodded sagely, then smiled as he sipped his brandy.

"And what, friend Orellana, were you looking for, hmmm? Knowing Pizarro as I do, I have to believe that he is on a quest to add riches to the coffers of the Spanish crown, not to mention perhaps lining his own pockets. Did he send you off to look for Curicuri, perhaps? The fabled golden cities of the Inca empire? I can't help but notice that you have posted a rather large force of guards on the deck of your *Señora de la Selva,* which I also notice is riding rather low in the water. Might that be due to a quantity of Inca gold secured in the vessel's hold?"

Orellana did not respond. He sat quietly, looking at the brandy snifter in his hands and the floor beyond before bringing his eyes up to lock with those of de Beas.

"I am insulted by your insinuations, Don José Jorge de Beas," he spat. "We do the work of the same crown, and as an officer of the royal navy I trust you and expect the same courtesy in return. Apparently this barbaric jungle life has eroded whatever social graces you possessed when you arrived here, so I will not report your insolence when I return. If you feel a need to inspect the hold of my ship, then by all means do so. If you are expecting to find a fortune in Inca gold, then you will be sorely disappointed. Shall I conduct the tour myself, then?"

His gaze continued to bore into De Beas' eyes, who returned the stare for several seconds.

Suddenly, de Beas broke the tension with a loud laugh. Raising his arm, he clicked his brandy snifter against that of Orellana, and said, "To the crown. May your journey home be safe and uneventful. And no, my friend, a tour of your boat will not be necessary. Forgive my impudence. Tomorrow, your men will rest, and we will provision you for the long journey home. When you are ready to take your leave of us, we will bid each other farewell as gentlemen." With that, he bade them goodnight and retired to his quarters.

"I don't trust that man, and I would recommend expanded guards on the ship," de la Cierva muttered, as they walked back to the dock. "It would not surprise me at all if he sent a raiding party tonight."

They walked on for a while before Orellana responded. "I don't trust him either, José Jorge, and I do plan to post extra guards. I don't, however, believe he'll strike tonight. I think he'll wait until tomorrow, after he has sent spies aboard as part of his provisioning crew to determine the nature of our cargo.

"Spread the word quietly, José Jorge: we sail tomorrow at midnight, under cover of darkness. I want to be well clear of this place before the dawn moon rises."

CHAPTER 16

The morning dawned dark and calm, with a threatening sky, and thunder rumbled across the water like cannon fire. The small harbor of Afuá was eerily flat, as if oiled. The air smelled fresh, and felt electric. Storms were coming.

Orellana and de la Cierva rose before first light and checked in with the guards. Nothing untoward had occurred during the night, yet Orellana felt unsettled. He supervised the changing of the guard of the watch, ate breakfast, then inspected the cargo. Below decks, he noticed that the hull was moist in places, but the rubber tree caulk seemed to be working well. There were no significant leaks.

At mid-morning, Orellana paid a visit to de Beas at his residence. The Alcalde received him cordially, offering food and drink on the terrace. While a young Indian servant poured rich dark coffee, de Beas asked Orellana about his plans for the trip.

"With your permission, Don José Jorge, we will avail ourselves of your hospitality for a few more days," he replied. "We've been wandering in the jungle so long now that I'm afraid a quick departure would precipitate a mutiny on the part of my men. If you have no objections, we'll rest a bit longer before sailing for Valencia. However, if your offer still holds, I'd like to go ahead and provision the ship so that we can balance the load prior to departure.

117

Do you have men who could assist us?"

De Beas responded to the question just a bit too quickly. "But of course, Capitán Orellana. In fact, I have handpicked a team of my best men to help with the loading process. They are prepared to begin whenever you are ready. Just give me the word."

Orellana smiled back at the man, but his eyes were hard. "Thank you, Don José. Please tell your men that we begin loading today after the midday meal. I will meet them on the dock with my first officer, and will conduct their orientation personally before beginning the loading process."

De Beas agreed, and Orellana took his leave of the Alcalde of Afuá.

As soon as Orellana disappeared beyond the low rise between de Beas' home and the dock area, the Alcalde sent a servant off to search for the leader of the team that would assist with the loading of the *Nuestra Señora de la Selva*. When the man arrived, de Beas pulled him aside.

"I believe that Orellana's ship is heavily loaded with Inca gold, but a thorough inspection is the only way we'll know. Do not tip your hand to the captain or any of his men: load the hold as they direct you, but look everywhere for sign. Orellana is not a stupid man, so I'm sure he has hidden his trove well. Return to me when the loading is complete and we will plan our next step."

He reached up and put his hands on the other man's shoulders. "Victor, this is a once-in-a-lifetime opportunity. If that ship carries what I believe it carries, then we may have found the means to buy our way out of this God-forsaken place. For all Pizarro will ever know, Orellana and his men died of rot in the jungle. Pity."

CHAPTER 17

Shortly after the midday meal, a party of Indian laborers led by a single Spanish soldier arrived at the dock. They carried barrels of salted meat, casks of water and rum, and sacks of potatoes, yams, dried cassava, and onions, which they piled on the dock before returning for more. Victor Casas introduced himself to Orellana and de la Cierva, placing himself and his men at their disposal to help with the provisioning of their vessel.

When the laborers returned, they added to the growing pile of provisions a cage filled with live chickens, a trussed pig, charcoal for the ship's cooking braziers, tobacco, dried fish, and woven baskets filled with fresh fruit.

Casas addressed the captain and his first officer. "Based on the small size of your crew, Capitán, we have provisioned you with enough food and drink to last six weeks. That should be enough to see you safely back to Spain. Is there anything else you can think of that you might need for the voyage?"

Orellana inspected the pile of provisions, mentally calculating the amount of food that his severely diminished crew would consume during the trip. He had no intention of sailing with the Indians that had accompanied him and his men during the overland trip; their absence would cut down on food consumption. Many had already disappeared into the jungle, and he felt certain that the rest would not be far behind. None spoke Spanish, and neither he, his men, nor any of de Beas' men spoke Nahuatl. He was not concerned that the Inca would reveal the contents of the ship.

"You are most generous, lieutenant," said Orellana, shaking Casas' hand. "This is more than enough for me and my men, and should indeed see us safely home. My men have prepared space in the hold for the stores, so if you are ready, we can begin the loading process. If you will permit me, I will introduce you to the interior of our humble vessel."

Bowing smartly, Casas headed up the gangplank, followed by Orellana and de la Cierva. They walked to the hatch before the mainmast and climbed down the ladder that had been placed there for the purpose.

As Casas' eyes grew accustomed to the darkness of the hold, he began to discern shapes along the curving walls of the hull. Casually, he walked toward those on the port side of the vessel, and saw that the shapes, whatever they were, were wrapped tightly in large, waxy leaves and firmly secured with hemp rope.

"Plenty of room down here for the stores, captain," he said, as he paused near one of the shapes. Slowly, he slid his foot under a bulge in the shape, and lifted, as he gazed off into the darkness of the hold. Whatever it was was hard, and far too heavy for something so small. It might be ballast stone, but he had his doubts.

"Over here if you please, Lieutenant Casas," directed Orellana, pointing to a vertical frame member. "If you would direct your men to begin loading from this fore post back toward the stern, my men and I will perform the load balancing over the course of the next few days."

Casas saluted. "*A sus ordenes, Capitán.* I will direct the men to begin loading immediately."

The laborers made trip after trip to the vessel, depositing their burdens on the deck. Orellana's own men then moved the provisions into the hold, positioning them carefully to balance the load before securely tying everything down. By the time night fell, the provisioning of the *Nuestra Señora de la Selva* was complete. Under orders from Orellana, de la Cierva supervised the process and kept a close eye on Victor Casas.

During the loading, Casas remained below decks, except for occasional excursions to check on the status of the shrinking pile of stores on the dock. Orellana had specifically instructed de la Cierva not to interfere with Casas, so he had largely left the man alone. Several times, though, as de la Cierva watched the man from a distance, he saw Casas surreptitiously stoop to examine their leaf-encased bounty, or probe it with the tip of his boot. No doubt about it, thought de la Cierva; Casas was on to their secret. They would have to get out before de Beas had a chance to impound their vessel—or worse.

CHAPTER 18

"So tell me, Don Francisco. Considering the capricious nature of the trade winds at this time of year, what is your planned route home?" Orellana and de la Cierva were seated at de Beas' table, enjoying a post-dinner brandy. They had dined on roast pork, greens, and fried manioc root, all prepared by Indian laborers.

"Our plan is relatively straightforward, Alcalde," replied Orellana. "We will cross the Caribbean, skirting along the southern and eastern edge of the *Banco Serranilla*. From there we will continue east and enter the greater Atlantic. Our plan is to sail due east to the Cape Verde Islands, then north past the Canaries to the mouth of the Mediterranean. From there we will sail to Valencia."

De Beas smiled. "And I assume the provisioning of your ship went well today?" he asked.

"Thanks to your man Casas and his team of laborers, everything was stored in record time," replied Orellana. "Unfortunately, the volume of your generosity taxes the hold of our little ship, so my men are rearranging and lashing down the stores as we speak to ensure that the vessel will sail straight and true on the open sea. Sometime within the next few days, we will take our leave of you. And you should know, Don José Jorge, that I intend to inform the commander of the Armada of the degree to which you have helped us in our mission. For that, I thank you."

De Beas inclined his head in a mock bow. "By all means, friend Orellana, by all means."

Pity you'll not have that chance, he thought.

CHAPTER 19

"Everything is in order, Captain," said de la Cierva, as he began his report to Orellana shortly after their return from dinner. "Everything is properly stowed and balanced in the hold, and other than the deck watch, the men have been confined to quarters. Furthermore, I sent the captain of the guard out to do a bit of surveillance for me; he reports that during the last two nights, only three guards have patrolled the dock area, and then no more than once every hour. If we time our departure properly, we should be able to slip out behind the island and be gone before anyone is the wiser."

Orellana nodded, considering what de la Cierva had just told him. "I believe that de Beas will strike tonight, but probably not until the long hours before dawn, when he expects us to be most vulnerable. Come, Antonio: We sail after midnight."

The night passed without incident. Like clockwork, a pair of soldiers walked the length of the deck on the hour, nodding to the watch commander aboard Orellana's ship. The dock creaked quietly in the deep, quick-moving delta current as de la Cierva's crew stealthily released and pulled in the mooring lines just after midnight. The patrol of soldiers had passed by less than ten minutes before; Orellana waited a few minutes for them to continue beyond hearing range before he gave the muffled command to his first officer to cast off.

Three things worked in their favor. First was the element of surprise. They had established an expectation among de Beas' men that they would remain as guests of Afuá for several more days. Second, there was no moon as yet, so the movement of the ship would be difficult to see. And finally, the sky was heavily overcast and a steady rain was falling, which they hoped would cloak both the sight and the sound of their departure.

Freed from her moorings, and with her rudder hard to port, the *Nuestra Señora de la Selva* turned slowly away from the dock and slipped quietly into the current. Neither Orellana nor de la Cierva, both watching closely from the deck, detected any sign of pursuit. For the moment they were safe; as soon as they were far enough downriver that the pop of the expanding mainsail wouldn't attract attention, Orellana would raise full sheets to the wind and sail away from Afuá and the treachery of the outpost's *Alcalde*.

He had lied to de Beas at dinner; he had no intention of sailing east toward Africa. Instead, he planned to leave the Amazon delta, then sail due west for a time to evade whatever raiding parties de Beas might send after them. The western Caribbean was reasonably well charted, and the waters of the southern sea were clear of obstacles. Once he had sailed far enough to the west and knew that he had evaded de Beas, he would make landfall on the coast of Panama and trek to the western coastline of the *Mar del Sur* to rendezvous with Pizarro and his contingent. With luck, they would still be there, awaiting Orellana's arrival.

Orellana's reverie was broken by the crack of musket fire. "They're onto us, Antonio," he said grimly. Turning to the open mouth of the hold, he yelled into the darkness. "All hands on deck with full armor and weapons! Hoist the main and prepare to sail. We are being pursued, gentlemen, so smartly if you please!"

Immediately, men began to swarm out of the open

hold, all well armed. They moved quickly to take up defensive positions along the rail or at hoist points for the mainsail. In less than a minute, the sail was up, and with a crack like a musket shot, it inflated. The *Nuestra Señora de la Selva* creaked in response to the full blow of the wind. She leaped forward, toward the open sea and freedom.

The rain was now coming down in torrential sheets, and between it and the darkness it was impossible to see more than a hundred meters beyond the stern rail. Orellana didn't know how far behind them the pursuing ships were, but he calculated that the element of surprise and the light, fast nature of their vessel, in spite of the fact that it was so heavily loaded, would give them a slim but crucial lead. The growing force of the storm drowned out all sounds of pursuit, and Orellana knew that if he could clear the mouth of the vast river, their chances of escape were reasonably good.

Peering into the wet, stygian blackness, Orellana made out a dark hulking shape in the distance that soon resolved into a large island. Thinking quickly, he called out to the rudder. "Rudder, turn hard to port quickly and run along the far side of this island that approaches!" The helm responded instantly, and Orellana felt the ship careen sharply as she turned north.

"Captain, not to question your command, but are you sure—"

Orellana interrupted de la Cierva in mid-sentence. "In their minds, we're headed for Spain, Francisco, which means that they will expect us to turn hard to the east once we clear the delta. With any luck, they'll sail in that direction, hoping to cut us off on the open sea. Meanwhile, we'll shelter behind this island and continue west after they have had plenty of time to clear the channel."

De la Cierva thought about it for a mere second before snapping a smart salute and giving the order.

They sailed behind the island, which was quite large and would someday be named Ilha Caviana by the Portuguese.

It was roughly oval-shaped, surrounded by vast clumps of reeds, and densely overgrown. Along its shores, deep, mangrove-lined channels pierced inward, affording protection and camouflage for the vessel, should it prove necessary. Hopefully, thought Orellana, they would be able to continue north and west in a matter of a few hours.

CHAPTER 20

It was a fluke that anyone saw the *Nuestra Señora de la Selva* sail away in the rainy darkness. Because of de Beas' suspicions about Orellana's cargo, the captain of the guard had decided to redouble the number of men patrolling the dock area. Shortly after Orellana and de la Cierva cast off their last mooring line and drifted silently away from the dock, a second pair of guards rounded the path from the garrison to the dock. They could not see the ship clearly through the rain, but the empty spot where she had been moored was glaringly obvious. Firing their weapons into the air, they screamed into the wind in vain for the ship to return.

The commotion at the docks awoke de Beas' guards, and they, in turn, woke him. He instinctively knew what had happened. He dispatched his personal guard to the garrison with orders that they should assemble at the *Plata*, armed and ready to sail in pursuit. Within minutes the soldiers were aboard, the mooring lines were released, and the mainsail was run up. The ship attacked the water when the sail filled, and her fore post bit deeply into the water before the wind.

"Helm, north and east!" cried de Beas over the noise of the storm. "He's running for open sea and Spain. Make way for the *Canal del Sur*—it's the fastest way out of the river delta. We'll intercept them before they're out of sight of land!" Heeling hard, the ship turned east and sailed in pursuit.

The *Nuestra Señora de la Selva* sat poised in a quiet estuary on the western side of the island, out of the shrieking wind and driving rain—and, more importantly, out of sight of the pursuing vessel. For four tense hours Orellana and his men sat immobile, straining to catch the strains of human voices or the sounds of a sailing vessel over the cacophony of the storm. They knew that if de Beas' ship rounded the island and spotted them, they would not have time to raise the sail and escape before the cannons took them apart.

Finally, after sending men out to scout the channel, Orellana gave the all clear and they cautiously raised anchor and sailed from behind the island. Orellana's ruse had worked: de Beas had sailed east, in pursuit of a ghost ship.

The water to the north and west was a maze of waterways that ran like a skein of hair among myriad tiny islands, and it took Orellana until dawn to clear the vast mouth of the river and sail into the open Caribbean. Once he had determined that there were no pursuers, he gave the order to sail north and west. Turning, the Caribbean winds filled the ship's mainsail and she headed northwest around the massive head of South America, then on toward the narrow isthmus of land that separated the Caribbean from the *Mar del Sur*.

CHAPTER 21

Aboard the *Plata,* dawn arrived to the sight of a great deal of water and little else. For more than seven storm-wracked hours, de Beas had scarcely moved from his position at the forward rail, growing angrier with every passing moment.

"Where could they have gone, damn them, where could they have gone?" he muttered angrily to his first officer. The officer, knowing his superior as he did, hesitated before tendering a reply.

"Given the severity of the storm," he began, "and the frail nature of their ship, it is conceivable that they broke apart and sank, Alcalde. We all know how unforgiving this ocean can be with our own vessels—and they are built for it. The *Nuestra Señora de la Selva,* after all, was built for the slow waters of the river, not the rigors of the Mar Atlántico."

De Beas nodded slowly, considering the logic of his lieutenant's words. "You make a good point, lieutenant. By now, we would have spotted them on the horizon if they were still afloat; yes, you are no doubt correct. Orellana and his crew must now rest with their gold on the bottom of the sea. Damn him for taking our salvation with him to his grave!" Looking to the distant horizon one more time, he spat disgustedly over the side before giving the order to turn back. As he disappeared below decks, the crew heaved a thankful sigh of relief. De Beas could be a driven maniac, and they didn't fancy a chase across the Atlantic in search of a ship that probably lay in pieces on the bottom of the sea.

* * *

Seven days later, Orellana and his tiny ship were far to the northwest of the Amazon delta, sailing close to shore before a stiff wind. The storm had abated quickly after their escape from Afuá, but squalls had continued off and on since that time, forcing them more than once to seek shelter. They had made good time, though, and a week later spotted the island that would someday be called Aruba off the port bow. There they stopped for several days to rest, hunt, and replenish their fresh water supply. The ship had held up well, and had not leaked in spite of the beating the storm and squalls had meted out.

"It would be easy to stay here, wouldn't it, Antonio?" said Orellana, addressing his lieutenant. "This place is beautiful, but we must get underway. Besides—" he looked up at the sky—"I think there's another storm coming, and the coast of this island shoals quickly is not particularly well protected. I want to be far offshore when it hits so that we can ride it out. Tell the men to get some rest: we sail at dawn."

And sail they did, heading due west under a dark and threatening sky that promised torrential rain. The banshee wind shrieked in protest through the rigging, randomly changing direction and putting the crew through their paces. At midday, they turned due west and headed for the narrow isthmus of land that they would cross to reach the *Mar del Sur* and hopefully, their colleagues. By late morning, however, it was clear to Orellana that they would not be going anywhere fast, at least not in the direction that they wished. Off to starboard they could see the eerie surface of the *Banco Serranilla*. A former atoll, it was known to sailing vessels as a mostly submerged reef, a 40-kilometer by 32-kilometer area with very little water covering it. It made its first appearance on Spanish maps in 1510, although it was known to hundreds of ill-fated sailors long before. Largely invisible to navigators unfamiliar with the area, many vessels under full sail had realized their fate too late, and piled up on the rocks of Serranilla, scattering cargo, men and wreckage across the barely submerged surface. When the tide was low, the remains of these vessels were clearly visible: as far as the eye could see, cannon, masts, anchors and other evidence of misfortune punctuated the surface, eerily appearing as if they were floating on the water.

The storm built into a frightening maelstrom. They were caught now in the full force of a gale, and the shrieking wind was blowing them inexorably to the west, away from the narrow isthmus that was their destination. They were taking water over the bow, and it was sheeting into the hold; Orellana screamed a command to his senior officers to drop the sail to keep the bow out of the water and attempt to save the ship, his men, and their valuable cargo.

Once they had carried out his command, the ship's pitching lessened somewhat, but they still had precious little rudder control. They were in too much water to deploy the sea anchors, and if they chanced navigating toward the distant coastline that they lay to the west, they ran the risk of running aground on any one of the many reefs that guarded the mainland. No, thought Orellana, our best chance is to ride it out and hope for the best. *Que Diós nos protega,* he thought—may God protect us.

The storm continued unabated for more than 20 hours, cruelly lashing the tiny vessel without surcease. The wind had blown them off course for hours, but had then turned to the south and was blowing them more or less in the direction of the narrow spit of land that they wished to reach.

In spite of the pains that they had taken to build a

seaworthy craft, the caulking began to fail by first light, and leaks began to appear in the hull. By morning they had lost two men to the teeth of the hungry sea, and the water in the hold was sloshing several inches above the men's ankles. The remains of the rigging hung in tattered sashes from the crosspieces of the mainmast, which now creaked ominously with every pitch and yaw of the ship. If this continues much longer, thought Orellana, the mast will pitch itself overboard, and soon thereafter, *Nuestra Señora de la Selva* will follow it to the bottom. Looking up, he grasped the small golden crucifix that hung around his neck and offered a prayer to the heavens for the salvation of his men and his vessel.

From his position near the bow, Orellana looked through the sheeting rain and the spray that skittered across the surface of the sea. The salt stung his face; squinting, he looked hard to port, where he though he saw the dark smear of a coastline. That could be a problem, he knew, if the weather took them in that direction, because where there was a coastline, there were inevitably reefs which would do everything they could to gut the *Señora's* belly. Looking again, he realized that the line was no illusion. There *was* a coastline over there, the storm *was* carrying them in that direction, and there was little they could do about it. Even if they had wanted to raise the sails, they couldn't; the conditions would tear the ship to pieces.

Yelling once again over the wind, Orellana called out to de la Cierva. "The storm is carrying us toward the coast there to the south," he pointed. "I can't see a barrier reef, but there may well be one, which means that we may break up before we make landfall. So spread the word to the men—prepare to abandon ship!"

The crew needed no further urging. Collecting their meager personal belongings, they gathered on deck, bracing for the horrible, wrenching and terribly final sound of the reef's teeth biting through the underbelly of their ship. Looking off to the south, they saw the coastline approaching far too fast, and as the bottom shoaled up, the frenetic pitching of the ship increased. It wouldn't be long now, thought Orellana; somewhere down there, not far below the surface, coral fangs lay waiting. Grimly, he held tightly to the rail and waited for the end.

But the end did not come, at least not the way he thought. Miraculously, the ship surfed through the shallows, and rode a huge following sea up the final green wall of the surf zone and crashed, nose-first, into the sand. She hung there for a moment, then slowly careened over onto her port side, lay down, and died. The men scattered across the deck like tenpins, falling and running for the sand of the upper beach. Fifty yards from the water, they fell to their knees, offering prayers of thanks for having survived the ordeal.

Orellana had not yet joined them, nor had de la Cierva. They stood in shock beside the damaged hull of their ship, watching it roll gently back and forth as the pounding surf washed under her and then withdrew.

"Gather your men," said Orellana to his lieutenant. "We have to rig the ship and pull her as far up the beach as we can. If the debris line up there is any indication, we're at mean low tide, which means that if we don't secure her, she'll float away when the tide comes. She'll never sail again, but we may be able to use her timbers for other purposes. Help me move her up the beach before she rolls and washes away."

Saluting his captain, de la Cierva turned and ran up the beach.

Four hours later, they had emptied the ship of her stores and priceless cargo and carried them to the safety of higher ground. Once emptied, the *Señora* was much lighter, and after rigging towlines, the men took up positions and began the onerous task of pulling the vessel slowly up the beach. It was backbreaking work in the raging storm, but thanks to the slowly rising tide and the ship's reduced weight, they finally succeeded in pulling her up to the drier part of the beach and securing her firmly to the trees. Once satisfied that the *Señora* would not leave the beach in the climbing tide, they began to set up camp and prepare a long-overdue hot meal. Orellana ordered a team of men to butcher the pig, while others gathered firewood. Under a quickly erected lean-to, they built a roaring fire to dry and warm themselves, then allowed the fire to settle down to a bed of very hot coals over which they roasted the now spitted pig. Shortly before the meat was done, they threw yams into the coals of the fire, which cooked quickly. Ravenous, they ate the pork, the yams, and handfuls of fresh fruit that they had rescued from the ship.

By the time they finished their meal, the storm had begun to abate, and the wind slowed, leaving a soft rain that fell from the glowering sky. Soon, it, too, ended. The storm was over.

At the end of the meal, the captain offered a cup of rum to all. They toasted their survival, the crown, and their continued success, then set off to explore their surroundings. Now that the storm had ended, they could see that the beach stretched, uninterrupted, as far as they could see in both directions. They had indeed been lucky: there were barrier reefs scattered randomly 100 yards offshore, and the *Señora* had managed to squeeze between two of them. In the jungle above the beach, they found banana trees which they climbed, and from them dropped entire bunches of the yellow fruit, much to the consternation of hordes of small monkeys that screamed at them from the relative safety of the treetops. Brilliant red, yellow and blue macaws shrieked from above, and one of the men jumped backward in surprise when a bird-eating spider, twice a man's hand across, jumped from a tree trunk onto his chest. Reflexively, he slapped it to the ground, cursing. *Qúe araña de miedo,* he muttered. Before he could crush it under his boot, it disappeared into the foliage.

Under the lean-to, Orellana and de la Cierva hovered over a chart, trying to ascertain their location. They knew that they had been blown past the headlands of Colombia, an area which had only been settled by Spanish explorers 30 years prior. Given their recent experience with the

Alcalde of Afuá, they decided that they would avoid contact with other settlements for the time being.

"It appears that we are somewhere here," offered de la Cierva, pointing to the narrow isthmus that connected Nueva Andalucía to its enormous neighbor to the north. "If that is in fact where we are, then we might be in a better place than we realized—and able to rejoin the rest of the party on the *Mar del Sur* side, although it will mean a longer overland trek than we had originally planned, carrying very heavy cargo. This jungle is dense, but we should be able to find a route through it that will be manageable. A northwest passage that will lead us back to Europe has long been rumored; perhaps our *compadres* have found it. If not, we will travel south through Tierra del Fuego, a longer trip but a known route. What are your thoughts, *mi Capitán?*"

Orellana agreed with de la Cierva. "We should send a small party of men into the jungle to see if it is feasible to cross this peninsula—if that is in fact where we are. When they return, we can make plans for a cross-country voyage, but until then, we rest here. We'll hide the cargo deep in the jungle until we are prepared to leave, and post a guard at all times. We don't know who inhabits this area, Antonio; until we do, or are ready to get underway, we must take precautions. Please see to it. Maintain an armed force and stress vigilance. We've come too far, and survived too much, to lose everything to complacency. Meanwhile, I will form a scouting party to seek a path to the *Mar del Sur.*"

Steven Shepard

CHAPTER 22

Two weeks passed. Orellana's men grew strong from their steady diet of fresh fruit, and from the seemingly endless supply of fish and shellfish that they netted from the sea and the meat provided by the troupes of monkeys that chattered endlessly in the treetops. The monkey meat was stringy and strong tasting, but far more edible than the dried fish that they had been provided by de Beas' men in Afuá.

To date they had heard nothing from the ten men that Orellana had dispatched into the forest with instructions to find a route to the *Mar del Sur*, but they were not yet concerned. If Orellana's estimates of their location were correct, then the total time to trek across the narrow isthmus, take stock of their location, search for signs of the other half of the exploration party, and return to the campsite, should take a minimum of two weeks, provided they did not run into difficulty or become lost in the heavy jungle. Meanwhile, de la Cierva took a small team of men into the forest, where they dug a hole and buried the gold that they had looted from Inca villages and carried with them from deep in the Amazon basin. He then posted two men to discretely guard the well-disguised site.

Three weeks to the day from their departure, the detachment of ten men returned from their expedition, none the worse for wear from their experience. Orellana, however, was astonished to see that his detachment had grown to twenty! They were in high spirits, for not only had they found a reasonable route across the isthmus and returned unscathed, they had news to report. Orellana received them warmly, offering them food and drink before hearing their story. While they ate, they told him of their journey. The trip through the jungle had been largely uneventful; they met few people along the way, and those they did encounter were friendly and curious about the oddly dressed strangers in their midst. They had found plenty of food, and had arrived at the *Mar del Sur* coast late on the afternoon of the sixth day. The sight of a broad, calm bay greeted them, and anchored there, much to their astonishment, was a European ship.

The Spaniards knew that a number of European countries had dispatched exploration parties to the new world, but from their vantage point they could not ascertain the flag under which this ship sailed. Crawling closer, they approached the shoreline, and were amazed to see that the ship was flying the Spanish flag. Furthermore, upon closer examination, they recognized the ship as one of the two belonging to their original expedition force.

"Once we cleared the jungle and arrived at the beach, we saw the smoke from a cook fire, rising from behind a dune," explained Tomás Garcia, the leader of the expedition. "We trekked across the sand until we came to the source of the smoke, and there we found a large detachment of our own soldiers, preparing their evening meal. Our appearance scared them out of several saints' lives—they were as surprised to see us as we were to find them.

"At any rate, they explained to us that Pizarro and the other two ships had sailed up the coast on an exploratory voyage in the hopes of finding an eastward passage that would avoid the hellish sail around Tierra del Fuego. They had put in on this beach to effect minor repairs to their ship, and planned to catch up with Pizarro and the others somewhere north. Pizarro had promised to light signal fires each night until they arrived.

"*Capitán,* they were astounded to hear our story, and informed us that Pizarro believed us dead. The priest has already held memorial services for us: won't they be surprised when we arrive, laden with the treasure that Pizarro sent us to find!"

Orellana was ecstatic. "What, then, is their intention with regard to us? Did they agree to wait for us to trek reach them?"

The man nodded vehemently. "Yes, captain. They agreed to wait until we return; they have plenty of room on their vessel for us and our cargo. I told them it would take perhaps 20 days to make the return journey, and the captain sent these additional men to help us pack and transport our stores to their ship."

Orellana heaved a sigh of relief. After anticipating a long, arduous journey back to Spain in the frail vessel that now lay canted and broken on the beach, this was very good news indeed. Providence had clearly smiled on him and his crew.

"Tomás García, you and your men have done well, and I extend my thanks to those of you who accompanied my men here. You are all a credit to the Spanish Crown." Orellana then turned to de la Cierva. "Antonio, tonight we celebrate our good fortune. Have the cooks prepare a meal to remember, after which we do damage to the remaining stocks of rum that our friend de Beas was so kind to include in our ship's stores. At first light, we will assemble the crew and prepare for our overland journey and a joyous reunion with our *compadres.*"

CHAPTER 23

The days flew by, as Orellana and his men prepared for the journey ahead. The distance to the far coast was not great, and while Garcia assured him that the trip was an easy one, he fretted. They had a considerable amount of heavy cargo to transport, much of it extremely valuable, and if they were ambushed in the forest they would have precious little ability to maneuver and defend themselves.

To begin, the men dismantled the hull of their beloved *Nuestra Señora de la Selva*. This part of their water journey was over; the ship would now be remade into a land ship of sorts, this time with wheels instead of a hull, men instead of wind-filled sails. From the timbers, Orellana's men fashioned large, sturdy carts, long and narrow, in which to transport their plunder and supplies. The towing mechanism was similar to that used for oxen, although there would be no oxen yoked to these wagons—instead, groups of men would take turns pulling the unwieldy vehicles through the jungle.

After eight days, they were ready. They excavated the gold from its hiding place, loaded it securely on two of the three wagons, and filled the third with their supplies—food, tools, water barrels, and an assortment of timbers from the ship to be used in case repairs were required on one of the wagons. Then, with a long, last look back at the skeletal remains of their ship, they lined up, took positions on the wagons, and began the arduous trek through the jungle to rejoin their expedition.

The trip across the isthmus went without incident, other than a broken axle on one of the wagons that stopped them for a day while repairs were made. As the men dragged the wagons through the dense jungle growth, others went ahead, clearing a trail and seeking the flattest route.

Ten days later, on a beautiful late afternoon, they stepped out of the jungle into the bright sunlight of the western coast. Beyond, the *Mar del Sur* sparkled blue and white in the hot tropical sun. In the bay to their left sat a large ship at anchor, the ship that would carry them safely home.

It took them until after midnight to load the cargo aboard the ship. Finally, the captain gave the all-clear signal to raise anchor. The sails filled with wind, the ship turned, and they were underway, heading north toward the rest of their expedition party and, hopefully, home. They would return to Spain, and there were strong rumors of a channel to the north that would get them there. Otherwise they faced a long and dangerous trip around the southern tip of América Sur, a trip that destroyed more ships than were allowed to pass. *Tierra del Fuego* was not to be taken lightly. For the chance to return to Spain, however, they would gladly risk the journey.

The voyage up the coast was uneventful, although the combination of tricky currents and strong winds made for exciting sailing. They proceeded up the coast of the Aztec Empire and continued north for many days, all the while looking for Gonzalo Pizarro's signal fires or any sign of another ship. They saw neither, and the farther up the coast they went, the more concerned they became. Perhaps a storm had forced them to retreat farther offshore? Or worse, perhaps they had been beaten by a storm and lay at the bottom of the sea. Neither Orellana nor the captain of the ship were willing to accept the latter explanation, and they continued their journey as planned.

For days they tacked back and forth, fighting the ever-changing winds and the capricious currents. Whales breached alongside the vessel, and black-and-white porpoises rode their bow wave. Gulls, terns, auks, cormorants and the occasional albatross wheeled above the sheets.

Finally, after ten days, a sign. It was late in the evening, and they were sailing approximately twenty furlongs offshore when the lookout called out that he could see what looked like a fire on the coast. Turning abruptly eastward, they sailed toward the rocky shore, and soon, all aboard could see the flickering light of a large bonfire. *At last,* thought Orellana. Writing in his Captain's log, he recorded the event, and then locked the leather-bound journal in the small trunk that contained his few personal items and that had traveled with him for the entire ill-fated journey.

The rudder fought to keep the ship on course. They sailed directly toward the uninterrupted rocky prominence of the coast, hoping to see a glimpse of a ship. Why, Orellana wondered, would Pizarro tie up and build a signal fire along a rocky coastline that clearly offered no protection from the elements? There had to be a reason, but it defied logic. Then he saw it.

From their position offshore, the coastline looked uninterrupted, but now, he realized that there was a harbor entrance before them, remarkably disguised by the position of two islands that, when juxtaposed against the mouth of the harbor, disguised the entrance perfectly. Apparently Pizarro had stumbled across this large bay, and the fire was kept burning to mark the entrance for them when they arrived. Orellana relayed his observations to the captain of the vessel, who immediately gave orders to steer for the harbor entrance. Soon, they would be reunited with the rest of their party. With any luck, their colleagues had located the alternate route that would carry them back to their beloved Spain.

It was fairly dark now, and they were close enough to

the coast to see people moving in front of the fire. The men on shore were clearly excited, a sign that they had spotted the vessel. The captain was sailing directly toward the narrow mouth of the harbor in a north-northeasterly direction. Orellana and de la Cierva stood at the bow, watching for signs of the other ships.

"There!" called Orellana, leaning over the rail and pointing into the harbor. "There, beyond those wash rocks! Pizarro's ships!" There they were, silhouetted against the dark background of a large island.

Just as de la Cierva turned to shake hands with Orellana, there was a sudden and violent deceleration of the ship, a horrible crash from below, and a terrible shuddering that passed through the vessel. Without warning, the ship began to heel obscenely to port. With a short distance to go to reach the safety of the harbor, they had run aground on a shallow reef, hidden below the dark, turbulent waters on the north side of the harbor mouth. Orellana and de la Cierva were thrown over the forward rail; they struck the water, and were carried by a powerful backwash toward the open sea. The dark water closed over Orellana's head, and he choked on the tartness of the cold, salty water that flooded over him.

His first thoughts were those of realization: the people on the beach that waved at them were not doing so in greeting; they were trying to warn them away from the savage teeth of the hidden reef. As the ship rose high and then crashed down upon him, smearing his lower body across the rocks, Orellana thought of Pizarro in his final, agony-filled moments. Damn the man, he cursed. Damn him to Hell for putting my men through such an ordeal.

His last thought was of his beloved Luisa. He hoped that they would one day be united in the hands of God.

Two sailors survived the wreck, and managed to swim to the safety of the rocks on the north shore of the harbor entrance before the whirlpool created by the dying ship's descent into the depths caught them and pulled them down. All other hands were lost, and in a matter of minutes the powerful current dragged the remains of the vessel to the edge of the reef, where she sank, her back broken and her hull irretrievably breached. Knowing Pizarro as they did, the two survivors chose not to mention the gold. Given his legendary temper, he might well have them horsewhipped—or worse—if he were to discover that an Inca fortune lay outside the harbor mouth, just beyond anyone's reach.

Some of the wreckage floated ashore, including rum barrels and Orellana's personal chest. In it were his journals, which Pizarro transported back to Spain. They were entrusted to a priest in Extremadura, and eventually, made their way to the National Archives.

Three days later, Pizarro and his remaining entourage turned and sailed south, heading to Tierra del Fuego—and home.

Steven Shepard

PART III

CHAPTER 24

Michael had no idea what to expect as he descended to where Billy was dredging away the silt of quadrant G4. There was a murky cloud surrounding the site, and as he passed through it he bumped directly into Billy's broad back. Billy started, then turned and grinned at Michael.

"What in the world are you hollering about?" asked Michael, swimming around to the front of the area where Billy was working. "Whatever you found—oh, my God!" Michael started, seeing the object cradled in Billy's arms.

There, in regal, golden splendor, was a carving of a ceremonial Inca raft, replete with a large godlike figure and a dozen smaller figures. The entire object was perhaps 30 inches long, and in the light of his flashlight, it was clear to Michael that it was gold. It was perfectly intact, except for one of the smaller figurines on the vessel's deck, which appeared deformed—crushed, most likely, when the ship carrying it went down.

"Where –" Michael began.

"Wait," ordered Billy. Turning, he reached in the dig site and retrieved a golden necklace covered with what looked like pearls; a golden drinking vessel, nearly 20 inches tall; and a pair of emerald-encrusted golden gloves, apparently ceremonial garb, perhaps stolen from the grave of a nobleman.

Michael was beyond speechless. All he could do was stare at the growing pile of riches as Billy continued to retrieve objects from the clay. A handful of golden beads. A tiny figurine, inlaid with the swirling opaline colors of abalone shell. A jade-encrusted statuette. A golden death mask. Looking at Billy, he shook his head in wonderment. It was several minutes before either of them could speak.

Finally, Billy broke the silence. "Bags. We've got to get bags to pack this stuff in. And they have to be big, to make room for cushioning. What have we got up in the boat?"

Michael thought for a moment before responding. "We've got the lift bags, we could use those. We also have clothes. In fact, we could wrap this stuff in the clothes, then stuff them in the bags. Are they fragile?"

Billy nodded. "Everything except the little boat and the abalone-covered statue is pretty solid; they're the only things that I'm worried about. If we wrap them in T-shirts, or maybe those rolls of neoprene patching material in the toolbox, I think they'll be OK. We can wrap the other stuff in the bags and pack them in the boat."

They wasted nearly fifteen minutes of precious air examining their find before they moved the artifacts to a designated holding area in the far corner of the gridded dig site, and then continued to excavate. They worked well into the dark of evening; Billy rigged a dive light on one of the rebar posts, and it illuminated the work area enough to allow them to continue to search the site in spite of the growing darkness.

Just as night fell, they completed the excavation of row G. In addition to the items that Billy had already found, their efforts yielded 36 heavy, cigar-shaped golden ingots, more than 100 marble-sized golden beads, and an ornately carved malachite bird. From the row's final quadrant, Billy retrieved the leather-covered haft of what looked like a sword of some kind. The leather was almost completely rotted away, and little remained of the blade. It was an interesting piece, and he laid it down carefully with the other artifacts.

Finally, he was finished. "That's it, Michael," he called to his partner, who was somewhere above him, watching the effluent at the screen. "That's the last quadrant; I say we call it a day and go do some celebrating. Besides, I have a feeling you want to share this with Lexie."

Michael's reply was immediate. "I didn't think you were ever going to finish, Billy. Let's get this stuff in the boat and get out of here. Besides, it's getting late, and I'm starved." They prepared to surface.

From the Achilles, they retrieved their shirts and sweatshirts, as well as all of the lift bags and the rolls of neoprene material. Descending once again to the excavation, they carefully wrapped all of the artifacts except for the golden boat in the clothing and neoprene, and placed them in the lift bags. They left the golden boat uncovered, out of fear that they might damage it in the process of trying to protect it.

They surfaced with their treasure, and upon arriving at the boat they looked around to ensure that they were alone and unobserved. Satisfied, they shed their SCUBA gear, temporarily hanging it from gear clips on the sides of the inflatable. Michael climbed into the boat, and Billy gently handed him the lift bags, followed by the exquisite golden vessel. Michael emptied the box that normally held weight belts and placed the artifact in the box on top of a spare pair of wetsuit pants, then covered the box with a wetsuit top to hide its contents.

Billy climbed aboard, retrieved the gear that was dangling below the boat, and started the small outboard so that it could warm up before they motored back to the marina. But after running the engine for about a minute or so, he turned it off, and turned to face Michael. Overhead, the lights of the Golden Gate were diffuse yellow blobs in the fog that enveloped them; the only sound was the surf breaking on the nearby rocks, and the distant sound of traffic on the bridge deck, 200 feet above them.

"Michael," he began, looking down at the bags that filled the bottom of the boat. "I—this—I mean, we—"

Michael laughed, and stood to join his friend on the starboard tube of the Achilles. Carefully stepping around the treasure on the floor, he sat down, and watched as a huge grin spread across Billy's face. High-fiving each other, they howled like hyenas into the night. Billy started the engine, and they turned the inflatable toward the bay and headed for Sausalito and home.

As they motored across the water, Michael tried to call Lexie to see if she was available that night for dinner, but her phone just rang, then went to voice mail. He tried several times with the same results.

"That's odd," he said to Billy. "Not answering."

Billy shrugged his shoulders. "She's probably running errands and didn't hear the phone ring. She'll call back, or we can swing by her place after we go by the shop."

Michael agreed, and they continued toward the marina.

CHAPTER 25

The week had been a bitch without Roland around.
Every day, Alan replaced zincs, cleaned hulls, fixed
moorings that had shifted, and made minor repairs to
outboards. He also paid careful attention to the coming
and going of Michael and Billy, noting that their days were
becoming longer as time went on. Most mornings they
arrived by 6 and didn't return until long after dark. He also
noticed something very, very interesting: every day for the
last week or so, they had unloaded their dive gear as they
always did, but they also unloaded something else: a very
large, very new Pelican case, the kind you can park a truck
on without damage, secured at all times with two very large
padlocks and sporting the Ocean Adventures logo. They
handled it like a newborn baby, and they never placed it in
the back of the van with the gear: it went into the front of
the van with them. Whatever they were working on down
there was valuable—he was sure of it. And he was just as
sure that there was something in that case that deserved his
attention.

The following Sunday, Alan woke early and waited for
Michael and Billy to leave the marina on their way to the
Potato Patch. Knowing that they would most likely be
diving until late evening, he waited until they were out of
sight and then jumped into the old work van that Roland
had left for him to use. He drove across the Golden Gate
Bridge, passed through the city and across the Bay Bridge,

went through the Caldecott Tunnel, and made his way to Walnut Creek, where he parked behind Ocean Enterprises. Wearing a baseball cap and sunglasses, he walked casually around the front to ensure that no one was there, looking in the shop windows as if he were a casual shopper. The lights were out; clearly, no one was inside.

Returning to the back of the shop he pulled a pry bar from the van and, after a few minutes, managed to carefully jimmy open the back door without damaging the lock. He knew from the brief time he had worked there that while the shop had an alarm system, it was rarely used. He quickly checked the repair area; he didn't think they'd put the case or whatever it contained in there, but he took a quick look. Finding nothing, he moved on.

The office door was open, so he went in and began to ransack the office, looking for … what? During the last few weeks that he had been surreptitiously watching them, he hadn't actually seen anything that they had recovered, because whatever they found they kept carefully hidden. He looked around the office, but didn't see anything out of the ordinary: SCUBA student certificates; a haphazard pile of business cards; a bookshelf with manuals, history books, a scattering of artifacts from various wrecks, an old French Underwater Industries camera housing, an old brass sextant. Opening the cabinets he dug through the files, but found nothing of interest.

He pulled open the center drawer of the desk, and there among the pencils and pens and other paraphernalia he spotted a gold medallion. He pocketed it; he didn't know that Michael had found it on a different wreck years before, and kept it around as a curiosity.

Turning slowly, Alan spotted the office safe in the corner, but it didn't take him long to realize that it was bolted into the wall and was for all intents and purposes impregnable. Nevertheless, he tried the pry bar on it, to no avail; it wouldn't budge. Chagrined, he looked around for something, anything, that he might use to open it. Maybe, he thought, the keys to the safe were hidden in the office somewhere.

Suddenly, he heard a sound from the front of the shop, the scrape of a key being inserted into the lock of the front door. He extinguished the office light and slid back into the darkness. Looking through the office door, he saw Michael's girlfriend enter the shop, her arms loaded with shopping bags. He waited until she had closed the door and headed into the shop to turn on the lights, then stepped out in front of her with a smirk on his face. Lexie saw him, froze for a moment, screamed, and began to quickly back away. Pulling her phone from her pocket she began to dial, but Alan was on her in an instant, knocking the phone from her hand and backhanding her across the face. She fell backward, striking her head on a tank standing behind her. She lay on the ground, unconscious, her lip split from the blow, a laceration from the tank seeping blood into her hair.

Moving quickly, Alan tied her feet and hands with duct tape from the shop and put another piece securely across her mouth before continuing his search. Knocking documents off the desk, he spotted a drawing that looked vaguely like the outline of a ship, with cryptic notes that made no sense. He stared at it for a while, then realized that in fact, it did make sense: It was an inventory. And holy shit, what a list. Every other fucking word was gold.

His immediate problem, however, was the girl. She was beginning to come around, a nasty bruise forming on the side of her face. He dragged her to the back door; looking out, he saw no one. Stepping into the alley and opening the back door of the vehicle, he returned to the shop, picked up the girl, and dropped her unceremoniously on the filthy floor of the van and slammed the door. She groaned in pain as she struck the hard metal floor. Closing the door of the shop, and with a final look around to make sure that he had not been observed, Alan started the van and casually drove away.

They had gold, he thought; I have their girl. Time to deal.

CHAPTER 26

The incessant bumping and shaking of the van woke Lexie from unconsciousness. Her head was pounding, and her lip throbbed painfully where Alan had split it when he struck her. Blood had sheeted down her face from the wound where she had struck her head against the tank. It had dried, gluing her left eye closed.

She realized that she was in trouble; struggling against the tape that bound her, she tried to free herself, to no avail. She kicked against the side of the van, over and over. From the front of the van Alan yelled, telling her to knock it off. "I'll split more than your fucking lip!" he threatened—and she didn't doubt it.

As they drove, Lexie took stock of her situation. Looking around the van she tried to find something— anything—that she could use to cut the tape, but other than a regulator and a locked toolbox, she found nothing that would help. Settling back, she decided to wait it out. She was scared: Whatever Alan wanted, he was willing to kidnap her to get it. And no one knew where she was.

Alan made his way back across the bay to Sausalito and the shop. Traffic was light; within an hour he pulled into the parking lot. Backing the van into one of the old repair bays, he closed the overhead door and opened the back of the vehicle where Lexie lay, glaring at him. He reached down and ripped off the tape covering her mouth, causing her to scream; he had ripped open her torn lip. It began to bleed again.

"Nobody knows where we are, and nobody will," he began, a look of emotionless malice on his unshaven face. "We can stay here as long as we have to, and nobody will know the difference."

Lexie was staring at the floor. And didn't respond. Alan reached out and painfully pinched her cheek, twisting until she screamed.

"Now I have your attention," he continued. "I want to know what your boyfriend and his friend have found out there—and believe me, you want to tell me."

Lexie thought for a minute, then pretended ignorance. "How the hell should I know?" she snapped. "I'm not a diver—go ask them!" Alan stood over her for a couple of seconds, then, without warning, slapped her again, hard. She felt her cheekbone crack and the side of her face went numb from the blow. Scared, her head reeling, she gasped, "Portholes. They found a wreck and they're pulling portholes off of it."

He sighed. Reaching out, he grabbed a handful of her hair and dragged her out of the van onto the hard concrete floor of the shop. She screamed, trying unsuccessfully to pull his hands off. She hit the floor and crawled away.

"We can do this all day, bitch—I've got all the time in the world. I don't believe they're scavenging portholes any more than I believe you're not a diver. I've seen that locked case they carry around—nobody padlocks a box that carries portholes."

Looking around, Alan's eyes settled on the old decompression chamber in the back corner of the shop. Reaching down, he roughly taped Lexie's mouth again, then dragged her by her feet to the chamber. There, he picked her up and dumped her on the wooden bench that lined one side. Closing the hatch, he dogged it down. She could scream all she wanted; the steel chamber was thick enough that nobody would hear her. And since Roland wouldn't be back any time soon, there was little chance that she'd be discovered. With luck, she'd scream until she used all the air in the sealed chamber and pass out—or die. That would certainly be more convenient for him.

Returning to the van, he drove up to the overlook above the Potato Patch, where he watched the almost empty Achilles bouncing on the waves. At 5 o'clock the divers surfaced and began to load gear into the inflatable. He hurried to the shop where he parked the van and then crossed the road to the marina, where he surreptitiously climbed a ladder into a sailboat, the *Veritas*, which was in the yard while repairs were made to her teak trim. From there he could see where Michael and Billy always parked their van and trailer.

Soon, they pulled into the ramp, pulled the inflatable onto its trailer, and began the process of unloading. From the boat they pulled diving gear, bags of tools, the ever-present Pelican case with its padlocks, and the storage tanks. There wasn't a porthole to be seen. Lying bitch. *What was in that case?*

Alan returned to the shop. Once again he pulled into the service bay, closed the door, and checked on the girl. He opened the chamber door and saw that she was lying on the steel floor of the tank, where she had presumably fallen. Her face was badly swollen, and covered with blood; one eye was closed. *Serves her right*, he thought. She was clearly pissed, screaming at him from behind the tape, but otherwise she appeared fine, other than the damage to her face. A thought struck him; reaching out, he snapped off the necklace she wore and stuffed it in his pocket before sealing the door of the chamber. Then he got into the van and made the one-hour trip back to Walnut Creek, where he parked in a spot near the dive shop where he could watch—and wait.

He didn't have to wait long. Billy and Michael arrived about 45 minutes later, pulling behind the shop to unload their gear. They entered through the back door and made several trips with their equipment, the Pelican case the first thing to be carried in.

After they had emptied the van and pulled the door closed, Alan made his way to the back door. He turned the knob carefully, found it unlocked, and quietly entered the shop. As he made his way from the back of the building to the front where the office was located, he heard them talking excitedly. He could see them in the office.

Michael, pointing perplexedly at the bags of groceries on the desk, said to Billy, "Lexie was here; there's a prescription here for allergy pills. What the hell happened in here? Did she surprise a thief? This place looks like a bomb went off in it."

Billy shook his head, looking around. "I don't think it was a thief," he mumbled; "nothing's missing. The safe's still here, but it looks like somebody might have tried to jimmy it open."

Michael stood stock still, looking around the ruined office. Where the hell was Lexie? What had happened to her? A feeling of dread began to spread through him as he contemplated the worst. Had she surprised a thief who was trying to rob the place?

"Billy, do you suppose somebody figured out what we've found out there and was looking for it? Is there any possible way someone could have seen—"

Before Billy could respond, Alan stepped out of the darkness, startling them. He was holding a cocked spear gun, its tip pointed at Michael's chest.

"As a matter of fact, I'd like to see what you found," he said to them, standing well back from Billy. "In fact, I want to see it all. I know you've found something down there because I've been watching you from the cliff above the bridge—I know you're working a wreck. And besides, I found this in your desk." He held up the medallion that Michael had recovered years before.

"Alan, what the hell? Put down the spear gun and listen to me. I don't know what you're talking about. I found that on a wreck in the Caribbean—I wrote an article about it in *Sport Diver*. You broke in and tossed the office for some stupid parts we took off a wreck? Are you out of your mind? And where the hell is Lexie?"

Alan gestured with the spear gun. "Nice try, Michael, but I know better. I've been watching you at the marina for days, and I've seen all the bottles you've gone through. I've also seen all the bags you've brought in and the Pelican case you carry around like it's full of explosives, the one with the padlocks. I think we'll start with that."

"You're full of shit, Alan," Billy replied. "What are you going to do, shoot us? That thing only has one spear, in case you haven't noticed. You can't get both of us."

Alan just smiled, and slowly reached into his pocket. "Actually," he replied, "you're right—I'm not going to shoot you. But I might shoot her," he said casually, tossing Lexie's necklace at Michael's chest.

Michael felt a chill course through him as he recognized the necklace. He turned toward Alan and began walking toward him. Leveling the spear gun, Alan shook his head. "Not a good idea, jerkoff. I've got her, and unless I walk out of here with the case and whatever is in it, I'll mail her back to you in pieces. So don't fuck with me, or I'll fuck with you."

Michael felt the anger boiling in his body. He knew he couldn't possibly reach Alan before he triggered the spear gun, but it took everything he had, every ounce of will, to stay put.

Billy slowly reached out and put a hand on his arm. "Easy…" he whispered.

"Yeah, good idea—listen to your friend, Michael," Alan said in a low voice. "Hand over the case and stay put. When I'm gone I'll call you and tell you where your girlfriend is—as long as I know you're not following me."

Michael was so angry he was shaking—but more than angry, he was scared. Lexie, his Lexie, was somewhere out there, maybe hurt, and there wasn't a single goddamn thing he could do for her.

"Whatever you want, scumbag," growled Michael. "I'll give you what we found, but not until I know she's okay. And listen to me now: you harm her in any way—ANY way—and I will find you, and I'll make you pay in ways you can't imagine." He never took his eyes off of Alan. Alan stared back, but his smile faltered.

Recovering, he gestured with the spear gun. "The case. Now. And by the way, you're in no position to tell me how this is going to go down. Remember who I've got locked up in a very nasty place that can get a whole lot nastier without much effort on my part. Now give me the fucking case."

Michael handed over the padlocked Pelican case. "Open it," Alan demanded.

Billy shook his head. "The keys are in the van," he said. "I'll go get 'em."

"Nope," said Alan. "You stay there—I don't trust you. I'll cut 'em off later. Now sit on the floor and don't move. If I see either one of you try to get up, the deal's off. I'll call you later and tell you where you can find your girlfriend."

Without taking their eyes off of Alan, they lowered themselves to the floor. Alan stood there for a moment, looking at them, shaking his head. "You fired me because I played grab-ass with a dive student? And smoked dope? Fuck you." Shaking his head in disgust, he grabbed the case and headed for the back door. They heard a car start and drive away.

CHAPTER 27

Earlier that afternoon, Jeff Bryer had come to the shop for a workout in the pool and to practice some of his SCUBA techniques. He was studying to be an instructor, and he knew that there was a lot riding on his ability to perform the skills flawlessly at the bottom of the pool. So he had done them, over and over, until he felt good about his ability to perform them well. Then he swam laps for an hour before crawling out of the pool and into the observation well, exhausted.

Wrapping a towel around himself, he stretched out on the bench and, after a few minutes, dozed off. He slept for an hour or so, but was awakened by voices coming from the office. Michael and Billy must be back from their dive, he mused. But before he got to the top of the stairs, he heard another voice, one he recognized—Alan, the asshole that Michael had fired a couple of weeks before. He could tell that it was not a friendly conversation.

Peering through a rack of rental wetsuits hanging on the wall, he had a clear line of sight to the office, where he could see Alan holding a spear gun pointed at Michael. He had no idea what they were talking about—gold? —but he was able to hear enough of their conversation to realize that the shithead had taken Lexie. Jeff remembered how he had treated her the day he'd been fired. The guy was a first class dickhead, and this was some serious shit.

Moving silently and unseen to the door behind the locker rooms, he grabbed his clothes and stole into the equipment room where the pumps and filters for the pool were housed. A door there led to the garage where they kept the Achilles, and from there, another door led to the back alley. Opening the door quietly, Jeff exited the shop. Once outside he climbed into his car, which was parked a short distance away, got dressed, and waited. He saw an old van parked in the alley behind the shop, and surmised that it was Alan's; from where he sat, he'd be able to see it pull away—if it did.

15 minutes later, the wait paid off. Alan came out of the back door carrying a Pelican case and got into the van. He pulled slowly out of the alley and casually drove away, just another guy headed to work. Jeff waited 30 seconds or so, then began to follow at a discrete distance. Luckily, his car—an older, light gray Taurus—didn't attract much attention.

The van headed west toward San Francisco on Highway 24; Jeff followed five or so cars behind, occasionally changing lanes to avoid (he hoped) detection. They crossed the Bay Bridge, wound their way through the maze of highways where Interstate 80 becomes northbound 101, then headed for the Golden Gate Bridge. Traffic was relatively light; the fog on the bridge was heavy, wet and wispy. Visibility dropped to a couple of hundred feet. On the one hand, this was good; it lowered the probability that Alan would recognize him. But it also made it difficult for Jeff to keep the van in sight.

After ten nerve-wracked minutes, the fog on the bridge thinned to the point that Jeff could see the van ahead without difficulty. They left the Golden Gate, passed through the Robin Williams Tunnel, and soon arrived in Sausalito, where Alan took an exit and wound his way past ridiculously expensive homes until he reached Bridgeway. He drove past the ferry landing, and just after the Sausalito Yacht Harbor he turned left into an industrial area that catered to the boat and its various marinas. It was a warren of chandlers, sail makers, fiberglass repair shops, small engine repair facilities, rope and line manufacturers, and commercial diving services. He pulled in front of what appeared to be an old gas station. Jeff continued on, resisting the urge to look out the window. He pulled into a parking place on the street about a block beyond the gas station. He took a deep breath, and exhaled loudly. Pulling out his phone, he sent a text to Michael.

* * *

Michael was still pacing back and forth across the showroom, trying to come up with a plan. He was beside himself with worry for Lexie. Twice, Billy had stopped him from calling the police.

Suddenly, Michael stopped pacing and pulled his phone from his pocket. Reading the text message that had just come in, he exclaimed, "What the hell?!?"

Billy walked over and looked to see what had caused his friend's reaction.

"It's Jeff—he's following Alan and says he's in Sausalito near the marina. How the hell did he—" Billy headed for the door as Michael tried to call Jeff. He speed-dialed the number; it rang for what seemed like an eternity, then went straight to voicemail. "Not answering," Michael muttered, as he followed Billy out of the shop.

"I'm going to cut off his head and shit down his throat," Billy muttered, pulling car keys from his pocket. "Let's go. I don't know how Jeff knew to follow Alan, or how he knows what's going on, but he's now on my Christmas card list." They looked at each other; their eyes said more than words ever could.

Billy grabbed Michael by the shoulder and stopped him before they reached the door. "We'll find her, Michael— we'll find her. I promise you that. And I'm going to kill that son of a bitch. But first, I'm going to hurt him. A lot."

* * *

Alan looked around carefully to make sure that nothing suspicious was going on before he got out of the van. Traffic was normal on the road in front of the shop, just the usual boaters, tourists and commercial vehicles. Backing the van into a space alongside the shop, he parked and waited, expecting to spot the two divers. After 30 minutes of waiting, he was satisfied that he hadn't been followed. He opened the overhead door and pulled the van inside, closing the door behind him. He placed the heavy Pelican case on a shelf under the window and then walked over to the decompression chamber. Looking in the inspection port he saw that Lexie had shifted her position in a vain attempt to free herself, but she was still securely tied—and more importantly, she still had the tape on her mouth. She glared back at him. He could feel the hatred coming off her in waves.

"You'll keep," he smirked.

Taking the Pelican case over to a workbench, he tried to cut through the hasp of the first padlock with a hacksaw. After several minutes of effort he had barely scratched the chrome. He clearly needed something different—bolt cutters, perhaps. He looked around for a set but couldn't find one; he knew, however, that the shop across the street at the marina would have everything he needed. Checking the hand wheel on the chamber one more time, he left the shop and walked across the street.

Watching from his car, Jeff saw Alan leave the shop and walk across the road to the marina. He quick-stepped down the sidewalk and turned casually into the industrial area as if he had business there. At the last minute he turned and headed to the front door of the building that Alan had just left.

The door was unlocked, and with a last look over his shoulder he opened it and entered the dark space beyond.

Closing the door quietly, he looked around. Jeff carried no weapon, other than a Buck knife on his hip. As his eyes grew accustomed to the gloom of the place, he was able to make out the layout of the room. What a mess, he thought; not only is the guy a pig, he's also a pig. From where he was standing he could see dive gear, piles of trash, a snarl of fishing equipment, welders, an old and partially disassembled band mask, a dozen or more tanks, hoses, salvage gear, a pile of half-rotten rubberized canvas lift bags, and back in the far corner, what appeared to be a giant hot water heater lying on its side, next to a pile of something covered with an old tarp. Jeff recognized the tank for what it was: an old decompression chamber, capable of holding about six people. Looking around, he shook his head at the mess. What a pigsty, he thought; the guy deserved to live in a gas station.

The place had an odd smell—a combination of rubber, oil, iodine, dust, and a faint patina of rot. Walking through the chaos, he thought he heard something—metallic, but muted. He stopped and listened, but the sound didn't repeat. Probably from the shipbuilding operation next door, he thought. Moving carefully around the piles of diving paraphernalia, stepping over unrecognizable pieces of hardware and piles of odorous trash, he stopped momentarily to admire an old wooden Hawaiian sling spear lying on a table. Then he heard the sound again: a muted metallic thumping, somewhere in the back of the shop. This time there was no mistaking it—the sound was coming from inside the building.

He walked to the back of the cavernous space, avoiding a mass of cobwebs that hung from an overhead beam. Spotting what appeared to be a glass viewing port on the chamber's side, he pressed his face to the glass and looked into the decompression chamber. Instantly, he saw Lexie struggling on the floor of the chamber, her arms and legs tied and a piece of tape covering her mouth. Her face was shockingly swollen and bloody, but she was alive.

Jeff knocked on the glass of the observation port, and Lexie looked up. At first she didn't recognize him and gave him a murderous glare. Then she realized who was staring back at her, and she began to struggle even more to free herself. There was no mistaking the look in those eyes. He was surprised that they hadn't melted a hole in the steel wall of the tank.

Moving to the front of the chamber where the hatch was located, he checked the gauges to make sure it wasn't pressurized. Spinning the hand wheel, he opened the access port and swung it open. Lexie looked at him with tears in her eyes. Entering the chamber he pulled his knife and sawed at the tape on Lexie's arms and legs, then carefully removed the piece across her mouth. She winced when the tape tugged at her lip, which still bled, then jumped up and hugged him tightly.

"Jesus, Lexie—are you okay?" he asked, looking her up and down, gently touching the wound on her head.

"I am now," she replied, rubbing her wrists and hugging him again. "Where is he? Did he leave? Have you told Michael where—"

Jeff put his hands on Lexie's shoulders and looked her in the eyes, trying to calm her down. She was frantic with worry.

"I sent Michael a text—he and Billy will be here any minute, I'm sure. For now, let's get out of here—we've got to call the police."

They stepped out of the chamber and picked their way across the minefield of equipment on the floor as they headed toward the front door of the old gas station. Lexie stumbled on a weight belt that protruded from under an equipment bag and went down on one knee. Jeff jumped to help her, and as he did, they heard the front door open. Looking up, they saw Alan standing in the doorway. He smiled—although his eyes did not. He moved toward them, holding a large pair of steel bolt cutters.

"So—the killer Marine has come to rescue the damsel in distress," he sneered, swinging the tool in his right hand.

Jeff gently pushed Lexie behind him. Looking around, he spotted the Hawaiian sling on the table and reached for it, but Alan was too fast. He brought the bolt cutters down on the table, narrowly missing Jeff's fingers. Jeff jumped back, frantically looking for a weapon. There was none to be had.

Feinting to the left, Jeff tried to draw Alan away from the spear gun. Alan anticipated the move, however, and swung the heavy cutters into Jeff's ribs like a baseball bat. Jeff felt and heard his ribs snap from the blow, and his vision shrank to pinpoints as he collapsed to the ground, writhing in agony. With every breath he could feel his ribs grinding; he wasn't sure how many Alan had broken, but he had never felt such paralyzing pain. He tried to rise, but Alan approached and kicked him savagely in the ribs where he had been struck. Jeff screamed, fighting the pain, but it was too much to bear. He passed out.

Alan stood above him with the bolt cutters at his side, breathing heavily. Hearing a noise behind him, he turned.

"Hey asshole," said Lexie, who now stood in front of him with a Bandido speargun pointed at his midsection. She had cocked it, the surgical tubing stretched tightly behind the spear. She looked like something out of a violent video game: her face was covered with blood, one eye was closed, and the entire side of her face was turning a violent purple. Her speech was slurred from the swelling of her jaw, and she wavered slightly on her feet. Her eyes, however, were set in a glare that never left his.

Alan smirked, raised the bolt cutters to his shoulder, and stared back. "You're bluffing," he sneered, swinging the tool at his side.

"Try me," she snapped back, her eyes fixed on his. Alan looked at her, thinking, calculating, deciding, assessing. He nodded. Then, in a burst of speed, he raised the heavy tool and leapt at her. Lexie didn't move, nor did the spear. Jeff, who had regained consciousness but was struggling to stand, would later describe the look in her eyes as something crystalline, hard, like diamonds. Alan

171

jumped at her like a club-wielding juggernaut, but she didn't move, and she never took her eyes off of Alan. Then she triggered the spear gun.

The spear, with a double-wing stainless steel rock tip mounted on the shaft, struck Alan's wrist just below the hand that wielded the bolt cutters. Powered by the two tightly stretched bands of powerful surgical tubing, the spear passed between the radius and ulna bones of his forearm and embedded itself in a wooden support post behind him. He screamed, the bolt cutters falling from his grasp, and fell against the post. Lexie walked slowly toward him and stopped. He looked up, groaning in agony, trying in vain to pull the spear from his wrist, and saw her staring. There was no smile on her face. "Fuck you!" he screamed, every movement sending waves of pain through his wounded arm. "Fuck—you!"

Jeff remembered the seconds that followed with absolute clarity. Lexie smiled slightly, inclined her head slightly to the right, and dropped the now discharged spear gun on the floor. Then, without warning, she kicked Alan as hard as she could in the groin. His eyes rolled back in his head, and with a mewling groan he dropped like a sack of rocks, hanging obscenely by his impaled wrist. "Not with that equipment, you won't," she said coldly, gesturing at his crotch.

Turning, she helped Jeff to his feet and, guiding him to a chair, helped him sit. She took his phone and called Michael, telling him where they were. Then she called 911 and asked for help, before sitting down on the floor beside Jeff. Then she passed out.

The hours that followed were a blur of activity. Within minutes of her emergency call, officers from Marin County and Sausalito P.D. converged on the old gas station, followed by a pair of ambulances. The police came in expecting the worst, clad in body armor and armed to the teeth. Once they determined that the threat, who now hung suspended from a wooden post by a spear, was no longer a threat, they allowed the paramedics to enter the building.

The paramedics carefully lifted Jeff onto a stretcher and placed him in the first ambulance so that he could be taken to Marin General for treatment. X-rays would reveal four badly broken ribs and some minor internal bleeding, which, once the pain began to fade, he reveled in. The second ambulance was for Lexie, and after examining her on-scene, the medics decided that her injuries were for the most part minor, other than the laceration on her head and the tear in her lip, both of which would require stitches. They transported her to the hospital as well to be treated and to be placed under observation because of the possibility of a concussion stemming from her head injury.

Alan was a different story. Once he regained consciousness he wouldn't stop screaming, which made it difficult for the firefighters to free him from the spear. At first they tried to unscrew the rock tip from the shaft, but that turned out to be futile. Not only was it was rusted onto the shaft of the spear, the tip was deeply embedded in the wooden post. Furthermore, the act of trying to turn the shaft in place caused Alan tremendous pain, based on the escalation of screaming that resulted. They briefly considered using a cutting torch on the shaft, but decided it would generate too much heat and burn the victim. A cop standing nearby who obviously had little sympathy for Alan suggested that they continue, offering the argument that it would cauterize the wound and stop the bleeding. They also tried a hacksaw, but the blade barely scratched the stainless steel shaft. And, the vibrations caused by the blade caused Alan to shriek even more, until he finally passed out, much to the relief of the paramedics who had to listen to his profanity-laced screaming. Ultimately they used a chainsaw to remove a section of the wooden post, after bracing the ceiling with a tall screw jack that they found leaning in a corner.

Shortly after the police arrived, Michael and Billy screeched into the parking lot. Rushing to the two ambulances, they found Lexie and Jeff, in pain but

Steven Shepard

otherwise fine. Michael went straight to Lexie, who collapsed into his arms and hugged him for a very long time.

Billy, after checking on Lexie, went straight to Jeff and lifted him off the ground in a bear hug. "Dude, you earned your pay today—and more. We're gonna take good care of you."

Jeff moaned and came very close to passing out again; his ribs couldn't take much more of Billy's kindness. One of the paramedics smacked Billy on the shoulder, telling him to give her back her patient.

"Sorry," said Billy, suitably chastised. He turned to Jeff. "We'll see you at the hospital, and I'll tell you what's really going on."

Alan was now lying strapped to a gurney, the steel shaft of the spear in his wrist immobilized to the stretcher by several feet of adhesive tape. Half of the shaft hung below the bed, while the other half stuck up in the air like a tent pole. It would have to be removed surgically, most likely under general anesthesia.

Putting on a face that spoke of grave concern, Billy walked over to the gurney and leaned in close. "I just want you to know that I'll be waiting for you when you get out, you worthless turd." With that he smiled, and, reaching below the gurney, gave the spear shaft a violent twist. Alan made a gurgling sound, his eyes rolled back in his head, and he passed out again. Billy looked at him for a moment, patted him on the cheek, and then went back to where Michael stood, his arm protectively around Lexie, a look of enormous relief on his face. Billy hugged them both.

One of the police officers motioned to Billy to join him in the dive shop. Billy knew the officer, because he and Michael maintained the Sausalito Marine Rescue boat and the officer was a member of the dive team. Motioning to a pile of regulators, he asked Billy, "Aren't those yours? They have the name of your shop engraved on them."

174

Billy explained that Alan had briefly worked for them in Walnut Creek until they had fired him for being an asshole, and that he must have stolen the gear while employed there.

"Take a look around," said the officer. Give me a list of what's yours and I'll photograph it for evidence. You can take it back to the shop with you."

Thanking him, Billy counted the regulators, put them into a separate pile, and told the officer to take his pictures. While this was going on, he casually picked up the Pelican case on the table near the window and held it in his hand as if he'd had it all along. Walking over to the door, he engaged another officer who was standing just outside in conversation, pointing out to him that his colleague had determined that some of the equipment in the shop was stolen, including at least five regulators that had their own Ocean Enterprises logo engraved on them.

Calling to the other officers, the young man explained what Billy had said, and as he did, Billy casually walked over and joined them, the case in his hand. They began to pepper him with questions about the stolen equipment. He was able to leave with the case after explaining what some of the gear did and how the police could recognize whether it was stolen or not. It turned out that much of it was, including a heap of outboard motors in the back of the shop hidden under the tarp that Jeff had spotted earlier. As it turned out, many of the motors had in fact been reported stolen. Billy explained that it was highly likely that Alan had visited the marina at night, donned SCUBA gear, entered the water, and disconnected the motors on the boats in their slips before carefully lowering them into the water and spiriting them away without being seen. They took careful notes and wrote down Billy's contact information. No one noticed the Pelican case.

Once the police had gathered as much information from Jeff and Lexie as they were going to get about the events of the day, and the ambulances carrying Lexie, Jeff and Alan had departed for Marin General, Michael and

Billy found themselves alone in the parking lot. Lexie had told them that she was fine, but she clearly wasn't: once they put her in the ambulance for transport they saw that she was trembling, obviously suffering from shock after her ordeal. They promised to follow her to the hospital shortly.

"Thank you, old friend," Michael said, pulling Billy into a bear hug. "So what is it you said to Alan when you went over to his ambulance before they took him away? I'm just curious because I heard him yell."

Billy smiled, but there was no humor in it. "I merely expressed my displeasure with the way he treated Lexie," he explained. "And I wanted to make sure he was comfortable."

Michael smirked. "Yeah, I saw how you rearranged the spear to make him more comfortable. Nice job."

Billy grinned widely. "Hey, he was in pain, you know? We couldn't have that, could we?"

CHAPTER 28

It was two weeks before the commotion surrounding Lexie's abduction settled down. She spent a night in the hospital under the care of a neurologist, but physical examinations and X-rays showed no concussion or fractures to her skull. The bruises on her face went from blue to gray to a sickly yellow-green, the swelling around the stitches in her lip and scalp shrank, and even though she insisted that she was fine, Michael tended to her as if she'd been grievously wounded.

Jeff spent a week in the hospital; he was ultimately diagnosed with four fractured ribs, a bruised spleen and a badly bruised kidney. The kidney caused the greatest concern; it appeared to be bleeding, but after several days of care the doctors decided that it was not, but they kept him in the hospital for a few more days just to be sure. When they finally released him they told him to take it very, very easy for a couple of weeks, a diagnosis with which he was not about to argue. His ribs were extremely painful, and the slightest twist at the waist caused such paralyzing pain that he came close to blacking out when it happened. Taking it easy was just the ticket, he decided.

Michael, Lexie and Billy visited him every day during his hospital stay, and treated him like royalty—especially Lexie, who wouldn't leave him alone. She brought him his favorite burgers from Fuddruckers, an endless supply of

177

diving magazines, and went to his house and picked up the mail—including the latest issue of Soldier of Fortune. The day before he was discharged she and Michael showed up for a visit, and from her purse she pulled a refrigerated roll of chocolate chip cookie dough, which he lit into as if he hadn't eaten in a week. When the nurse realized what it was, she tried to relieve him of it, but Lexie intervened. With a stern look that hid a smile, the nurse relented.

When they finally let him go home, Billy picked Jeff up at the hospital and drove him to the shop, where he was met with a hero's welcome. By now the news had gotten out about Alan's abduction of Lexie, although the motive remained murky. He had never managed to get the Pelican case open and had therefore never seen the gold within, and besides, Billy had walked away with the case—so it was never entered into evidence as part of the scene. Michael speculated to the investigating detectives that Alan was upset over being fired from his job and wanted what he believed was back pay owed to him, and took what were obviously extreme and desperate measures to convince Michael to pay up. Michael and Billy were able to demonstrate that they had paid him in full, so that aspect of the investigation was closed quickly.

As for Alan, the police executed a search warrant on the garage, and in the middle of the search, Roland returned from Berkeley to find his place swarming with police. Once they calmed him down and explained why his place was being torn apart, and after he explained that he rented the space to Alan, he was soon cleared of any involvement.

During the search they uncovered evidence of dozens of thefts. There were more than 30 outboard motors piled under the tarp in the back of the shop, all stolen and most of them later reunited with their rightful owners, thanks to their serial numbers. The police found rental dive gear from a handful of Bay Area shops, a stolen welder, a pistol (which in and of itself was enough to send the convicted felon away for damn near forever), and more than fifty pounds of fresh abalone in a freezer, most of them too small and still in their shells, a serious violation of

California Fish and Game regulations. The crowning blow came when a deputy accidentally knocked over an 80 cubic foot SCUBA tank that was standing in a corner of the shop. Its valve had been removed, presumably for an internal inspection, and the mouth of the bottle was covered with tape to prevent contaminants from entering. But when it landed on its side on the cement floor, instead of the customary 'clang!' that a falling tank normally makes, it landed with a dull 'thunk'—as if it were full of something. As it turned out, it was—about ten pounds of marijuana, sealed in dozens of baggies, ready for sale. As Billy gleefully pointed out, between the kidnapping and assault charges, the stolen property, the Fish and Game violations, the pistol, and the drugs, Alan would be locked away so long that he'd have to attach a SCUBA tank to his wheelchair if he ever wanted to dive again. "I'm still going to be waiting for him when he gets out, though—with a nice fruit basket," he added.

Michael and Billy sat down with Jeff and told him that they had indeed found a valuable wreck, and that he was the first person after Lexie to know about it. He understood the reason for the secrecy, but wanted to be involved in whatever capacity he could be. They made it clear to him that he was now family—because of him they had been able to rescue Lexie—and that he would certainly share in the spoils of their find. His injuries were far too painful to allow him to dive with them, which they were secretly happy about, since he had no experience with salvage diving and wasn't really prepared for the rigors of the Potato Patch. Instead, they assigned him the role of site security and swore him to absolute secrecy. They posted him on the road above the Golden Gate in the same spot where Alan had first seen their inflatable, far below on the Potato Patch. His job was to notify them of any suspicious activity in the area, a job that he took to with zeal. They didn't show him any of the gold they had found, but promised to, once they had excavated the entire site.

"Hey guys," he replied solemnly, "your secret is safe—

you know I have your backs." Dropping his tone and his head ever so slightly, he continued, "After all, you put up with my stories; not too many people would do that and still let me come back into the shop as much as you have." Michael was taken back, wondering if Jeff had overheard some of their comments. At the bottom of it all, he was a hard worker, a surprisingly steady learner, and it struck Michael that he would miss the little guy if he wasn't around.

Billy looked at Michael and then back at Jeff. "We both know that, dude, and you're as much a part of this place as we are. But for right now, we have some places to go, so you take care of yourself and we'll check on you tomorrow." With that he tugged at Michael's arm and drew him toward the door.

As they walked down the hallway, Michael remarked to no one in particular, "I think our little brother grew up just a bit today."

Billy smiled back with just the slightest twinkle in his eye. "He's not the only one. Come on—we've got some planning to do. We've got a sea floor to dig up!"

As they drove out of the parking lot, they discussed the fact that they had also not yet had the opportunity to show the extent of their find to Lexie. They decided to complete the excavation first, then show her everything—it would be a huge surprise. It was driving her nuts, because she knew they had found something big, but she played along—although she made it clear that her patience was growing thin with all the secrecy. And besides, neither Michael nor Billy would leave her side—they practically followed her into the bathroom. So after two weeks, Lexie put her foot down and ordered them back to the dive site. They were driving her crazy, she told them; she was fine, she insisted. And besides, she reminded them, winter was coming, and once it arrived they would have even greater difficulty dealing with the rougher waters outside the Gate.

Reluctantly, they agreed, and on Friday morning, three weeks to the day after Alan had come into the shop and taken Lexie away, they returned to Sausalito, loaded up the Achilles, and headed back to the wreck.

CHAPTER 29

"Hi Lexie, it's Michael. You up for dinner tonight?" He was with Billy in the inflatable, floating above the wreck site.

He could barely contain himself—he wanted to tell her everything, but he didn't dare do it over the phone. "We just finished, and we're on our way back to the dock now. If you're up for a quick bite, meet us at the shop in about an hour. We have some things that we need to talk with you about." He waited for her knowing reply before signing off.

"I love you too, babe. See you at the shop." Michael turned to Billy, grinning. "She knows," he said. "I could tell from her voice that she knew why I was calling. I'll bet you dinner tonight that she's already in her car and on her way over." They both laughed, knowing that that was *one* bet that neither of them would take. They knew Lexie far too well.

"Do you have any idea what this stuff is worth?" asked Billy, starting the engine and turning the inflatable toward shore to avoid a large party boat on its way out of the Gate. "I mean, the gold alone has to weigh close to a hundred pounds. At about $1,000 an ounce, that's more than a million-and-a-half dollars, and we've only dug up about a third of the area."

Michael interrupted him. "And don't forget the historical value," he interjected. "That has to be worth more to a collector than the raw value of the gold. I mean, who are we to quibble over a million dollars, but if we can get more than that—"

Billy finished his sentence for him. "...Then we should. After all, who knows what else is down there?"

They sat quietly, contemplating everything that had happened, listening to the dull rattle of the little outboard as it pushed the overloaded Achilles through the small swells of late afternoon, knowing that their lives had changed in profound ways. They had dreamt of this day for years, but rarely spoke about it, and then only as a joke between them. Now, it wasn't a joke at all. They had found a treasure trove of unimaginable value, and now faced a series of decisions that would have inconceivable impacts on the rest of their lives.

They arrived at the marina and were thankful that the place was largely empty, other than a few people walking the floating docks, going to and from their boats. No one paid them any particular interest, other than one older gentleman, a regular customer of their hull inspection and cleaning business who waved from his sailboat. Nonchalantly, they waved back.

"I'll get the van, you stay here with the boat. I'll be right back." Billy ran up the ramp, a massive knot of keys clutched in his hand. Michael smiled after his friend. Billy's keychain was as big as his wallet, which was easily an inch thick and contained every piece of paper, it seemed, that had ever been stuffed in it. Michael didn't understand why Billy didn't have some kind of nerve damage in his leg from having the massive thing pressed against it all day long.

In a matter of minutes, Billy was back. He expertly backed the trailer down the ramp into the water, and Michael hopped overboard and walked the inflatable onto the trailer. After tying it down, he signaled to Billy, who put the van in gear and drove up to the distant corner of the parking lot, far from any other vehicles. There, Michael joined him, and they quickly unloaded the boat, placing everything in the cargo area of the van. They transferred the box of artifacts and the lift bags that were wrapped around their latest haul of precious cargo first, stowing them between the two front seats. Next they tied down the storage and SCUBA tanks, packed up the wet gear, and closed the rear doors. As they did, the manager of the marina came trotting over, asking about Lexie and Alan. They reassured him that she was fine and that they would give her the man's regards; he then expressed regret for having hired Alan in the first place. No worries, they told him; after all, they had hired him as well, and he had seemed like a good choice at the time. They shook hands, and after checking the boat one last time, they pulled out of the parking lot, made their way back to the highway and headed for the East Bay.

Traffic was still heavy through San Francisco, but by the time they reached the Bay Bridge it had died down somewhat. They moved quickly past Berkeley and Oakland to the Caldecott Tunnel, then passed Orinda and Lafayette, watching tendrils of fog spill over the tops of the Berkeley Hills behind them, glowing in the fading sunlight. By the time they reached their exit it was nearly dark. They pulled into the alley behind the shop and unloaded the equipment, stacking it just inside the back door.

As Michael fumbled in his pocket for the key to the door, it burst open, and there was Lexie, looking extraordinarily beautiful—and impatient.

"Where have you two been?" she demanded, hugging both of them. "You smell like rubber. Get inside and take a shower, and then you can tell me what's so important. I've been here since an hour after you called, and after that much time with Jeff, you owe me dinner big time."

Billy hesitated as he unloaded the last piece of equipment from the back of the van. "Is he still here?" he asked her.

"No," she replied. "He left about half an hour ago—

seems he has a date tonight, although I can't imagine who with. Why?"

Billy and Michael looked at each other. "Uh…Lexie, let's go inside. We have to get this stuff moved into the shop, and then we'll meet you in the office. We'll be there in five minutes, I promise. And since the shop is closed, would you mind ringing off the cash register while we bring in the gear?" She looked at both of them, and then shook her head with a smile.

"This is all very mysterious, gentlemen. You better have a good reason for dragging me all the way down here, and you better pay off with dinner at Chevy's or I'll go find a better offer. Get cleaned up. I'll meet you in the office." With that, she turned and disappeared into the hallway that led to the retail floor of the shop. Soon, they heard the clicking of keystrokes as she closed the register and ran the daily sales reports.

They dragged the dive equipment into the rental area to be washed later, and took the tanks into the compressor room. While Michael hooked the tanks to the fill hoses and started the compressor, Billy retrieved the lift bags and the box from the van. Then, he disconnected the boat trailer, raised the rollup garage door adjacent to the rear entrance to the shop, and pushed the boat into the space. After closing the garage door, he locked the van and reentered the shop, where Michael was finishing the task of putting the gear away. He had already hung up the wetsuits and was in the process of hosing them down when Billy entered.

"We better get in there before she comes looking for us again," he said, grinning at Michael. "If she does, it won't be pretty. Here, take two of these bags; I'll get the box and the other bag."

Michael double-checked the doors to ensure that they were locked. By sheer coincidence there were no dive classes that night; every other evening there were two going on simultaneously, one in the classroom upstairs and one in the pool.

They entered the office, where Lexie sat patiently behind the desk, reading a copy of *Food and Wine* Magazine. "I'm getting hungrier…" she mumbled, not taking her eyes off the magazine. She hadn't noticed the bags or the box they brought in with them. Reaching into the box, Billy carefully extracted the small golden boat and placed it quietly on the desk in front of her.

"Maybe this will help you focus on something else," he said softly. Putting down the magazine, she looked at the artifact. Her eyes grew impossibly wide, but she said nothing. She reached out to touch it, slowly, as if it would disappear at the slightest touch, like smoke. She looked up at them, her eyes filled with wonder, and still she said nothing. She looked at them quizzically, her mouth moving but making no sound.

"You look like a trout," said Billy. She smacked him on the shoulder without taking her eyes off the golden object before her.

Finally, leaning close to the boat and gazing at it intently, she spoke. "How—where—" she shook her head impatiently, as if the words wouldn't come to her.

"Our wreck," came the simple reply. Michael moved beside her and pulled the desk lamp over so that it illuminated the rich, golden relic. It glowed faintly in the overhead light, lambent, as if lit from within.

Kissing her lightly on the cheek, he explained. "That's just the beginning."

Billy was already unpacking the bags and bringing the heavy cargo wrapped in wet t-shirts over to the desk, where he placed them carefully on the floor. Clearing away the office paraphernalia on the desktop, he unfolded a large sheet of dry neoprene and then carefully transferred their finds to the desktop. Water drooled down the sides of the desk, soaking the carpet in tiny puddles. He carefully unwrapped the first shirt, revealing ingots and what looked like five double handfuls of solid, three-quarter-inch gold beads. One of them rolled off the shirt and fell to the carpet, but no one moved to pick it up. The next package revealed the mother-of-pearl encrusted statue, the pearl-covered gold necklace, and the life-size golden death mask. Next came a sweatshirt, which cradled the emerald and gold ceremonial gloves, and four more ingots.

The desk was now covered with gold. By the time Billy and Michael finished unpacking the lift bags, there were stacks of ingots at all four corners of the desk, a plastic basket filled with gold beads, and a collection of statuettes, gloves, and other artifacts in the center of the desk, along with the badly corroded knife.

Lexie was still speechless. "Do you have any idea what you have here?" she asked them repeatedly. "This must be a hundred pounds of gold. I don't remember what gold trades for these days—maybe $700 an ounce or so—but even at that, we're talking about millions of dollars here, just in raw gold. But Michael—Billy—the real money is in the historical value of these things. There are collectors out there that will pay five or six times the value of the gold, just to have pieces like these. Believe me, I know; I run into them all the time at Bancroft." She paused as she picked up and examined the encrusted statuette.

"So the question now is this: what do you want to do with this stuff? How much of it do you want to sell, and how much do you want to keep? And just as important, where do you propose to store it while you decide?"

She shook her head and rubbed her face with her hands, before peeking above her fingers to make sure that the things she had seen on the desk were still there and not part of a cruel dream. "I suggest you get a very large safe deposit box before you do anything else. They're hard to get, so until you find one, I can store most of it, if you like, in my artifact vault at Bancroft—I think it will fit there.

"What I'm going to do is photograph these pieces," She continued, "and try to identify them from the historical record. I have a feeling I may have been right—they may be part of Orellana's cargo, and he may have gone down right here outside the Gate. I won't know until

I have a chance to compare these things to some of the pictures I have in my office and to records in the Spanish National Archives, but what I do know is this: you two will never have to work another day in your lives. You can count on that. Now take me to dinner so I can decide which one of you I'm going to marry. Hell, maybe I'll marry both of you. You're already married to each other."

They packed the artifacts back in the safe and turned out the lights. As he closed and locked the door of the shop, Billy looked back in the darkened storefront and, smiling, let out a low whistle. "Zowie," he whispered.

CHAPTER 30

Very early the next morning, Michael and Lexie carefully packed and loaded the gold into two nondescript backpacks, an equally nondescript canvas gym bag, and a briefcase, and took it to the Berkeley campus, where they placed it in the artifact safe in Lexie's office. The only thing that did not comfortably fit was the golden boat; they could have jammed it into the safe, but by the time everything else was inside, space was tight and they worried about possible damage. Instead, Michael took it with him back to the shop in a box inside the duffel and locked it in the safe there, where it fit comfortably.

Before Michael left, Lexie locked her office door, set up her digital archival camera and sunlight-balanced LED lights, and carefully photographed the boat against a neutral background from all angles, making detailed notes along the way. She examined every square inch of its surface for identifiable markings that could help to establish its provenance. After carefully packing the relic for transport in the box and bag, they said goodbye, and as soon as Michael had left she once again closed and locked the door, opened her safe, and painstakingly photographed the other pieces, storing the images on her personal laptop and backing them up on a thumb drive, which she placed in a zippered pocket in her purse. When she finished, she returned the pieces to the safe and locked it. By now, people were beginning to arrive for work, and she didn't want the artifacts in sight, even with the door locked. She couldn't risk someone seeing them.

Her next task was to attempt to categorize and identify the pieces. Thanks to her position at Bancroft, she had a number of unique resources at her disposal. The museum possessed a significant collection of data on the activities of 16th century Spanish explorers, including Inca codices that detailed the plunder of wealth by the Spaniards and the decline of the Inca Empire in the 16th century. The Spanish National Archives had holdings that dwarfed those of the Bancroft, and thanks to both her and Michael's contacts there, they had extensive access to them. Online, the Archaeological Institute of America provided hooks into databases worldwide, some of which would contain information germane to her investigation.

Taking a deep breath, she exhaled slowly. Better get started, she thought; this was going to take awhile. Brewing a cup of coffee from the Nespresso machine on her desk—a gift from Billy—she sat down at the computer, brought up Lightroom, and imported the images from her digital camera. Then she picked up the phone and started to make calls.

By five PM, she had made two calls to Cuzco, Peru and three to the National Archives in Madrid. Her calls to Peru yielded little that she didn't already know, but the calls to Spain proved fruitful. Rafael Santoro, a senior archivist and close friend of Michael's, provided her with a significant amount of information about shipping manifests from the same period during which Orellana apparently met his demise. She had never met Santoro, but after a few vague inquiries about Spanish shipping activities along the Pacific coast during the 16th century and about the activities of one Francisco de Orellana, he sent digital images to Lexie of a series of original paleographic documents stored at the Archives, which contained detailed data about cargo shipped from the New World to Spain during the 16th and early 17th centuries. She spoke passable modern Spanish, but that didn't help her with these documents. They were written in the fine, flowery hand of a scribe who lived and written centuries before, and were indecipherable to most people, even those fluent in modern Spanish. Michael, however, had spent considerable time with documents identical to these, and could read them as easily as most people read a daily newspaper. She would take them to him to be interpreted.

"We have considerably more than this in our holdings, Alejandra," he explained to her, "That haven't yet been examined or catalogued. If you can find your way to Madrid, I can provide you with visiting scholar access and make them available to you." She thanked him, promised to call soon, and disconnected.

Earlier that morning, Lexie had called a friend in the Berkeley paleontology department. She explained that she had a sample that she needed to have radiocarbon dated. The friend agreed to perform the test, and because her schedule was currently light, she told Lexie that she could most likely have results in a couple of days. Lexie explained that the sample was a piece of wood, but didn't reveal the source; this was not unusual and raised no suspicions, because the museum routinely sent over scrapings or tiny samples of artifacts to be dated. "Your timing is perfect," her friend explained. "We just finished installing and testing our new Accelerator Mass Spectrometry system, and I'm looking for projects. You're in."

Lexie thanked her and agreed to call in a couple of days to check on the results.

CHAPTER 31

Este Manifiesto consta de los contenidos de cinco barcos recién llegados desde las tierras nuevas del oeste, incluso el Perú, las tierras Ecuadorianas desconocidas al sur, las selvas Colombianas, y las aldeas en la boca del grán río Amazonas en Brasilia.

Encargado de esta flota el Sr. Francisco Pizarro, quién se marchó de España con ocho barcos en el mes de Abril, año 1527 para comenzar las exploraciones y descubrimientos del nuevo mundo en el nombre del Rey. Tres de los ocho barcos no volvieron a causa de naufrágio, que Diós los bendiga, incluso el nao bajo el comando del Capitán Francisco de Orellana, perdido a causa de tormenta furiosa en la boca del Río Amazonas en el año 1545.

Sigue la lista detallada –

Arturo Hoz

Contador del Rey

Badajoz, 1560

Manifiesto

52 barras de oro de 400 gramos cada una de peso en forma de huevo

2,355 abalorios de oro, con diámetro promedio de 3,5 centímetros

Varias estatuas (cantidad 181) de oro encrustados con gemas preciosas incluso
esmeraldas, perlas, rubíes, y nácar con altura promedia de 30 centímetros

Varios platos, bandejas, y medallones, todos artesanados y en oro, con peso total
de 303 Kilogramos

También hay una colección amplia de joyas de tipo, no detalladas aquí

Michael sat back and adjusted the lamp on the desk, rubbing his eyes. Spread before him were the original manifest documents sent to Lexie by Santoro, and Michael's translation of the elaborate and hard-to-read 16th

century text into modern Spanish. "Well, I'm not sure how much this is going to help us, but here goes," he commented to Billy and Lexie, who sat on the couch. "It certainly tracks with what we've found so far, but I don't see anything yet that provides us with a clear provenance.

"The document is a manifest listing the contents of a bunch of ships that came back from the new world. What it says is this: "This manifest consists of the contents of five recently-returned boats from the new lands to the west, including Peru, the unknown southern lands of Ecuador, the jungles of Colombia, and the villages at the mouth of the Amazon River.

"In charge of this fleet was Francisco Pizarro, who left Spain with eight boats in April of 1527 to begin exploring the new world in the name of the king. Three of the eight boats didn't return because of shipwrecks, God bless them, including one under the command of Francisco de Orellana, which was lost in a violent storm at the mouth of the Amazon River in 1545.

"A detailed list follows. Signed, Arturo Hoz, King's Accountant, Badajoz, 1560."

He put the paper down and turned to them. "Orellana's mentioned here, but only as having been lost somewhere in the Amazon. We need more than that, especially if we still believe that this is his ship we're excavating. If he went down following a storm in the Caribbean, then I can't imagine how his stuff showed up outside the Golden Gate."

Lexie nodded. "According to Santoro, there are still hundreds of documents in the Archives in Madrid from that period that haven't yet been catalogued, which means that the only way we can get access to them is to go there and see them firsthand. It may come to that, you know."

Billy smiled at her. "Yeah, as if Mikey needs an excuse to go bopping off to Spain." They all laughed; Michael's intense love of all things Spanish was well known.

"Before we go bopping off anywhere," Michael

offered, "Perhaps I should finish this translation. It goes on to list the contents: 52 egg-shaped gold bars weighing 400 grams apiece; 2,355 gold beads; a collection of 181 assorted statuettes, made of gold but covered with precious stones including emeralds, pearls, rubies, and mother-of-pearl, with an average height of 30 centimeters; a variety of gold plates, platters and medallions, all engraved—I think that's what the scribe means by 'artesanados'—with a total weight of—get this—303 kilos; and finally, a wide collection of jewelry, not detailed here."

303 kilos, they realized, was about six times the weight of the gold they had found on the site so far. *And they had barely begun to excavate.*

Michael looked at them. "That's it," he concluded. "So if there's anything here that ties our wreck to this stuff, I don't see it. Lexie, did anything else come out of your research that might shed some light?"

Lexie nodded as she opened the folder on her lap. "I have a stack of photographs here that Rafael sent me with the manifest; they're pictures of a lot of the stuff that you just described, and as you can see"—she tossed the pictures on the desk in front of Michael—"they match the things you two found pretty closely. Unfortunately, there's nothing in any of this stuff that directly ties your find to Orellana, and obviously that's what I'd like to be able to do."

Michael poured himself and Lexie a cup of coffee, and grabbed a Diet Coke from the fridge for Billy. "As you both point out, I'd never turn down a chance to go to Spain, but this time it looks like we may have no choice. If we can find documents in the Archives in Madrid that will conclusively tie our find to Orellana, then we'll have our provenance for historical purposes, and the stuff will be worth that much more because of its proven authenticity. I think we should wrap up the dig in the next couple of weeks and then go to Madrid to do a little research. What do you say?"

Lexie was the first to respond. "You've been promising

to take me there for what seems like forever, Michael, so here's your chance. Not only will I get a chance to actually meet and work with some of the people at the Archives that I've been in touch with for so long by mail, computer, and telephone, but I'll actually be able to do some real field work for a change. I've been buried in an office too long." She was clearly excited at the prospect.

"You two are going to have to do this one on your own, I'm afraid," replied Billy. "I've got the Cook salvage job starting up offshore in three weeks, and since I'm the project manager, I can't very well take off. Besides, somebody has to stay here and keep Jeff from burning the shop down while you're gone. You two go ahead and have a good time. Besides, that's your area of expertise, not mine. Bring me a surprise: five feet nine, beautiful, smart, and rich will do fine. English is optional."

Lexie leaned over and hugged him. "I'll see what I can do, Billy," she offered. "I can't guarantee the good looking señorita, but I can guarantee that the rich part won't be an issue for you."

CHAPTER 32

For the next ten days, Michael and Billy worked long hours to complete the dig, while Jeff patrolled above them, binoculars in hand, pretending to be bird watching. This was the season when hawks migrated along the Pacific Flyway, so it provided a good cover story.

They had excavated 40 of the 96 quadrants, and by now were entirely comfortable with the process of overburden removal, sorting, searching, and removal. They averaged four quadrants per day, starting at sunrise and often finishing long after the sun had set beyond the Farallon Islands on the distant western horizon. The early darkness of autumn soon proved to be a problem, so Billy constructed a four-bulb, 12-volt light array, mounted in a cage of PVC pipe and connected to 100 feet of waterproof cable. A deep-discharge marine battery powered the lights, and while it wouldn't power them for more than a few hours of constant use, by rigging a switch to the unit he could turn them on and off as required, using handheld dive lights as an alternative. The water was so murky that the brilliant illumination from the light array wasn't visible from the surface.

They used the lights to illuminate the work site and extend their working time each evening until the batteries died, and were richly rewarded for their efforts. By the time they completed the final quadrant in the grid, they had found 121 additional ingots, more than 300 gold beads, three gold death masks, two golden sacrificial daggers, and 12 sets of what looked like huge, ornate earrings—in addition to a surprising array of bottles, fishing lures, a folding chair, a tragically ruined Nikon SLR camera, a radio, and an anchor.

On the tenth day, they completed the excavation of all 96 quadrants, and then moved outside the grid, where they excavated random areas around the perimeter of the debris field. This yielded no additional treasure, leading them to conclude that they had placed their grid well. When they finished, they packed up their equipment and bid a fond farewell to the work site that had consumed them for weeks and yielded so much. They left the grid in place, in case they needed to return to the site for any reason.

By the time they pulled up the anchor and headed back to the marina in Sausalito on that final night, it was dark. The fog had receded far out to sea, as it usually did in the fall, and legions of stars pierced the blackness. Billy's hand moved to the pull cord to start the engine, but for some unspoken reason, he didn't pull it. Instead, he looked over at Michael, smiled, and extended his hand. Michael took it and shook it warmly, then pulled Billy over, enveloping him in a bear hug. They both laughed, hugging and slapping each other on the back.

"Oh man, oh man, oh man," Michael laughed. "We must have done something right, I guess, 'cause somebody's definitely watching out for us."

Billy nodded, smiling. "How about a little celebration before we head in?" he asked Michael. Reaching into the ice chest, he dug deep and pulled out a split of Freixenet champagne. He pulled off the top, filled two plastic glasses that he had hidden in his dive bag, and offered one to his friend.

They clicked the glasses together, and Michael proffered a toast: "To the future, my friend. To a bright and shining future together."

They drank to the future, to their friendship and to their continued venture, then stretched out along the tubes of the inflatable and watched the stars. After 15 minutes of companionable silence, Billy started the engine, and they headed for the marina.

CHAPTER 33

While Michael and Billy completed the excavation, Lexie continued her research. As they brought her a steady stream of new artifacts, she photographed and catalogued them, and prepared for the upcoming trip to Spain with Michael. She made plane and hotel reservations for them and notified Rafael that they were coming. He was delighted. She also rented two large safe deposit boxes at a local bank and surreptitiously moved all the gold, including the boat, to them.

A week after submitting the wood sample, she visited her friend in the Paleontology lab, who informed her that the wood was between four and five hundred years old. This tracked with her belief that the treasure site was a 16th century vessel.

The night before they left for Spain, Lexie prepared dinner for Michael and Billy. They ate seared ahi steaks with hot papaya chutney, Australian warrigal greens that she bought at Trader Joes, a nutty rice pilaf, and hot, fresh-baked bread as they discussed their plans for the next few weeks.

During their absence, Billy would keep the dive shop and commercial side of the business on track, while Michael and Lexie attempted to uncover the secret of the wreck site and establish a provenance for the relics it had yielded. They anticipated that they would be gone for no more than three weeks; that should be plenty of time to do whatever research was required. If they failed to find the information they needed within three weeks, they would relegate it to a back burner and proceed with other priorities, specifically the quiet identification of potential buyers. During the two weeks that Michael and Billy completed the excavation, Lexie had spoken confidentially with a number of companies, including Christie's, Lloyd's, and Sotheby's. In every case they assured her that locating buyers for such rare pieces would be a simple task—speaking theoretically, of course.

Over Lexie's chocolate decadence and the fine Australian red that she had purchased, they talked long into the night. The treasure had opened doors onto opportunities that they had dared not dream of, but that were now tantalizingly real. Both Billy and Michael knew that the ocean was an inextricable part of their lives; they needed to regularly submerge themselves in its cool depths the way most people needed to breathe air. The diving business, they agreed, was a good way to pay the bills, share their passion for the ocean with students, and give them excuses to go diving, but it was as much a chore as it was a money generator. Now that they were on the verge of becoming—hopefully—independently wealthy, they realized that they were about to be presented with a difficult choice. Would they keep the dive shop, or would they leave it behind and do full time salvage work? It was a somewhat unsettling prospect; the shop had been a part of their lives for a long time, and selling it would be like selling a child. On the other hand, their combined professional expertise in seamanship, history, engineering, archaeology, and marine sciences clearly pointed them toward careers that would make better use of their skills and knowledge. Undecided, they opted to leave that decision for another day.

The next morning, Michael and Lexie flew out of San Francisco International Airport on a USAirways flight to Philadelphia, where they waited three hours for their 7:45 connection to Madrid. They landed at 9:10 the next morning at Barajas International Airport northeast of the city, where they collected their bags, cleared customs, and caught a cab into the city. Michael was in heaven, chatting with the cab driver as he gave him instructions to take them to the Meliá Madrid Hotel on the Calle Princesa. *He's like a little kid at Christmas*, thought Lexie, as she watched him grow more and more excited with every familiar landmark he spotted as they drove down the Avenida de las Américas toward the center of Madrid.

By the time they reached the tall, modern hotel downtown, jetlag had set in and they were exhausted. They checked in, went up to their room, took a quick shower, and fell into bed. They slept soundly for about five hours, at which time they awoke, still groggy but feeling immensely better. They took a long, hot shower, dressed, and went out for a stroll along Princesa, one of the busiest streets in Madrid. Michael guided Lexie down the street to the left, toward the Plaza de España. They window-shopped along the way, winding their way through the crowd, and before long had arrived at the massive statue of Don Quixote, Sancho Panza and Cervantes that marked the spot where Princesa ended and Gran Vía began. They crossed the street and walked around the statue, ultimately finding a vacant stone bench beside the reflecting pool. They sat down, and Lexie immediately threw her arms around Michael and hugged him tightly to her, refusing to let go. He hugged her back, chuckling.

"What's this for?" he asked. She hugged him tighter. "Just because I love you so much," she responded, kissing him fiercely on the lips. "I can't believe we're here together, by ourselves. You've told me about Madrid for so long that I feel like I've seen all this before. I know how much this place means to you, and it's really special that you're sharing it with me."

They looked at each other for a long time before anyone spoke. "Lexie, there's no one I'd rather share it with. You're so much a part of who I am now that I can't imagine being here without you. And besides, this is just as special to me. I know it sounds kind of corny, but I've wanted to share Spain with you for so long that this is a dream come true for me."

Michael paused for a moment, looking deeply into her crystalline blue eyes. "God, I love you so much. I'm so lucky to have you."

Lexie hugged him again, and whispered in his ear. "I'm so lucky to have you, too, Michael. Thank you."

With that, he kissed her on the lips, stroked her hair gently, and pulled her to her feet. "Come on, there's something I want to show you."

They walked up Gran Vía to Plaza Callao, the roundabout that reminded Michael of Piccadilly Square in London. From Callao they turned and walked down Calle Preciados to the Puerta del Sol, the oblong plaza that was once the center of the ancient city. From Sol, Michael guided Lexie down Calle Mayor to the Calle de Felipe III, which led them to the northeast corner of the Plaza Mayor, Michael's favorite place in the entire city. Begun in 1618, the enclosed Plaza was opened in 1620 to celebrate the canonization of five Spanish saints—Santa Teresa de Ávila, San Ignacio de Loyola, San Francisco Xavier, San Isidro, and San Felipe Neri. Throughout the 1800s and 1900s, it had seen bullfights, jousting competitions, marriages, royal assemblages, and open-air markets.

"Oh, Michael," breathed Lexie. "This is wonderful!"

They emerged from the shaded archway that led into the plaza proper. It was a massive, square structure that enclosed a vast cobblestone plaza surrounded by five story walls with towers perched at each corner. Delicate archways marched around the inner perimeter, setting off the shaded store entries behind them from the plaza itself. In the center sat a massive statue of Felipe III on horseback, looking down upon the goings-on. He was covered with sparrows.

"Years ago," said Michael, "They realized that they needed a parking lot around here because of all the tourist traffic. So they moved the statue, pulled up all the cobblestones, numbered each and every one of them, dug a huge hole, built an underground parking lot, and put the stones and statue back exactly as they were before. Unbelievable job." They walked across the cobbles toward the statue. They paused for a moment, looking up at the king.

"When I was here as a kid," Michael recalled, "my friends and I would always meet right here on Friday night. We'd tell each other, 'See you under the horse's ass!'"

After a minute or so, they continued across to the other side of the Plaza. Lexie pointed to a dense gathering of people beneath the arches. "What are all those people doing over there?" she asked.

Michael smiled. "That's the stamp and coin market," he replied. "Vendors come out to sell old coins, bills, and stamps to collectors. The stamps and bills are genuine, but most of the 'Roman and Greek' coins are forgeries. They stamp them out of copper blanks, bury them for a while, pound 'em with a hammer, then sell them as centuries-old artifacts. They're fun to collect, though. I have a whole box of 'em in my closet; up until now, they're the only treasure I've ever had—except for you, of course." Lexie punched him in the shoulder.

They walked past the street vendors under the shaded, arched promenade, looking at the bewildering array for sale there. A gnarled gypsy approached from an arched doorway with a baby, muttering, begging for money; Michael gently pushed her aside and guided Lexie to an outdoor café, where they sat at a small table under a parasol. The table rocked gently on the cobbles.

"How may I help you?" inquired the waiter who magically appeared from nowhere, dressed in a white jacket and black bowtie. In flawless, staccato Spanish, Michael replied. *"Calamares fritos, dos lonchas de tortilla, aceitunas, y dos horchatas, por favor."* The waiter smiled, impressed. "Si, señor, right away." He turned, weaving his way through the warren of tables, most of them occupied by other diners.

"You really are in your element, aren't you?" laughed Lexie. "I've never seen you so excited."

Michael grinned back at her. "This is like home, Lex. I have sort of an—I don't know, I guess a kind of psychic link with this place, and it's really comforting to be here. I really meant what I said earlier—it's incredibly special to be in Spain with you."

She took his hand and squeezed it. "It's just as special for me, Michael. I'm really glad we're doing this together."

Michael went silent for a time, staring down at the tabletop long enough that Lexie became concerned and asked if he was all right.

"I'm fine, Lexie," he responded. "I'm just thinking. I really am 'in my element,' as you said; this place makes me feel complete. The only thing missing is—well, this ..." he reached into his pocket and withdrew a small hinged velvet box. Lexie immediately recognized it for what it was, and the lambent light from the candle on the table made the tears that gathered on her face glisten. "I've wanted to ask you this for a very long time, but didn't feel like I had enough to offer you and was afraid you'd—"

Lexie reached across the table and grabbed his hand. "Yes, Michael—yes. I've loved you since the day we met, and yes, I will marry you. I'm assuming, of course, that there's an engagement ring in that box? And that I haven't just made a fool of myself?"

Michael smiled slowly, and dropping to one knee, much to the surprise of the other guests nearby, he opened the box and withdrew an exquisite Varna Tzarina ring, which he carefully placed on her finger. "Let's make this official. Will you marry me, Lexie?"

She covered her face with her hands, still crying, and nodded. The crowd around them, which had gone silent during Michael's proposal, broke out in spontaneous applause, and the gentleman at the next table called out to the waiter for champagne. Michael stood, pulled Lexie from her chair, and kissed her, then enveloped her in a hug. Toasts rang out all around them, and more than a half hour passed before they were able to eat. Every guest at every table came over to congratulate them. Michael ended up ordering several additional bottles of champagne to share with their fellow diners, as a spontaneous party atmosphere settled over the café.

By the time the waiter arrived with their food they were starving, and they ate with relish. The calamares were cooked perfectly, hot and sweet and tender, and the tortilla was exactly as Michael remembered it—sweet with the taste of caramelized onions and rich with potato and egg. He watched as Lexie tasted horchata for the first time, the sweet, milky liquid made from chufa beans. Her eyes lit up.

"This is really good!" she exclaimed. "I can't believe you can't get this in the States!"

"Actually, you can," Michael replied, "but only in Hispanic markets. Sometimes I buy it down south of Mission in San Francisco. I just love the stuff."

Lexie nodded. "It's kind of chalky, but really refreshing."

They continued their meal, and when they were finished, Michael paid the waiter, thanked all of their newfound friends for helping to make the evening so special, and then guided Lexie across the Plaza to the Arco de Cuchilleros, which led down a steep stairway to the narrow, winding streets of Old Madrid. There, time ran more slowly. The streets, narrow and cobbled, were lined with tiny specialty shops that each sold a single product: wooden dishware, straw products, rope, grain, barrels, wine. Each was owned and operated by ageless, time-creased men and women who chatted openly with all comers. Michael stopped and talked for several minutes with a little old man who sharpened knives, his peddle-powered grinding wheel mounted on the handlebars of his bicycle. He announced his imminent arrival to the neighborhood by blowing a tuneless, rhythm-free melody on a panpipe; residents would come out of their homes with their knives and wait patiently in line to have them sharpened.

They strolled around Old Madrid for several hours, and by the time evening fell were pleasantly exhausted. They stopped in a small *tasca* to have dinner, which consisted of several plates of *tapas,* washed down with tiny glasses of harsh red wine. To cap off the evening, they walked back to the hotel and stopped at an outdoor restaurant at the pedestrian-packed corner of Princesa and Grán Vía. There, Michael invited Lexie to try a special treat: cinnamon ice cream, the specialty of the restaurant there. They sat in chairs on the sidewalk, watching the crowds of people go by and eating the spicy, cold dessert.

"We used to sit here on Friday and Saturday nights when I was in high school," said Michael. "We saw all sorts of people go by. Madrid was a real happening town back then, and there were all sorts of Hollywood people here. It was lots of fun."

The ice cream finished, they strolled back to the hotel with their arms around each other. Once there, they showered, and shortly after Michael climbed into bed Lexie joined him, smelling of Maja soap. The scent took him back to his high school days in Madrid. She leaned over and gave him a long, lingering kiss before sliding on top of him.

"I guess you are excited to be here," she whispered huskily. She softly kissed his eyelids, nose, forehead, cheeks, and worked her way to his neck, which she licked before moving on to his ear, sending shivers down his spine.

"Welcome to Spain," he smiled.

CHAPTER 34

The next morning, Lexie and Michael rose early and ate breakfast at a *churrería* around the corner from the hotel. They consumed fresh, hot churros and the thick hot chocolate so characteristic of Spain. It was more like pudding, Lexie observed.

After eating, they caught a cab and directed the driver to Paseo de Recoletos 20-22, the address of the *Biblioteca Nacional*—the Spanish National Library. They had plans to meet Rafael Santoro at nine o'clock to begin their research into the mystery of their shipwreck.

Santoro met them in the cavernous lobby of the prestigious building. He was a short, dark, balding man dressed to sartorial perfection, and upon seeing Michael, he broke into a broad grin and hugged him, planting kisses on both cheeks. In heavily accented but otherwise perfect English, he took Lexie's outstretched hand and brushed the back of it with his lips, bowing as he said to her, "Had I known that you were as beautiful as Michael intimated, I would have brought the information you requested personally—or perhaps suggested that you come alone."

Lexie giggled, and turning to Michael, said, "I think I could grow to like it here. In about five minutes."

Michael just smiled and shook his head.

Santoro gestured with a wide sweep of his arm, and

they followed him to an elevator that took them to his office, a large cluttered room with precious little space for a human being among the stacks of books, article offprints, videotapes, stacks of DVDs and artifact cases. Deep in the chaos was a cavern carved among the stalagmites of paper, where they found a desk, two chairs, and a lawyer's bookcase, in which was a collection of books that were clearly very, very old. On top of the desk perched a massive flat screen computer monitor, the only indication that the modern world had made its way into Santoro's sanctum sanctorum, and behind it a coffee pot was just gurgling to a finish. The smell of fresh-brewed coffee was overpowering, and Santoro poured three mugs.

"I took the liberty of reserving a study room for you while you are here, and had the archivist move all of the relevant documents in our collection in there for you. You are free to peruse them as you require, provided you use standard paleographic techniques to handle them. You're quite lucky: Michael spent so much time here in the past that the staff all know him. That helped me *immensely* when I requested access for you, and Alejandra, your affiliation with Bancroft—how do you say—sealed the deal."

"Orellana is something of an enigma to us," he continued. "There's precious little in the known history about him regarding what he did after leaving Pizarro and heading off to the Amazon, and what we do have is often conflicting. Some say he headed down the Madre de Diós River, while other accounts have him drifting interminably down the Napo. One account says that he made it all the way to the mouth of the Amazon and continued on to the Spanish outpost in Trinidad to report on his findings and re-provision before heading back up the Amazon, while others have him never leaving the Amazon before he disappeared in what was apparently a rather nasty storm. The one thing we *do* know is that he apparently gave the Amazon River its name.

According to legend, he and his party were apparently attacked by a village that as near as he could tell comprised nothing but women. They sent him and his followers, brave soldiers all, fleeing for their lives."

Lexie smiled at this, which Santoro picked up on immediately.

Looking at Michael, he said, "If those women were half as beautiful as this one, I can't imagine why they fled. I would have gladly died in their arms."

Lexie laughed, and Michael retorted, "Rafael, you haven't changed a bit. Once a charmer, always a charmer." Santoro smiled enigmatically and shrugged his shoulders as if to say, 'What can I say? I'm Spanish!'

"You'll have to forgive me, but I have a series of meetings that I must attend if I am to continue to be paid by this august organization," he continued. "Come with me and I'll show you to your temporary quarters."

He led them down the long hallway before stopping at a solid wooden door. "Here are the keys, one for each of you." He handed them over. "You know where my office is; please call on me any time. And Miss Moliner, if you can lose this fellow, I can lose my meetings." With that, he bowed, winked at Lexie, embraced Michael, and walked off down the hall.

"Is he always like that?" laughed Lexie, shaking her head.

"I'm afraid so," sighed Michael. "Nature of the beast. Shall we get started?"

* * *

By noon, they had made a cursory examination of all of the material that Santoro had left for them. They organized it as best they could into piles categorized by topic: shipping manifests, log entries, clerical documentation, and so on. It was clear that they were the first researchers to examine many of the documents, based on the lack of organization of the materials and the haphazard manner in which they were stacked. Some documents were not marked, and were relegated to a "For Later Examination" pile. Michael took the shipping manifests, which were in a collection of document boxes and difficult to read, since they were written by hand and by dozens of different people, all of whom seemed to have their own special spelling rules. Lexie, meanwhile, began to plow through the clerical documentation, which was somewhat easier to read since clerics all seemed to follow some sort of canonical standard for the written word. And while her Spanish was not as good as Michael's, she could wade her way through most of the text; what she didn't understand she asked Michael to interpret for her.

By the end of the day they had read all of the shipping manifests and most of the clerical documents without discovering anything of consequence. There were occasional mentions of Orellana, particularly in the documents that came back with the Pizarro expeditions, but they were scant at best, offering little in the way of insight. The clerical material yielded one passing reference to the man, but only in the context of his intentions to convert the Indians he encountered during his voyage across the South American continent to Catholicism. Otherwise, Orellana remained a mystery.

At seven o'clock, they quit for the day, told Rafael that they would be back a bit later, and left to eat. They returned to the hotel, cleaned up, and took a cab to José Luis, a steak house that Michael knew. The restaurant was nowhere near ready to serve dinner, which in Madrid begins no earlier than nine o'clock, so they sat at the bar, ate tapas, and had a sherry while they waited. Finally, the maitre d' came over and led them to a table. Michael ordered a bottle of Marqués de Riscal, and *solomillo* with roasted potatoes and asparagus for both of them. They were famished, having worked through lunch, and they ate ravenously. For dessert, they had flan and espresso.

They took a cab back to the library, but it was nearly ten thirty by the time they arrived, so they agreed to work for an hour before calling it a night. They went through the remainder of the clerical documentation, but again, found nothing. Resigned, they returned to the hotel and went to bed.

The next morning they rose early, ate breakfast in the hotel, and once again took a cab to the Library, where Rafael greeted them warmly in his office. They explained that they had not yet found anything that would help them with their research, but still had a great deal of documentation to go through.

"Much of that material has not yet even been catalogued," Santoro explained apologetically. "There is so much in our collection, and our archival staff is so limited, that it will be many years before we have the luxury of a completely catalogued archive. It would not surprise me if you run across something important that we do not yet have recorded, so if you do, please let me know so that I can make note of it. In that regard, you are helping us as much as we are helping you." They spoke for a few more minutes, then, after agreeing to meet for lunch, they bid Santoro farewell.

They returned to their temporary quarters, and while Michael plowed through the log entries from the captains and first officers of the many ships that had sailed back and forth between Spain and the New World during the 16th century, Lexie tackled the "For Later Examination" boxes. They contained single sheets of scrawl-covered paper, partially completed maps, and dozens of books that had no title. Many had been exposed to moisture over the years, and had pages that were inseparable and would require careful conservation efforts to open. Others had been feasted upon by insects, as evidenced by the tiny, random tunnels that meandered through their pages. All had the same wonderful smell of archival knowledge.

Many of the books turned out to be religious treatises, offering little to their search. One was completely blank, other than a name on the first page, written in ink long turned to brown: Maimonides Cásaro. She set it aside and picked up the next book in the first box. It was large,

perhaps thirty centimeters by twenty, and covered with a
stained leather cover, shiny from handling. Placing it on
the table, she opened the book to reveal a large, pressed
flower, faded almost white from age. Written below it were
these words:

Diario de Nuestra Señora de la Selva
Capitán Francisco de Orellana
Primer Oficial de A Bordo Antonio de la Cierva
A.N.S. 1545

Lexie rubbed her eyes and read the words again. If her
Spanish served her properly, this book was the ship's log
from some vessel called "Our Lady of the Jungle,"
captained by Orellana. She guessed that the next line
referred to the first officer, Antonio de la Cierva, followed
by A.N.S.—Año de Nuestro Señor, Year of Our Lord—
1545. She carefully turned the pages, and found that the
book was filled with long, wandering passages written by a
skilled, flowing hand, and shorter, more informational
entries written by a less careful diarist. The signature at the
bottom of one of the long entries made it clear that
Orellana was the more careful writer, while first officer de
la Cierva was less concerned with neatness. The book had
gotten wet at some point in the past, because many of the
pages were stuck together, sometimes in thick blocks of
twenty sheets or more. She did not attempt to separate
them.

Turning to the list of holdings that Rafael had provided,
she scanned the entries. There was nothing about the book
listed. "Michael, you'd better look at this," she whispered.
"I think I've found something."

Michael turned from the log he was perusing and rolled
his chair over to where Lexie was working. "What've you
got, babe?" he asked, bored with his own work. He saw

that she had a large hand-written book in front of her, and he felt his pulse pick up just a bit.

She turned to him, pointing to the cover page. "This is Orellana's log from some voyage he took down a river, and based on what we know about him, the only river journey he ever took was the one we're interested in. I just checked the list of holdings that Rafael gave us, and this book isn't listed. I don't think it's ever been logged into the collection."

Michael looked closely, turning the pages quickly to get a sense of what it contained. "Damn, Lex, I think you're right," he replied, excitedly. "We're going to have to read this thing cover to cover, and if we're lucky, it'll mention something that we can match to what we found. How did I ever get along without you, anyway?" he asked, kissing her loudly on the cheek.

She smiled at him, and replied, "Just keep that in mind when you get the urge to start shopping around for a little señorita."

He just shook his head. "Never happen. Scoot over, let's take a look."

She made room for his chair, and together, they began to wade through the journal of a journey that led them from the Andean Altiplano to the Amazon River basin and beyond. Michael read the entries out loud in Spanish for a brief time, then began to translate them for Lexie who was having trouble keeping up with him. It was difficult going, particularly because they had to read the book in patches, since so many of the pages were inaccessible to them.

Steven Shepard

CHAPTER 35

4 April 1545

*We have left the relative comfort of the high
mountains to begin our exploration of the jungle
lands that lie to the south and east of here.
Gonzalo Pizarro has instructed us to search for
what the Indians refer to as Curicuri, a lost city
where the rivers flow with gold and riches. I
remain skeptical, but for the glory of Spain will
undertake the journey. It has been nearly a year
since I saw my wife Luisa and my son Miguel
Angel; I trust that it will not be much longer
before I am reunited with them. I miss them very
much.*

Lexie shook her head. "You know, I've read everything
we have on Orellana, but I've never seen any reference to
his wife or children," she began. "In fact, I wasn't even
aware he *had* a family until now. Life must have been pretty
crappy for him to have left a family behind for a couple of
years without much hope of coming back."

"You hit the nail on the head, Lexie," responded
Michael. "Remember the time period we're talking about
here. It's mid-16th century, and Spain has been in a steady
economic and cultural decline since 1492, when the

Catholic Kings made the colossally stupid mistake of kicking the Jews out of the country in the name of the Inquisition and all that was believed to be Holy. The Sephardic Jews represented the merchant class; they *were* the economy. So when they left, they took the economy with them. Also, remember that Spain's military power is starting to fade by now, as well. This was written in 1545; three years later, Sir Francis Drake sank the Armada, putting the final nail in Spain's coffin. So it wasn't really that much of a leap for these men to take. The country was in disrepair; there were no jobs; and most of them came from Extremadura, the poorest part of the country, way down in the southwest. Men tend to be far more adventurous when they have nothing to lose. And it's clear that many of them felt that way."

He turned the page and read on.

10 April 1545

We lost a man today when he was set upon and bitten by a large spider that fell from a tree. In spite of all ministrations by the priest, he expired, shaking as if with palsy. The creatures in this jungle are devil sent. Even the monkeys in the trees bedevil us, pelting us as we pass with excrement from their own bodies.

"That is just plain gross!" Lexie exclaimed.

Michael laughed. "You obviously haven't been to the Primate Center at the San Francisco Zoo lately. There's a gorilla there that spends his day pelting tourists with gorilla shit with unerring accuracy. He's become such an attraction that people get there early to set up their video cameras."

Lexie just looked at him. "You would know that," she retorted.

14 April 1545

We spoke today with a group of heathen Indians that we came upon. They told us that there was gold to be found farther inland. We had them lead us to their village, where we found much gold. We killed their tribal leader as punishment for misleading us, and took all of the gold we could find. It did not amount to a great deal, but perhaps there will be more.

21 April 1545

The insects in this jungle cannot be escaped, and they bite without surcease. In some cases the clouds of mosquitoes are so dense that they send men screaming into the jungle, looking for water in which to immerse themselves. I have been so tempted on more than one occasion. Some of the men have taken to smearing themselves with mud to prevent the worst of the bites. It occasionally works. Luisa, I would give anything to hold you now.

22 April 1545

Today we came upon a large village in the foothills of the mountains that appeared to have been abandoned. There were buildings aplenty, but they were empty and did not appear to have been used for quite some time. In one building we found a cache of golden icons, religious items perhaps, which we confiscated. We have still seen no sign of Curicuri, but remain confident that we are on the proper course.

As we left the village, one of the soldiers spotted a face peering at us from the edge of the jungle. However, when we investigated, there was nothing there. I suspect that it was a mere hallucination.

"Sounds like he's starting to lose it," Michael commented.

Lexie shook her head. "I don't think so," she replied. "I think he's just getting disgusted, and beginning to wonder if the gold is worth all the headaches it's causing them. Read on."

30 April 1545

We fought a skirmish today with the residents of a small village that attacked us from the safety of the jungle as we passed their village. They threw spears and killed two men with stones flung from slings. We were victorious in the battle but lost seven men by the time it was over. The captain grew angry and frustrated, as we do not appear to be any closer to his goal than when we started the journey.

Two men are dead sick with spider bites.

"So this is the first time we hear from someone other than Orellana," mused Lexie. "De la Cierva speaks. He sounds pretty together, and is obviously watching out for his captain. It's interesting how neither of them have said much of anything about the morality of what they were doing, looting villages."

Michael nodded. "There wasn't much room for questioning during that time," he explained. "You didn't question the morals or reasons for the actions of the Inquisition; you just accepted it and did what they said to do. Besides, they probably had a priest along for the ride, and those guys typically served as spies for the powers of the Inquisition back home. Any transgressions would be reported, and the consequences could be—well, less than pleasant."

8 May 1545

*A most strange thing happened today. We came
upon a small river, along which were boats carved
from a soft wood. The boats reeked of fish.
Alongside the river was a small village, and the
residents of the village came out to meet us as we
approached. Wonder of wonders, one of the older
men spoke a form of Spanish that allowed us to
communicate in something close to the tongue of
the realm. He explained to us that he had spent
some considerable time with the Priests when they
arrived in Peru, but had left after many months
to return here, to his village. He told us that there
was in fact a village, farther downriver, where we
would find that all implements of eating, cleaning,
and daily routine were of the purest gold. A few
days travel, he allowed, and we would come upon
it. We left his village with a joyous demeanor,
secure in the belief that we were now close to our
goal.*

18 May 1545

*It is the cruelest trick of God that keeps us here,
lost in this verdant Hell. It has been ten days
since the village elder told us of the golden city, yet
we find no sign of its existence. It is true that
various small settlements have given up their gold
to us, and we now transport more riches than we
can scarce carry. The gold, however, begins to pale
in value as we consider the depth to which we have
penetrated this jungle. We know not how much
farther it is to civilization, and as a man of the
sea I would give anything for a glimpse of the
ocean. Thankfully we travel alongside a large,
slowly flowing river; its water gives me strength.*

Antonio has been my salvation throughout our

*ordeal. He helps to keep the men healthy and
sane, works with the priest to provide for their
spiritual needs, and keeps my own spirits as high
as they can be. They flag with regularity, but I
must hide my own feelings, as that would cause
grief for the men who now fight their own demons.*

*Luisa María, a small golden medallion has
found its way into my possession. It is perhaps the
size of a falcon's egg, inlaid with a surround of
the tiniest of pearls, and bears the raised outline
of an Inca god of sorts. One of our men is an
artisan, and I had him mark it with your
initials. Its beauty will be enhanced when it hangs
on a chain around your beautiful neck, the neck I
long to kiss.*

Lexie reached for the photographs she had made of the
artifacts just as Michael finished reading the passage. She
fanned them out on the desktop and searched through
them frantically. Finding the one she was looking for, she
extracted it from the pile, brushed the others aside, and
looked at the close-up of the medallion that Michael and
Billy had found. It was, indeed, inlaid with tiny pearls, and
bore the embossed image of a deity. More important,
however, was the photograph of the back of the medallion.
There, in the center of the smooth gold, clearly visible in
the close-up photograph, were engraved the initials
LMO—Luisa María de Orellana.

"That's it!" Michael exclaimed. "We've got it, Lexie!
We've got our provenance! This really is Orellana's ship
that we've found, and now we can prove it!"

Lexie jumped and hugged him. "Do you know what
this means?" she asked, hugging him tighter. "The value of
what you found just went up by several orders of
magnitude. This isn't just a treasure—it's *Orellana's*
treasure! Collectors *kill* for artifacts that come with proof
of provenance!"

They held each other for several minutes before sitting back down and returning to the book. The rest of the narrative was now inconsequential as far as their original reason for coming to Spain was concerned, but they felt compelled to finish the journey with this man that had gone so far and who had brought them so much. Michael read on.

25 May 1545

We have come to the confluence of two great rivers, the one we have been following and another, much larger one. It is so wide that it appears to be standing still, it moves so slowly.

A most strange thing occurred as we arrived at this spot. We have decided to remain here for some number of days to provision our stores and give the men some time to rest, and were in the process of setting up a camp when we were descended upon by a great horde of scantily clad women, dressed as warriors and armed as equally as men. They were fierce, and drove us far downriver from where we had intended to make camp. Three men succumbed to their weapons, and four others remain unaccounted for. They attacked us without respite for more than an hour before disappearing into the forest.

As much damage as they caused us I cannot help but be impressed with their courage, valor and ferocity. I have named this mighty river 'Amazon,' to honor our fierce foes and to serve as a warning to those who might follow.

"It's a reasonably well-known fact that Orellana is the guy who gave the Amazon its name, and this is why," effused Lexie. "What a fantastic document this is. To date, the only accounts we have of this voyage are second-hand logs from clerics and oral histories collected from some of the soldiers in bits and pieces. Here we have the actual log entry from the day he named the Amazon. Incredible!"

Michael agreed. "We'll have to share this with Santoro eventually, but not until you have a chance to publish your paper. This is going to make your name in the field, isn't it?"

Lexie nodded. "Yes it will, Michael. This is the kind of discovery that archaeologists work their entire lives for and rarely ever find. I'm already thinking about the paper, but don't worry—I won't get near a publisher until you and Billy have established ownership of the artifacts."

1 June 1545

We have decided to take a bold step, and have taken to it with vigor. The task of cutting a track through this jungle is arduous and fraught with peril, as there are in addition to the fierce human warriors that we must contend with a dangerous collection of serpents, jaguars, biting insects that carry various diseases that continue to take my men with frightening regularity, and poisonous plants that bleed saps and juices that blind and burn. We have therefore decided to build a vessel upon which we will travel downriver in a manner that we are far more accustomed to. If we can accomplish this we will be less susceptible to attack, free from most of the insects, and able to travel considerably farther in a day's time than we can possibly accomplish on foot.

10 June 1545

Work on the vessel continues apace. There are plentiful hard and softwoods in the forest, and among the troops there are many skilled in carpentry. Antonio once again distinguishes himself as a natural leader among the men, and

*under his guidance the ship will be complete in
short order. He has organized the men into work
groups; some have felled trees, others have been
tasked with cutting strength members and planks
from them, while others have the arduous task of
cutting nails from the horseshoes that we brought
for the horses. It is onerous but necessary work, if
we are to ever leave this place.*

29 June 1545

*We have launched our vessel, and she floats
proudly upon the water! We christened her
Nuestra Señora de la Selva with a splash of rum
across her forebow, and pray that she will take us
out of here. Her planks are caulked with the
white, rubbery sap of a succulent that grows in
quantity in the jungle, a strange liquid that dries
into rubber. Tomorrow, we sail downriver.*

*For just a moment this evening, I swear that I
smelled a faint taste of the sea upon the breeze,
just before sunset. I take it as a good omen, and
while I strained to regain that wonderful smell, it
did not return.*

Unfortunately, the pages that followed this entry were
cemented together in a thick block, probably by water.
Michael tried for several minutes to tease the pages apart,
but succeeded only in fraying the corner of the page.

"Rafael will kill me if I tear this. These can be pulled
apart, but it requires special equipment that we don't have
here. We'll just have to turn over to the next part that isn't
stuck together and wait for the paleographers to do the
restoration work for us. It's a shame, but we already have
what we need."

Lexie nodded. "You're right, but I'm really enjoying
this. I feel like I'm inside this man's mind, and we're taking

part in a novel. I really want to know what happens next!"

The pages of the journal were not numbered in any way, and it was therefore impossible to tell with any accuracy how many they were forced to skip. Michael turned to the next section of the book where the pages were free, adjusted the desk light, and continued to read. The first page was a continuation from an entry begun on the previous page.

> ... and neither I nor Antonio trust him. I intend to sail from here under cover of darkness at the first opportunity, because after what we saw yesterday I believe that he intends to take our treasure for his own purposes. As for his intentions toward us, I can only assume the worst. We will therefore take our leave of this place as soon as the darkness of the moon permits.
>
> 22 August 1545
>
> Tonight is the night. We leave Afuá and the treachery of de Beas after midnight. The moon and the promise of rain will perhaps help us to slip away.

"Who do you suppose this de Beas character is?" mused Lexie.

Michael shook his head. "Don't know…let's keep reading, maybe we'll figure it out. Otherwise we'll find out when we get the book restored."

> 31 August 1545
>
> We managed to evade the pursuing ships of de Beas, but the teeth of a hungry storm have seized us and now toss us about the sea as a terrier tosses a rat. I worry about the integrity of our tiny ship; she was, after all, built for the calm of the

river, not the rages of the open sea. I must now repair to the foredeck to help Antonio stand watch, as many of the men are sick. May God preserve us.

10 September 1545

We are wrecked upon the sandy shore of an isthmus of land far to the west of the mouth of the great river that spit us into the sea. I have written 10 September although that is merely a guess, as the ability to track the comings and goings of the days and nights during the storm that tossed us here was difficult. However, we are now safe upon the sand, although our salvation, Nuestra Señora de la Selva, lies with a broken back and stove sides before us in the surf. She is pitiful, like a whale cast upon the beach. We must salvage her before the tide takes her away.

12 September 1545

The men have come together and recovered from the storm's fury and their anger at being shipwrecked after enduring such an ordeal for so many months. We have set up a camp of sorts, and have managed to salvage most of what was on our ship. Once she was unloaded, we managed to rig lines and pull her up the beach away from the clutching hands of the sea. I remain pessimistic about our ability to repair her, as she is mortally damaged; however, I have other plans. I believe that we are aground on a narrow spit of land that can be crossed in a matter of days. The other side of the spit is washed by the Mar del Sur, and if we can reach it, then perhaps we can rendezvous with Pizarro farther south. I have therefore dispatched a team of men to trek into the jungle and probe its depths. Hopefully they will return with news that the Mar del Sur lies not far away.

7 October 1545

The Captain drinks rum with the men as his beliefs have borne fruit. His expedition force has returned after 21 days away with wondrous news. Not only did they find the Mar del Sur, but God was watching out for them as He saw fit to send a small cadre of Pizarro's ships northward where by sheer coincidence they met up with the expedition team. They have agreed to wait for us to trek across the Isthmus, where we will load our cargo aboard the vessels and sail northward, where we are to rendezvous with Gonzalo Pizarro, who has sailed ahead in search of that which he pursues ceaselessly. Thanks be to God!

18 October 1545

We are once again aboard a fine ship, and are underway. The trek through the jungle took place without incident and we now sail northward. We have been instructed to look for Pizarro, who will leave a signal fire burning at night. I look forward to our reunion with much anticipation, as we have much to present him for the king's treasury.

20 November 1545

We have been sailing now for nearly 30 days since leaving shore, but to date have seen no sign of Pizarro. One of the men on watch thought he saw the mast of a ship on the horizon, but was not sure. Luisa, I can almost feel you in my arms. Soon, my darling, we will be together and I will never leave you again. Never.

22 November 1545

*I write this entry by lantern light, as it is dusk
and the light fails me. To our west, there is a
small chain of islands that are shown on the map
as the Faralones; they are home to thousands of
sea birds, and earlier the captain gave orders to
anchor and sent a party ashore to collect eggs.
Now we sail due east, as the watch spotted a
signal fire along the cliffs of the coastline. We are
now close enough that I can see the flames clearly.
Soon we will be reunited with the rest of our
expedition, and with our treasure will sail for
Spain. I salute the King and praise God.*

Michael turned the page, but much to his dismay, the
remaining pages were blank. He flipped through the entire
book, but found nothing else written there. He felt a chill
as he realized that this was the last entry Orellana made
before his ship piled up on the reef, leaving a trove that
would lie hidden in the thick mud of the sea floor until he
and Billy found it 500 years later.

This was almost too much for him to accept. Not only
had he and Billy found a treasure of incomprehensible
value, Lexie had now found the provenance that detailed
the gold's identity, its age, and how it came to be buried
under the Golden Gate. And, he realized something else:
somewhere down there, near where he and Billy had
excavated the sea floor, Orellana's bones continued to rest.

"This is so strange," he said, standing up and
stretching. "I feel like I'm having a dream, and any minute
now I'm going to wake up. But it isn't, is it? This is all
real?"

Lexie laughed and hugged him. "Yes, Michael, it's real.
The gold is real, the provenance is real, and this"—
gesturing at Orellana's log—"is real. You guys have really
done it. Do you realize what this means? Do you realize

how wealthy you're going to be, and how this is going to change your life? This is as big a find as the Atocha, and from what I've seen, may be worth more, both historically and monetarily. You and Billy can now do all the things you've talked about for so long."

Michael looked down at her, then reached out and took her in his arms. "This is real too, Lexie, you and me. I found my treasure a long time ago. The gold's icing on the cake. It's a hell of a cake, but it's just icing."

She hugged him back as she spoke. "Like I said, now that you're rich and soon-to-be-famous, keep me in mind when all those dark-eyed señoritas start chasing you. Remember" she said, flashing her ring in his face, "You're mine now, and I don't share."

He hugged her back. "Your job is to chase them all away," he replied.

CHAPTER 36

They quickly went through the remaining documents, but found nothing else of value, certainly nothing that could compare to what Orellana's log had revealed to them. They turned the logbook over to Santoro, explaining that they had found some items of interest in other documents but that the key to their research lay in the pages of Orellana's logbook. Santoro was immensely pleased that Lexie had identified the document, and promised to have the paleographers separate the pages and send her digital images of the entire book within two weeks.

"This is an important document, Rafael," she explained to him. "There is very little available on the life of Captain Orellana, and this fills in many of the holes in what we know. Thank you for sending copies as soon as possible." Santoro promised he would, and that evening he and his wife Dolores took them to dinner at Bajamar, a renowned seafood restaurant on the Paseo de Castellana.

They visited long into the night, and finally bid each other farewell at two in the morning. Michael and Lexie caught a cab back to the hotel, where they fell into a deep sleep. The next morning they woke, showered and dressed, and ate churros for breakfast before renting a car.

Michael had promised Lexie that he would show her the country before going home, so they took off in the tiny vehicle and spent the next five days touring the places that were so deeply emblazoned in Michael's memory. They went to Toledo, where they stopped the car beside the Puerta del Sol, the gateway into the ancient walled city that was built in the first century, to buy olives and churros from the street vendors there. The olives were ladled from huge, earthenware crocks; the churros were cooked in hot oil and strung on reeds picked at the nearby river. They munched on these as they walked through the town, taking in the spectacular view of the city from the road that wound above the Tagus River before touring the Bermejo Steel Factory, where the dress swords for most of the world's militaries are made. In the town square, they ate lunch at a sidewalk café before walking through the massive, hushed cathedral.

From Toledo, they continued on to Segovia, where they visited the Alcázar and paid homage to the Spanish kings that sent people like Pizarro and Orellana off to explore the new world. Lexie smacked Michael hard on the butt when she saw the massive, seven-story Roman aqueduct that divided the town and listened to his tale about crawling across the top of it with a group of friends when he was in high school, only to discover that it didn't end at the other side of the plaza: They had to continue crawling for almost a kilometer until it dropped low enough that they could jump into a pile of hay.

For the remainder of the five days, they went to Ávila, El Escorial, the windmills of La Mancha, and Seville, before continuing on to Granada. There, they toured the Alhambra and the Generalife, spent the night in a parador, and rose early on the last morning to return to Madrid. That evening they dined with Manuel Quirós, an old friend of Michael's who had become one of Spain's best-known surrealist artists. They spent their last night at the Meliá before catching the noon flight to Philadelphia the next day, arriving back in San Francisco at 8:30 that evening.

Billy met them at the airport and took them to Lexie's apartment, where they visited for an hour, filling Billy in on all that had happened. Needless to say, he was as stunned as they had been, but that quickly gave way to euphoria.

"I knew it!" he cried, laughing. "I knew we'd be able to get something a little bigger than the Achilles!"

Michael laughed as well. "Hey, don't knock the inflatable. If it weren't for that, we wouldn't have what we do."

Finally, Billy left for home, and Michael and Lexie fell into bed without even bothering to unpack. They had agreed to meet Billy for breakfast late the next morning, and at ten o'clock, they strolled into the Village Inn Café in Orinda, where Billy already had a table.

"About time," he grumbled. "I've been sitting here for half an hour already, and I'm starving to death. I already ordered, but Kathy's been waiting to turn it in until you got here." He motioned to Kathy, who smiled and gave him a thumbs-up before putting their order on the wheel. She was Lexie's oldest and dearest friend, and as soon as she turned in the order she came over and gave them all hugs. They visited for a few minutes before she went back to her other customers.

"So tell me where we are with all this," Billy asked, excitedly. They had told him the basics the night before, but today had to fill him in on the details of their trip. They went back through the description of all the documents they had examined, concluding with Lexie's discovery of the logbook from Orellana's ill-fated final voyage.

"So what you're telling me," he said in a hushed voice, "Is that we've got our provenance, and now all we have to do is figure out what to do about the—you know."

Michael nodded. "Yeah, that's right, except that we've got to be very, very careful from here on out. Nobody—and I mean, nobody—knows what we've found out there, and we have to keep it that way until we figure out what our next steps are. I'm not all that good on Admiralty Law, so I don't know if we can legally own the gold, or if Spain will come after it, or if Peru will come after it, or California, or what. We need to get a lawyer, and we need to get one that's discrete and good at—lawyering."

They looked at each other for a full five seconds before they smiled at each other and spoke in unison.

"Rich."

CHAPTER 37

"This is almost too much for me to get my head around, Michael," said Rich, gazing intently at him across the wide expanse of desk. "It's certainly more than I can process with my tiny little lawyer's brain."

Rich's office looked like the medieval armor display room in a large museum. Collections of swords hung in glass cases on two walls; a suit of armor stood in one corner with a halberd at port arms; and a chain mail shirt lay draped across a wooden stand beside the desk, just in case its owner needed it for a casual encounter on the street. He was a lawyer, after all.

Looking down at the photographs with which Lexie had paved the surface of his desk, he shook his head in disbelief. "You're telling me that you found this stuff practically under the Golden Gate? I mean, people spend their entire lives digging up the sea floor in search of a single coin, and you walk away with the Inca treasury because you were looking for a porthole. There's just no justice in this world."

Billy leaned over. "Spoken like a true lawyer, Rich. So what do we know about our claim to the artifacts?"

Rich stood up and walked to the window, which looked down on the Oakland Estuary and a small fleet of tugboats.

"The Law of Salvage is pretty fluffy," he began, "and always has been. You have an interesting situation here. First of all, we're not talking about a silver coin. We're talking about a lot of gold, with no allowance made for the artistic and historical value of the stuff."

Billy interrupted him. "You have no idea, Rich. By the time, we finished excavating the wreck, we found that we had more than—"

Rich interrupted him. "Don't say any more, Billy. At this point, I don't need to know how much you have. In fact, I don't *want* to know, because if we end up having to do what I think we will, it's better that I not know."

Billy nodded. "Gotcha. Sorry."

Rich smiled. "No problem. I'll explain in a minute. Now where was I: oh, yeah. Second, while you have a provenance for the gold, you can count on the fact that the Spaniards will lay claim when they hear about it. And third, it wouldn't surprise me at all if Peru, Bolivia, Brazil, and Ecuador, not to mention Colombia and Panama, try to get a little skin in the game.

"The fact is, your best bet is probably to keep your discovery as quiet as possible, and sell it off anonymously to collectors. I have plenty of contacts to help facilitate that, but before we go down that road, let me give you a bit of background on the subject, because there may be another option that I want to discuss with you. I do plenty of salvage law, but it usually deals with stuff that sank or became disabled last Thursday, not 500 years ago. So consider this deep background—no pun intended. I want you to have all the facts in hand before you decide what you're going to do.

"There are a number of precedent-setting cases out there that I can tell you about that may guide your decision about what to do. The best known of them is probably the story of the *Atlantic*. She was an American built and owned side wheel steamship, 267 feet long, that went down in August of 1852 in Lake Erie, in Canadian waters, after colliding with the Ogdensburg, an American steamship. She sank in about 65 feet of water and was not insured.

"In September of 1984, a Canadian diver from Ontario named Michael Fletcher found the wreck and removed a number of artifacts from her: the ship's bell, the telegraph, and some dishes, I think. Now, Fletcher is an amateur archaeologist, so he immediately turned the things he found over to Canada's receiver of wrecks to protect them under the Canadian Shipping Act.

"Meanwhile, a commercial salvage company from California called the Mar Dive Group located the wreck, thanks to the buoy that Fletcher had placed on it. They took a bunch of stuff from the wreck, and filed an unopposed salvage claim in a California court. They maintained that they were acting with the blessing of the Canadian government, that the wreck was in U.S. waters, and that the wreck was legally abandoned.

"Predictably, the sovereign Ontario government decided to get involved, and claimed the vessel for themselves as a historically important site. So now we have three claims to the wreck.

"Fletcher bailed out of the proceedings early on and settled up with the Ontario government. Under the Law of Finds, he would have become the legal owner of the wreck, had the Canadian government not stepped in and claimed the wreck for themselves. The Americans from California were disqualified early on, if for no other reason than that American law has no applicability in Canada. Court decisions made in California have no teeth in Canada, unless Canada decides to accept them. Besides: it turns out that the wreck was indeed seven miles inside Canadian territorial waters. So, back to the drawing board."

They had all been listening carefully, and when Rich finished, no one spoke for some seconds. Finally, Michael asked a question.

"I understand Canada's right to exercise territorial prerogative. But what about laws here in the States? Is there anything that speaks to the potential ownership conflicts that are going to spring up, if our find becomes public?"

Rich nodded. "Sort of, Michael. I know that's not much of an answer, but unfortunately, it's the best I can give you. There are a considerable number of laws on the state books about shipwreck rights, but most of them are rather fuzzy—by design. Generally speaking, a vessel will have hull insurance that's paid for by the ship's owner, while the cargo that it carries is covered under something called 'marine' insurance, regardless of whether it's transported by ship, airplane, truck, rail or horse-drawn carriage—it's still called marine insurance. And the marine coverage is typically purchased by either the shipper of the cargo for FOB—freight on board—or by the purchaser of the freight who arranged the transport.

"As it turns out, North Carolina has the most advanced laws on the books about shipwrecks and ownership protection, because they have so many vessels off their coast. But forget about state law for a minute, and take a look at the federal Abandoned Shipwreck Act."

He handed them each a copy of a multipage document. "The feds have staked a claim to three types of shipwrecks: those that are abandoned and embedded in a state's underwater land; those that are abandoned and embedded in coral reefs on state underwater lands; and any wrecks that sit on land that qualifies to be included in the National Registry of Historic Places.

"Now: historically, once the Feds beat their chests and assert title to a wreck, they typically turn around and give control of it to the individual states to administer.

"Your wreck sits smack dab in the middle of the Golden Gate National Recreation Area and four other designated areas that could easily allow the State of California to presume ownership. In a court of law, you wouldn't stand a chance. You'd recover the cost of salvage, but that's about it."

They sat in uncomfortable silence for a moment before Michael finally spoke up with a sigh.

"Okay, Rich, so what do we do? The last thing I want is to turn this stuff over to any government, state, federal, or otherwise. Right now, the only people on earth that know about this are those in this room and Jeff, so let's talk candidly. Needless to say—I feel like some sort of Mafioso saying this—we'll take care of you in exchange for getting us through this. I mean, based on the amount of gold we found, there's more than we can ever even *think* about spending, so a significant chunk of it will find its way into your pocket."

Rich smiled and chuckled. "Consider yourselves long-established, existing clients, Mike. Everything said here is under the protection of attorney-client privilege, so not to worry about confidentiality. To be perfectly mercenary about it, it's in my best interest to help you get through this, so enough with the butterfly dance.

"I think I know how we can keep you guys ridiculously wealthy and still make the Feds, if not California, happy. Let me walk you through my thinking. And Billy, this is why it's important that I not know, at least for now, what all you have."

He walked over to a display case on the far side of the wall and took down a replica of El Cid's Tizón, a massive broadsword, and swung it back and forth experimentally as if he were chopping the legs off of Moorish horses. "OK, here's the deal…"

He spoke for fifteen minutes without interruption. They listened intently, and when he finished, he turned to them and raised one eyebrow. "So? What do you think? Workable?"

Michael looked at Billy, then at Lexie. They smiled, then nodded their agreement. Michael was the first to speak.

"Rich, I underestimated you. I tend to think of you as my friend the dive instructor. I keep forgetting that you're also my friend the lawyer, as evidenced by today's performance. So: What do we do next?"

CHAPTER 38

Six months later, on a bright Saturday morning, the story hit the papers.

DIVERS FIND SPANISH TREASURE

Archaeological find of the century, say experts

SAN FRANCISCO (AP)

Two local divers have found a 16th-century wreck believed to belong to Francisco de Orellana, a Spanish explorer credited with naming the Amazon River. The wreck, found in shallow water off the coast, has proved to be a treasure trove. The divers pulled more than 500 pounds of Inca gold off the wreck, and believe that there is more to be found.

"It really is an extraordinary find," says Rich Meyersonn, attorney for Michael McCain and

William McAdam, the divers who located the wreck. Meyersonn, a specialist in maritime law, described the nature of his clients' find in a press conference Tuesday afternoon.

"When Michael and Billy happened across the wreck, they knew that they were onto something quite extraordinary," he explained to the large group that had assembled in front of the San Francisco Maritime Museum at the foot of Hyde Street. With several vintage vessels lying at anchor behind him, he asked McCain and McAdam to join him at the podium to describe the events that led to their finding the ship. "We have always been interested in marine archaeology, and for years have searched for and salvaged the remains of vessels lost at sea," began McCain. "As many of you know, there are more than 600 known wrecks off the California coast. We've done salvage work for many years now; many of the artifacts we've collected are in museums throughout the Bay Area. We were actually in the middle of surveying a modern wreck—1950s, as near as we were able to tell—when Billy found the first golden artifact. It was clear to us that this was an extraordinary find, so we used standard archaeological techniques to establish the debris field (the area over which the remains of the ship can be expected to be found, given currents, water depth, etc.). Once we determined the extent of the field, we laid out an excavation grid and proceeded to excavate each square. It took us more than two months to document and complete the dig, but we're sure glad we took the time."

Meyersonn explained that McCain and McAdam had refrained from telling anyone about the find until they were finished with the dig, because of the danger of the site being overrun by amateur treasure divers. He went on to explain that the site had been turned over to state and Federal archaeologists, and that McCain and McAdam had spent a considerable amount of time with them at the site. He declined to tell the group the actual location.

"My clients have placed the artifacts taken from the shipwreck in the capable hands of Alejandra Moliner, curator of Mesoamerican history at the Bancroft Archives on the UC Berkeley campus. Ms. Moliner is an expert in Inca culture, and will prepare a complete briefing document for the press as soon as she has catalogued the artifacts. However, we know that there is considerable interest in the nature of the find. I have therefore been authorized to describe, in general terms, the nature of what my clients found.

"First of all, it is a Spanish ship from the mid-16th century. It was carrying what appears to be Inca gold, including more than 150 inlaid statues, a collection of plates, goblets, and medallions, all solid gold, a wide variety of jewelry, a number of golden death masks, and several exquisite pieces that can only be described as works of art, including models of ships."

McCain and McAdam own Ocean Adventures, a commercial (Continued on page A4)

Michael finished the article and put down the paper. "Nice job, Rich," he said, turning to the attorney. They were sitting in the office at the shop, having come in the back door to avoid the crowds of reporters and bystanders that were already gathering on the grass out front.

"We're not done yet, Michael," countered Rich, pouring another cup of coffee. "Things are going to be rather exciting around here for the next few weeks, and all of you are going to become celebrities whether you like it or not—in fact, based on the crowd outside, I'd say you already are. We seem to have appeased the state with the artifacts that have been turned over to Bancroft; they're already talking about a wing at the De Young to display some of the stuff. If I were you I'd throw together a quick course on treasure diving. Given the current interest, you might make more money on that than you will on the gold."

Just as Meyersonn had predicted, Spain, the U.S. Government, the State of California, Brazil and Peru all made claims to the treasure that Billy and Michael had pulled from the sea floor, claiming that historical precedent gave them each right of ownership. The pending legal battle was far too complex for Michael and Billy, but Rich Meyersonn, with his vast knowledge of maritime law, put together a chess game of sorts in which he played the various claimants against one other. In secret negotiations with each claimant country, he worked a behind-the-scenes deal in which the U. S. Government agreed to pay an unfettered $10 million to Michael and Billy in return for ownership of the gold—with specific conditions. In return, the government agreed to pursue trade deals and other economic incentives with the other claimant countries, some of which were already underway, in exchange for each of them giving up their claim to the treasure. Meyersonn was able to make a compelling argument that the value of the gold was eclipsed by the long-term value of a trade deal with the U. S.

As a condition of the initial stage of the agreement, Michael, Billy, Lexie and Jeff agreed to sign gag orders which prevented them from publically describing (for a time) the details of their find.

Once the government had the opportunity to begin its various commitments to the other parties, they were free to display the golden artifacts, and Lexie was able to publish a full report of the history of the wreck and its contents, in which each of the claimant countries played a major role. The agreement also called for the gold to become a permanent element of the holdings of the

Bancroft Archives, but would visit the world's museums as part of a traveling exhibit. Already, exhibitions were being planned in Spain, Holland, Peru, and the UK, and others would soon follow. As a private part of the agreement, Spain—specifically, the National Archives—received a substantial grant, to be managed by Rafael Santoro, to complete its curation of the Orellana collection.

Suddenly, there was a commotion as the front door opened. Billy and Lexie came in, fighting off hordes of reporters. Balancing a box of bagels in one hand, Billy pushed the door closed and locked it, shutting off the cacophony of questions. "Jesus!" said Lexie. "It's bad enough that they're all over me at home and on campus. I can't get away from them!"

* * *

Michael smiled as he gave her a kiss. "Rich tells me that it's going to be that way for awhile, so we might as well get used to it. How's the briefing document going?"

Lexie poured herself a cup of coffee and plopped down on the couch next to Rich. "It's finished. In fact, I have it with me, so Rich can read it before I release it. It has everything in it that we discussed, so it should be fine." She fished around in her small briefcase and handed the stack of papers over. Rich took them and began to read.

"So, what's the plan for today?" asked Billy, biting into a bagel. "I mean, it looks like the morning is going to be pretty busy," he said, gesturing to the growing crowd outside.

Rich nodded. "This looks fine, Lexie," he offered, handing the papers back to her. "We're going to do another press conference out front, Lexie's going to read her manifest paper, you two are going to answer general questions about the dig just as we discussed, and that's it. As I said before, you can expect this to go on for weeks before the excitement dies down, so make the most of it."

Billy laughed. "Based on the calls we're getting to be on talk shows, I have to go out and buy a suit. I don't think they want me showing up in neoprene."

"Don't be so sure," Rich observed with a wink and a smile. "Between Evening Magazine, the Today Show and Entertainment Tonight, a hunk in a wetsuit would be in big demand."

"Billy's elected!" Lexie gleefully shouted.

At ten o'clock sharp, they opened the front door of the shop. Rich announced that they would make a brief statement to the press and would then take questions, but that first they had to make room through their ranks for the shop's regular customers. This was, after all, a business.

The crowd was hushed as Lexie read her carefully crafted briefing document. There were gasps as the magnitude of the find began to dawn on the collected group, and when she held up one of the ruby-encrusted statues, they pressed in close to see. The local police had provided an armed escort for Lexie, given the value of the artifact she held; they stood quietly in the background, watching the crowd closely.

At noon, Rich declared to the press that the conference was over, and squired his clients back into the dive shop and quickly out the back door, leaving things in Jeff's hands temporarily. They promised to be back by early afternoon, but knew that Jeff would enjoy the attention that was now centered on the shop. He also knew that Jeff was going to make out just fine; Michael had pulled him aside earlier that week and told him about the check that he would soon be given. The only place Jeff had ever seen anywhere near that many zeroes was on a burger joint sign, advertising how many burgers they'd sold. And thanks to some clever legal maneuvering on Rich's part, the taxes were already covered. Jeff was also grateful that Michael didn't try to repeat Billy's bear hug—his ribcage was still tender, although he would never publicly admit to an inferior defect in his perfect human machine.

They ate lunch at Jack London Square, then proceeded to Rich's office. The office was closed, but that didn't stop the crowds from gathering. They avoided most of them by driving into the underground garage and riding up in a private elevator, avoiding the lobby. While Rich organized the documents they needed to discuss, Michael prepared a pot of coffee. Billy and Lexie stood at the floor-to-ceiling window and watched the tugboats do their thing in the estuary below.

"OK, gather around and let me bring you up to date on where we are," Rich began. You have turned over all of the artifacts that we have discussed, which means that as far as I know, you are no longer in possession of anything that legally belongs to the State of California or the Federal Government. We all know that there is considerably more in your possession, but I do not know, nor do I *want* to know, anything about that. I'm starting to think I should change my name to Saul.

"Anyway, Michael, at your request, I have contacted a colleague in Austria who has agreed to talk to you about the brokerage of items that you and Billy have collected over the years. I assume that we're talking about portholes, so I plan to send you a hefty bill for my services as soon as you sell them. After all, the scrap price for brass is pretty steep these days.

"Meanwhile, it's business as usual. Go to work, dive, teach. Let the hoopla die down before you head off to Graz, and do *not* discuss your porthole collection at the shop or in any text, email, Skype, SnapChat, whatever, anywhere, anytime. All of those things can be found by anyone determined enough to look for them, and they will look, repeatedly. Assume that there are ears everywhere, even when there aren't. Work with the government as much as they require, and do it eagerly. Let them know that you are anxious to preserve the site as much as they are, and that the preservation of historical sanctity is paramount. Hell, give them the equipment if they need it."

CHAPTER 39

MORE TREASURE FOUND

Dig complete, says State

SAN FRANCISCO (AP)

After finding more than 40 additional Inca artifacts at the now-famous shipwreck site outside the Golden Gate, California state underwater archaeologists have finally declared the dig complete. Salvage divers Michael McCain and William McAdam, who pulled more than 500 pounds of gold from the site, discovered the shipwreck over a year ago. The wreck, now known to have been a sailing vessel transporting Spanish explorer Francisco de Orellana, was apparently en-route to meet Gonzalo Pizarro on the Northern California coast when it struck a reef and sank with all hands. "It was a tragic end to a fascinating story," says Alejandra Moliner, a historian at UC Berkeley's Bancroft Archives and curator of the Orellana collection, now on display at the Bancroft Archives. Orellana's journey, which started in the Andes and ended at the Golden Gate, is beautifully recreated in Moliner's "Over Land, Over Sea: The Tragic Journey of Francisco de Orellana." The book chronicles Orellana's gold-plundering voyage down South

America's rivers from the Andes to the mouth of the Amazon, then on to the Strait of Panama, where he and his men were shipwrecked. There, they tore apart their ship and built wagons, which they loaded with the gold they collected along the way and pulled across the strait to the Pacific. Later, they rendezvoused with one of Pizarro's ships, which took them and their cargo aboard, only to sink several weeks later.

McCain and McAdam own Ocean Adventures, a sport and commercial diving operation in Walnut Creek, California. They have worked closely with state and federal authorities throughout the excavation and are confident that all artifacts have now been recovered.

PART IV

CHAPTER 40

Banco Serranilla, five years later

They were on-station, southeast of the Banco Serranilla, halfway between Panama and Cuba, and the early morning sun had turned the sea into a sheet of beaten gold. The area was stunning and bizarre, but after three weeks they had grown accustomed to the scene that stretched into the distance just off the starboard bow. It was a remarkable sight: at low tide, the water over the reef was so shallow that bronze cannon and careened anchors protruded eerily from the water. The place was a graveyard: over the centuries, hundreds of ships had broken up here. There was no reason why early vessels should be cautious, after all; the reef was 90 miles from the nearest landfall, and since few of the ships that encountered Serranilla survived to warn others, the frail wooden vessels continued to scatter themselves and their cargo across the reef's stony teeth for the better part of two centuries. Michael smiled as a memory came to him from long ago. The kids had an expression for someone who "crashed and burned" while skiing, scattering equipment all over the slope. They called it a yard sale. This, he thought, was one hell of a yard sale.

The Grunt rolled gently in the early morning sea as the swells lapped quietly against the gleaming white sides of her three hulls. Somewhere off in the unseen distance, a fish slapped the water; the only other sound was the soft whisper of the anchor line as it rubbed against its stay.

Michael listened to the familiar sounds of the *Grunt* as she gently rocked and tugged at her tether. She was aptly named, he mused. She was a working boat, and in the five years that she had been the team's home away from home, she had proven to be hard working, reliable, and plenty comfortable. The *Grunt* was a 65-foot trimaran, and had earned her name during her initial shakedown cruise off the Monterey coastline. During that voyage, a large rubber cushion between the center deck and the middle hull had begun to squeal and grunt happily in cadence with the swells that rocked her. It sounded like a pig rooting around in the mud, and since Billy loved pigs, the cushion was never repaired, and the vessel's name was changed from *Monterey Dream* to *Grunt*.

She was remarkably stable. The boat had weathered all manner of conditions, and other than a few cosmetic marks in her hulls, she had never suffered any major damage. The *Grunt* was a beamy boat for her length, 48 feet across at the widest part of her deck. She ran seven feet of freeboard when anchored, and was powered by twin Perkins diesels that could move her along at a handy clip of 13 knots in calm seas, grunting happily all the while.

When Michael and Billy found her, she was nothing more than a bare set of hulls with decking tying the three together. Where most people would have seen a derelict in the sorry-looking vessel, Michael and Billy saw the answer to their collective vision: a sound hull that was the right size and had the right performance characteristics for their intended task. They purchased her with cash and hired a harbor tug to move the vessel to the Seaside Marina, where Michael's brother John ran a marine repair operation that was unrivaled on the northern California coast. There, they stripped her to bare glass, sanded and varnished her decking, and applied layer after layer of resin until she gleamed like white porcelain.

Meanwhile, yard workers were busy below decks, rebuilding the massive engines and installing twin gensets, compressors and other equipment that Michael and Billy envisioned they would need. At the same time, carpenters converted the remaining space into first-class living quarters, with private staterooms for all team members and three guests, four fully appointed heads with freshwater showers, a small conference room, a spacious salon, and a well-designed and fully-stocked galley. The superstructure, such as it was, housed the bridge, radio room and navigation bay. Equipped with the most modern navigation complement possible, including GPS, the *Grunt* could be piloted automatically to virtually any port in her considerable database by satellite navigation. And although he had not yet had the courage to do it, Billy knew that he could program the vessel's computer to take her right into a slip if he wanted to.

Michael sipped a steaming mug of coffee as he enjoyed the early morning smell of the ocean and the far-off cries of gulls wheeling off the stern. He felt a presence behind him just as a pair of hands rose up his chest, hugging him tightly. Smiling, he set the cup down on the rail and turned around. "Morning, Lexie," he said, embracing her in a bear hug.

"Morning, sweetie," she replied. "More coffee?" She filled his cup from a galley pot, then stood in front of him at the rail, snuggling against him and drawing his arm around her. He hugged her tightly, and they gazed across the broad expanse of water that lay between the vessel and the reef to the northwest. Around her neck was the tiny gold medallion with its inlaid pearls that Michael and Billy took from the Potato Patch wreck. She never took it off.

"It's going well so far, isn't it?" asked Lexie, looking up at him. They had been married for five years, and she became more beautiful to him with every passing year. She was an indispensable member of the team. In addition to serving as historian and divemaster, she was a phenomenal cook, and always ensured that no one on the crew lost weight while they were on a project—although she and Billy fought endlessly over the galley, its many utensils and the food they prepared. Her inquisitive spirit served her well: as a historian, Lexie's meticulous eye to detail had often meant the difference between the success and failure of a project.

As divemaster, what Lexie said was inviolable law. Her logging tasks kept track of the number of daily dives each person made, the number of team members that were in the water at any point in time, and countless other details that a less meticulous person might miss. As a consequence, there had never been a serious accident aboard the *Grunt,* and if Lexie had anything to say about it, there never *would.* She remembered all too well the pleasure trip that she, Michael, Jeff and Billy had taken on a live-aboard dive vessel years before. There were 38 divers on board; they discovered too late that no official divemaster had been appointed to track activities on or around the boat.

During the second evening of the trip, a group jumped overboard for a night dive. They finished at 11 PM, and at 11:15, the boat weighed anchor and moved four miles west to another site on the backside of the island, unwittingly leaving two divers in the water. The divers surfaced 20 minutes later to the sight of a flat sea and no dive boat. They were forced to swim to the island, which was uninhabited except for a small Coast Guard station. They had to hike all night to the other end of the island before they could call for help. Needless to say, the Coast Guard found other uses for the pilot's charter license.

Michael and Lexie's reverie was interrupted by two huge, hairy arms that enveloped them in a cold, clammy embrace.

"Ah, what a fine morning!" bellowed Carl Leonidas, the arms' owner. Unnoticed, he had climbed out of the water from the diving platform at the stern of the boat after an early morning dive and had snuck up behind them. Planting a loud, sloppy kiss first on Lexie's cheek, then on Michael's, Carl turned to Lexie with a big grin. "So, what's for breakfast?" he asked, swinging a small grouper on a pole spear in front of her.

"Get that disgusting thing out of my face, you animal!" she flared at him, giving Carl a shove that toppled him off balance and nearly sent him over the rail. "If you want grouper for breakfast, you can sit up here by yourself and eat it raw. I'm making pancakes." With that, she planted a kiss on Michael's cheek, then one on Carl's, and disappeared below decks.

"Guess she doesn't like fish," laughed Carl. He was one of Billy's oldest friends, and had been with the crew longer than anyone could remember. Built like a bulldog, he was a well-known authority on 16th and 17th century shipping practices, and was an accomplished salvage diver and underwater archaeologist.

"So how's life with wingnut?" asked Carl. Michael smiled at the reference to the team's current client, who was still asleep in his cabin.

"It's okay," he replied. "He's a bit more intense than I like my diving partners to be, but I can write that off to personality, I guess. I'm still not convinced he really knows what he's looking for down there, or that he really knows what he's doing, but since he's diving with Billy, I'm not worried."

Carl smirked. "The guy's just a little bit too tightly wound for my taste," he replied. "Diving's supposed to be fun, and this guy's never learned that. He's gonna get somebody hurt if he's not careful. And if he looks cross-eyed at Lexie again, I'm going to be the one doing the hurting."

Michael chuckled. After Billy, Carl was Lexie's greatest protector, and was always looking out for her. It was a responsibility that he and Billy shared; they were the big brothers she never had, and woe be to the person who looked at her the wrong way if one of them was nearby.

"Just don't put a shark dart in the guy until after he pays us, okay? Besides, we only have a few more days with him and then we're done. He thinks he's close, and if so, we should be heading home in a week or so."

Carl scowled. "Sorry, Mikey, but he's a scumbag. I can smell scumbags, and I've smelled him since he stepped on board. I just don't trust the guy, and I want him gone, payment or not. We've got plenty of other clients out there that help pay the bills—not that we need help with that— but we really don't need him."

Michael was inclined to agree. Lee Graves had called Michael eight months before about the current expedition, and wanted to hire the *Grunt* and the team to help him locate and salvage a wreck that he was convinced had a fortune on-board. After agreeing to the terms of the contract, which included rights to a percentage of the take and verification that he had a legal right to salvage on the Serranilla—none of them wanted to mess with the Colombians without the proper paperwork—they had researched the wrecked vessel extensively, and while there was a good chance that some items of value could be recovered from the ship, there was no guarantee. There never was in this business. Michael and his friends had learned long ago that fully 95% of all wrecks yielded little more than an entertaining dive, but if a client wanted to pay them for their services, they were more than willing to accommodate, provided the activities were legal and safe. Modern wrecks really weren't their bailiwick – they preferred the excitement of searching for older vessels – but this was, after all, their business, and they didn't want to be too picky.

"Why don't you go down and dry off, and I'll meet you in the galley," suggested Michael. "I can smell breakfast cooking, which means that Billy and Lexie are doing battle. And if you'll clean that," motioning to the grouper, "I'm sure one of them will put it on ice for dinner."

Carl agreed, and headed for the fish cleaning station on the stern while Michael disappeared below decks.

The *Grunt's* dining room, which also served as a conference room, was big enough to seat twelve, but the galley itself was relatively small—it fit two people comfortably, but not many more. As Michael predicted,

Lexie and Billy were in the process of preparing something that smelled heavenly, but as usual, they were deep in an argument about the ingredients of whatever it was they were cooking when he strolled in.

The image that presented itself to Michael would have caused anyone else to head for the upper deck, but to Michael, it was just another day with his wife and best friend. While Billy brandished a chef's knife to argue his points, Lexie was in Billy's face with a kitchen whisk. Amused, Michael listened to the conversation for the better part of a minute before clearing his throat.

"I'm sure that the future of the free world depends on the outcome of this argument," he interjected, "but Carl and I are starving. Not to mention the fact that I'm sure you two have managed to wake up everyone in the Caribbean Basin."

They both turned to him, grinning. "Morning, boss!" boomed Billy, still gesturing with the knife. "You're just in time for breakfast. How about apple pancakes and ham? They're my own special recipe—"

Lexie swatted him in the butt with the kitchen whisk. "They are *not* your recipe! They're *my* apfel pfannkuchen, which you stole the recipe for. Tell the truth!" Her eyes blazed with indignation, but Michael noticed that she couldn't hide the tiniest smile that crept into her eyes and the corners of her mouth. She and Billy both loved to cook, and were perpetually at odds with each other over the culinary affairs that took place aboard the Grunt.

"Apple pancakes with ham sound great. And Billy, she's pretty good with that whisk, so I'd be careful the next time you go looking for recipes."

Billy just grinned. He hadn't changed much in the years since the Potato Patch adventure, other than the profusion of gray hair that now covered his head. He was the backbone of the team.

Michael looked around the well-appointed galley. It was appointed in oak, finely crafted, as nice as anything found on land. Professional appliances had been installed at the request— demand, really—of Lexie and Billy, including a commercial stove and oven, a massive refrigerator and chest freezer, an overhead pot rack, and every small utensil they could ever need. One thing could be said about their trips: they occasionally came home without salvage, but they never came home hungry.

Michael's reverie was interrupted by voices at the top of the galley way. Seconds later, Carl and Lee, the client, strolled in. Carl immediately walked over to Lexie with the freshly cleaned fish, and, dropping to one knee, bowed his head and said, "Oh goddess of the galley, I submit to you and bring this meager offering as a token of my esteem and love. Would you be so charitable as to allow this unworthy vassal to place it in the freezer, that we might later sup upon it?"

Lexie looked at him seriously for five seconds before exploding. Taking the fish from him, she placed it on each of his shoulders, then on top of his head, laughing, "I dub thee Sir Grouper. Rise and place your offering in the refrigerator. I shall marinate it appropriately as befits such an offering." He stood as Michael, Lexie and Billy applauded; Lee just stood there, baffled by the performance.

"I'm ready to go, as soon as you are," he interrupted. I'd like to dive as soon as possible today."

Carl walked over and put a massive arm around his shoulders, guiding him to the table and forcing him to sit. "You need to eat something, my friend," he said. "You don't want to be in the water with Billy if he hasn't eaten – he gets cranky. So relax, have some coffee, and a plate of Lexie's apple-fan-kootchie-whatever-they-ares. Besides, it's only 7:30; we've got plenty of time."

Lee sat quietly for several seconds, then stood. He was a small man, bearded, and very intense. "I'm going to go get my gear ready. As soon as you're ready to go, I'll be on deck," he replied, and headed for the stairs.

Carl moved to stop him. "Not so fast, chief," he said, blocking Lee's passage. "That boat has been down there for a lot of years, and it's not going anywhere in the next hour, so relax. You have to eat, because Billy won't let you in the water if you don't. You guys are going to be working hard down there, and you're going to need your energy. We've never had an accident on this boat, and I'm not going to start now. So come on—have some breakfast."

The room was silent, as the two stared at each other. Finally, Lee broke the tension. Smiling, he sat down. "You're right," he said, sheepishly, reaching for the coffee pot. "It's just that we're so close I can feel it, and I want to get down there."

Carl sat down next to him and clapped him on the back. "I know, my friend, I know," he said, as Billy slid plates of pancakes and massive slabs of ham in front of them. "You'll be down there before you know it. Now, did I ever tell you about the time my friend Michael here…"

CHAPTER 41

By 9 AM, they were ready to dive. Billy, Carl, Michael and Lee moved to the equipment locker at the stern of the center hull. After donning thin, one-piece wetsuits and loose fitting jeans over them, Michael and Carl helped Billy and Lee into their backpacks, and watched carefully as they secured their equipment. Carrying masks and fins, they walked down the stairway to the water-level dive platform. There, they slipped into the water.

"You two be careful down there," said Michael, before noticing that Lee had already disappeared. Shaking his head, he continued. "OK, Billy, then *you* be careful down there. You've spent the most time diving with Graves, so you know him better than anybody. Just stay out of his way."

Billy just smiled and nodded. "No problem. See you for lunch." And with that, he slipped quietly below the surface.

Passing under the Grunt's massive hulls, he swam to the anchor line and descended. There, he found Graves waiting impatiently. Giving him a thumbs-up, Billy followed as Lee led the way to the shipwreck, its bulk dimly visible in the distance.

They swam to the canted deck of the Carla V and found the entry point they had used throughout the operation. When the vessel sank, it settled on its starboard side in 120 feet of clear blue water. Upon striking the bottom, the entire superstructure sheared off, leaving a gaping hole in the deck. The superstructure now lay some 50 yards south of the hull at the end of a debris field. That hole was a blessing in disguise of sorts, because it gave them access to the innards of the vessel without having to swim down the long passageways that they would otherwise have to navigate. They had to be extremely careful, however: the wreck was a chaos of sharp, rusty metal, especially at their entry point. They wore jeans over their wetsuits, because the hostile environment in which they would be working would make short shrift of the neoprene.

Nodding at Billy, Lee disappeared into the maw of the vessel. Shaking his head, Billy followed him into the darkness.

CHAPTER 42

Peruvian jungle south of Cuzco, November 1533

"Faster, child! And quietly – we must be away from here before the sun crests the mountains!"

The old man patted the young girl on the back as she hastened past him with her heavy burden. She was tall and slender, tall as all the Inca children were, but under the weight of the basket hanging from the strap around her forehead, she stumbled often as she trotted down the steep trail into the dense jungle beyond. The elder watched as she disappeared into the underbrush, one of a long phalanx of similarly burdened children, all carrying Inca gold. Ahead of them, long since disappeared into the jungle, a train of llamas carried even more of the treasure, leading the way for the young ones.

The old man shook his head in sorrow and disgust as he thought of the ongoing destruction of the Inca Empire by the invading Spaniards. As a people and civilization, the Inca were older than human thought, and the fact that the beauty, religion, science, and architecture of the Inca would be destroyed for the want of *gold* was inconceivable to him.

A month before, the Spaniards had captured the Supreme Inca, Atahualpa, and threatened to kill him. After much negotiation, the Inca agreed to provide the Spaniards with a room filled with gold, in exchange for the life of their leader. They did so, stacking golden bars, plates, ceremonial masks, and ingots as high as the ceiling of the treasure room. In return, the Spaniards agreed to free him immediately, but instead, they garroted him, cut off his head, and displayed it atop a pike in the central square of Cuzco. The fierce Inca warriors declared war on the invaders, but their arrows, spears and fierce hand-to-hand combat skills were no match for the Spanish harquebus. It was a tragically lopsided battle; because of armor and superior weaponry, 180 well-armed Spaniards were able to defeat an Inca army of nearly 20,000. After days of skirmish and death, the Inca withdrew to the jungle, disappearing into the infinity of green. The Spaniards celebrated the cowardice of their opponents; meanwhile, the Inca planned their counterattack. Knowing that they were militarily outmatched, they changed their strategy, deciding to attack the Spaniards where it would hurt them the worst.

They waited ten days. By then, the Conquistadores had reached the fatally wrong conclusion that the Inca had fled for good, and the guards became complacent. Late in the dark, moonless night of the tenth day, a small contingent of Inca warriors slipped silently into Cuzco to the building where the Spaniards were hoarding the gold. The building was located at the extreme eastern edge of the city; a major thoroughfare ran before it, but it backed up against the emerald density of the Peruvian jungle.

Three Spaniards guarded the treasury; in the darkness, Inca warriors approached soundlessly and overpowered them before cutting their throats with razor-sharp obsidian knives. Hot Spanish blood pulsed from severed arteries and splashed on the floor. One man tried feebly to scream, but his severed trachea allowed nothing more than a rush of air to escape into the night. The bodies twitched convulsively, then lay quiet.

After dragging the bodies of the guards deep into the jungle and leaving them for the jaguars, the warriors carefully surveyed the surrounding buildings for any sign that they had been detected. Finding none, one of the men went to the door at the back of the building and whistled softly into the trees. Within seconds, men began to emerge silently from the jungle growth. All carried large, woven baskets which they passed empty into the treasury, bucket brigade fashion. Minutes later, the baskets began to emerge from the building, heavily loaded with gold. These were quickly dispatched into the gloom of the jungle. Once they were far from the building, the contents of the baskets were repacked into larger baskets on the backs of llamas.

"*Sssst!*" hissed Condori, the Inca guard they had posted just inside the front door of the treasury. "Someone approaches!"

Immediately all activity in the building ceased, and everyone lapsed into silence. Footsteps announced the imminent arrival of an uninvited guest.

From outside, a voice called out in Spanish. "*¿Juan Antonio? ¿Estás ahí?*" Silence greeted the question. Sticking his head cautiously into the treasury, the man who had called out looked around, realizing too late that the shadow on the floor was not a shadow at all but was in fact a spreading pool of blood surrounding the head of his friend. "*¿Qué pasó aqui —*" he began, but the sound was cut off by the obsidian blade that pierced his trachea, just before it was jerked upward to sever the carotid artery and jugular vein. Blood covered the hand of the silent assassin, and pulsed down the front of the Spaniard's tunic as he died.

"*Quickly!*" Condori called out. "Others may come!" He looked out the door, but there were no signs of suspicious activity. Giving the all-clear sign, he returned to his lookout position while the others redoubled their efforts.

They worked long into the night, spiriting away a seemingly endless supply of gold from the treasury. Other than occasional changes of the guard, who were quickly and quietly dispatched with the deadly obsidian blades, they were not disturbed, and no suspicions arose. Finally, after more than five hours of work, they had emptied the room. Piles of Inca gold were replaced with piles of

Spanish bodies, victims of Inca rage.

The last of the gold now gone, the remaining warriors slipped from the back of the building and disappeared into the jungle. Dawn was breaking; the sun was just creeping over the tops of the impossibly tall mountains, flushing the town the color of the gold that had been spirited away and the blood that now covered the floor of the empty room.

CHAPTER 43

Banco Serranilla

The penetration of the wreck had been long and difficult. Now, wedged as he was in a stairway that connected adjacent decks, Graves once again wondered, as he had many times, if it was worth the effort. Ahead of him, beyond the pile of rusted metal that now blocked his passage, the captain's safe waited, beckoning, the contents his for the taking. All he had to do was get beyond this junk pile without slicing himself and contracting blood poisoning or having the pile collapse on him. The way things had been going, both would probably happen.

Squeezing his tanks against the rotten pipe that formed the bulk of the blockage, he pushed with his legs, listening for the sounds that would indicate that whatever lay above was about to come down on top of him. The rusted pipe shed brown rust flakes the size of potato chips, and finally, with a sustained groan, moved far enough to allow him to pass.

The effort strained him, and he was breathing hard; looking down, he located his pressure gauge and saw that 2700 pounds of air remained in the twin 80s. Better take it easy, he thought; it's tough to do an out-of-air free ascent from inside a wreck. Looking back, he watched as Billy squeezed through the narrow opening that he had created. As soon as Billy was clear, Lee moved forward, and the two of them continued down the passage toward the captain's cabin, deep in the hulk of the ship.

Graves had been on the trail of the Carla V for six years. An Italian luxury liner that sank off Serranilla following a fire that flashed through the ship, it had gone down so suddenly that, while all passengers escaped unscathed, most of their valuables remained on board. Opportunistic divers had already plundered most of the loose items; the captain's safe, however, had so far evaded all efforts to reach it. The main reason was its location. The captain's cabin was located so deep inside the ship that getting to it required extensive planning, commercial salvage skills and more than a small dose of insanity. Several divers had reached the deck where the cabin was located, but no one, other than Lee, had yet reached the cabin itself. He intended to be the first, and he had no intention of returning empty-handed.

He had first heard rumors of the safe and its purported contents in a bar on San Salvador Island in the Bahamas. A group of locals were discussing the wreck with the former captain of the ship, who had retired on the island. The captain had apparently confided to somebody that a small fortune waited for whoever popped the safe.

Lee had left the bar intrigued, and had done a bit of research upon returning to his home in California. The captain, who had annoyingly died of an alcohol-induced stroke a few months after the conversation in San Salvador, had taken the combination of the safe with him. As near as Lee could tell, though, the man had been wealthy, and there was nothing to dispute the general belief that the strongbox held riches of one kind or another. Since then, he had worked toward this day, the day when he would know whether the captain's story was based in truth.

Exhaustive research and responses to dozens of letters yielded the name of the manufacturer of the safe, a French concern located in Lyon. Citing the salvage laws of the sea, Lee had contacted the safe's manufacturer and demanded the combination. After much legal haggling, he had finally left Lyon with the combination in-hand, as well as an assurance that the heavy paint on the safe would most likely have protected the metal it covered from corrosion. With luck, he would be able to open the safe door by dialing in the right numbers. Otherwise, more drastic means would be required, means that could damage the contents within.

At this depth, the Carla V's white-painted hull was gray, and her angle on the bottom made her look more like a stranded whale than a cruise ship. The angle made diving on her difficult, as well: stairways ran horizontally throughout the vessel instead of vertically, while companionways and cross-corridors rose like chimney flues. To a diver, this was at best disorienting, at worst, deadly; the topsy-turvy aspect of a canted ship made wrong turns inevitable.

Every time Lee entered a wreck, he performed a conscious safety check as he remembered the story of the ill-fated cave divers in Florida that he had heard about a few years before. The divers had never been on a cave dive, and to make matters worse, had not undertaken any of the special training required for such dangerous diving. As a consequence, they had taken none of the necessary precautions that cave diving requires, such as tethered safety lines and a bailout bottle for out-of-air emergencies. Like most freshwater cave systems, this one offered crystal clear water, as long as divers stayed away from the silt-covered bottom. Unfortunately, one of the divers kicked too close and raised an inky brown cloud that reduced visibility in the cave to zero. In the confusion that followed, one of the divers managed to turn around and return to the surface, where he waited anxiously for his buddy. He never arrived. The diver's body was found in a dead-end passage; on his slate he had written,

SHIT I'M LOST

Not me, thought Lee. Last year, when he had finally completed the mapping of the ship and had determined the location of the captain's cabin, he had permanently rigged a heavy nylon line from his habitual entry point into the bowels of the ship. The line ended at the third deck, where he knew the cabin to be; in fact, he had been in the cabin, and had seen the safe. It was deceptively small, measuring no more than 20 inches on a side, but big enough to hold—who knew what?

Rounding a corner, he swam down a crazily canted stairway, spooking the large parrotfish that always lingered there. Shadows on the walls danced crazily, an aboriginal frenzy, as Billy's light moved about. Ahead, Lee could see the yellow Pelican Float that indicated the end of the rope, and below it, the two 80s that he had left behind as part of their safety plan. The tanks ensured the availability of air should they overstay their welcome in the depths of the vessel. Reaching the end of the rope, Lee stopped and floated, suspended like an astronaut between the four walls of the companionway. Signaling to Billy, they compared pressure gauges; about 2650 PSI each, easily enough for the job ahead. They pushed on, their goal almost in sight.

CHAPTER 44

Juli, Peru, western shore of Lake Titicaca

Present Day

The outboard motor on the barge roared to life as the captain pulled the starter cord for the fifth time. *¡Bestia!* He cursed. The motor belched a cloud of oily blue smoke, sputtered, then settled down to a burbling, uncomfortable rumble. From the starboard rail, Jessica Cutter watched as the small outboard slowly moved the enormous bulk of the barge away from the dock and onto the lake. This is ridiculous, she thought; this thing is way too big for that motor.

Indeed, the 150 HP Yamaha did seem ridiculously small for the vessel it was now propelling into the Uinamarca Basin; the wooden barge was currently carrying two full-size buses, two automobiles, and an assortment of kayaks and inflatables, all at the whim of the sputtering outboard. After a few minutes, though, the motor settled down to the task and began to make headway against the wind that blew into their faces from the southwest.

Cutter and her friends were on their way to the Strait of Tiquina, the narrow body of water that connected Uinamarca with Chucuito, the northern and southern basins of Peru's Lake Titicaca. As exchange students at the University of Cuzco, they had spent the previous 11 weeks in an intensive Spanish language and Peruvian history and culture program. Now that the term was over, a group of them had decided to see a bit more of the country. After examining the brochures that the tourist office gave them, they had decided on a guided trek along the shore of the lake, followed by a boat tour complete with a resident naturalist to point out what the brochure called "multitudinous wildlifes." So far, the only "wildlifes" they had seen were birds, unless they chose to count the captain and crew of this barge, who spent most of their time leering at her legs.

A mixed crowd of people surrounded her. Most of them were from a Road Scholar group that had arrived in buses the night before, and were now being ferried across the lake to continue their journey to who knows where. The rest were a mixed bag of 1960s hippie types who had stepped out of a time warp somewhere, and a group of hardcore birdwatchers who lined the rusted rails of the barge with enormous binoculars and called out the names of whatever they saw to colleagues, who promptly wrote them down in little notebooks. Every once in a while they would spot something that was apparently unusual, because upon announcing it they jumped up and down and clapped their hands in excitement. Get a life, she laughed. I like birds as much as the next person, but geez!

The barge was now running almost full into the wind, and it picked up some chop. The flat-bottomed vessel slapped its way across the lake toward the narrow strait, where it would stop briefly to let passengers disembark. Jessica and her friends planned to spend the day swimming and exploring the dense brush that lined the shore there. The naturalist would stay with the barge and the other tourists, but told them that the vessel would be back before nightfall to pick them up and return them to the parking lot, where a bus would meet them to transport them back to their hotel. That would give them most of the day to enjoy themselves and relax.

As they approached the narrow passage that formed the decidedly figure-eight shape of the lake, the vessel, aptly named *La Tortuga* (the tortoise), slowed as it approached the makeshift floating dock that jutted into the water. As the vessel slowed to a crawl, Jessica and her friends gathered their belongings and negotiated their way to the rail, where a deckhand waited to help them ashore. As soon as the hull squealed against the old tires that were nailed to the dock, they jumped ashore, carrying their duffels.

Jessica was an experienced free diver, and she planned to spend the day exploring the waters around the rocky strait. From where she stood, however, the water didn't look all that appetizing. The shore was lined with wads of greenish-brown weeds in thick mats that washed in and out to a distance of about ten feet from the shore. She recognized them as totora reeds, the same plants that the local Indians used to build the boats that they paddled up and down the lake. She would have to swim through them to get to the clear water beyond, and grimaced at the thought.

"Let's set up over there by those rocks," suggested her friend Sarah Roig, motioning to the cluster of low boulders that lined one side of the narrow peninsula. Walking over, they decided it was a good place. The flat rocks provided a place to sit, and the water behind them was relatively clear of weeds.

This I can deal with, thought Jessica. The gaps in the floating weeds showed that the water beneath them was relatively clear, and the bottom seemed to drop off quickly. She could see small fish darting among the rocks below as the sun glinted off their silvery sides; this would be fine.

"Anybody for a swim?" she asked the group. No one answered; they were all unpacking. "Hey, come on, guys, how about a swim? Anybody game?" This time there was at least one response to her question.

"I think I'll eat first, Jess," responded Dan Wilson, another member of the group who had taken a liking to her soon after they had met in Cuzco. She liked him too, although they had never really connected other than via the drawn out flirtation that had gone on between them for the last several weeks. Even the other members of the group had noticed, and seemed to be growing more tired of it than Jess and Dan.

"Get on with it," advised Sarah. "Jump his bones. He's just waiting for it, and face it – you want his skinny little ass!" Jess had responded by gently shoving her friend, but she had blushed at the thought and decided that Dan's bones were probably worth jumping. That was about a week ago; she was hoping that this trip would give her the opportunity to maneuver herself into a rendezvous with him. She was pretty sure that he felt the same way that she did, but who could tell? He was a typical guy, good looking, fun to be with, but often seemed to be more interested in his Frisbee or the local kids who came up to him than he was in her. Oh well, she sighed; she could fix the Frisbee thing, and his interactions with the kids always made her smile.

"OK," she responded. "I think I'll take a quick dip, and you can join me after you've eaten. Don't eat too much, though; I'll see you in the water."

"No," he said, smiling and raising his eyebrows as she slipped out of her cutoffs and T-shirt, revealing the tiny bikini she wore underneath. "*I'll* see *you* in the water!"

He continued to watch her as she put on her shorty wetsuit, gloves and wetsuit boots, and didn't go back to rummaging around in the ice chest until she sat down to put on her fins. Shuffling backward, she sat down on a round boulder and swished her mask in the water. Pouring it out, she spit into it—She hated that part—and rubbed the saliva all over the inside of the mask to prevent the glass from fogging. She had a bottle of commercial defogging solution in her bag, but she rarely used it; she smiled as she remembered that her SCUBA instructor had told her that those bottles were filled by college students, hired during the summer to fill them with spit. Rinsing the mask in the lake, she put it on, adjusted its position, and inhaled through her nose to ensure that it made a tight seal against her face.

After pulling an errant skein of hair out of the mask, it finally sealed. Standing, she closed the Velcro strap that attached the capillary depth gauge to her wrist, strung a waterproof flashlight below it, and wrestled on the ten-pound weight belt with its attached goodie bag. Then she turned so that she was facing away from the lake. Stepping backward, she carefully negotiated the rocks at the shoreline until she reached the edge of the water.

The place she had chosen provided a perfect entry point. There, a large, relatively flat rock protruded out over the water, which as near as she could tell was about eight feet deep – at least, that's how far down she could see before the light was absorbed in the green depths. She decided on a Hawaiian roll entry, which was the safest way to enter the water under the circumstances. Turning, Jess faced the lake. Placing one hand over her weight belt buckle to secure it, she placed the snorkel in her mouth with the other. After drawing a few deep breaths, she launched herself out over the water. As she left the ground, she rolled over in mid-air so that she landed in the water on her back. Divers making their entries from the tops of reefs use this technique, developed in Hawaii. When the surge washes in over the reef and the water is therefore at its deepest, they launch themselves. By landing on their backs, divers avoid the possibility of serious injury, should they time their entries improperly. After all, a poorly timed jump could land a diver on the reef itself if the surge pulled back sooner than expected.

Jess struck the water and forced herself to relax as she hit. It was cold on her arms and legs, but the shorty prevented the water from striking her torso. Instead, it seeped in gradually and was soon warmed to body temperature and kept there by the insulating properties of the neoprene. She allowed herself to sink into the surprisingly clear water, watching the dance of bubbles around her as they traveled back to the surface.

She had been swimming since she was an infant, and a

childhood spent in Southern California had allowed her to while away her summers at the beach, swimming, body surfing and snorkeling. For her 14th birthday her parents gave her SCUBA lessons, and she was entranced from the first moment she looked into the water. She became a dive shop groupie and was soon assisting in classes. She dove every chance she got, was active in her university diving community, and planned to become an instructor at some point, just to have an excuse to spend more time in the water. In fact, as soon as her Cuzco educational experience was over, she was scheduled to return to Santa Cruz to attend an Instructor Training Course to get her license to teach.

Looking around, she saw that the water was indeed deep here; she had submerged to about fifteen feet and could see the stone cliff behind her descending into the green depths of the lake. It wasn't really a cliff, she noticed; it was more like an enormous jumble of stones of all sizes. Close to the surface they were small, about the size of bowling balls. But as she looked down she saw that they grew steadily bigger. The largest ones that she could see were about ten feet below her, and were quite large – some of them twenty feet or more in diameter. In most places they appeared to be cemented together by thick deposits of lake silt, but in others the shape of the boulders resulted in gaps between them that were large enough to easily swim through.

Surfacing, she blew water out of her snorkel and looked toward the shore. Dan, Sarah and the others were seated in a loose circle on top of a large boulder eating lunch. Looking up, Dan spotted her and waved. She responded with the standard diving response, the fingers of one hand touching the top of her head. After resting for about a minute, she took three deep breaths and executed a perfect surface dive that drove her deep into the water. Kicking powerfully, she dove deep, equalizing the pressure in her ears as she did so by pinching her nose and blowing gently.

Checking her depth gauge, she passed 25 feet as the intense feeling of freedom washed over her that she always felt when diving. Rolling over, she looked up at the beams of sunlight that pulsed through the water like searching fingers, illuminating the motes of sediment suspended in the water. Tipping her head back, she blew a series of bubble rings that expanded as they rose, scattering a school of tiny silver fish. Surfacing, she rested again, hyperventilated for a time, and once again dove into the green depths of Titicaca. This time, as she passed 25 feet, she continued deeper, and was rewarded by the site of a large turtle that swam leisurely out of one of the crevices. It looked like a softshell with its long snout, but she wasn't sure. As it swam past, it turned and looked at her, wondering, no doubt, about this strange creature that had invaded its home. Turning, it dove deep and disappeared into the gloom.

By now, Jess was getting into the rhythm of the dive. Her breath-hold ability was excellent. She could stay submerged for slightly more than two minutes if she didn't exert herself too greatly. Turning, she swam toward the boulders that made up the rim of the lake and poked her head into the four-foot gap between two of them. Because of the depth she could see very little, so she turned on the Pelican Lite that she carried on a lanyard on her wrist and shined its intense beam into the crevice behind the boulders, illuminating a small cave about four feet across. There, floating close to the ceiling, was a group of what appeared to be bass, their gill covers opening and closing, their mouths open as if in surprise. They did nothing in response to the light, and would do nothing unless she disturbed the water column. Looking around, she saw nothing else of interest; a thick coating of silt as fine as flour covered everything. Careful not to disturb it or the fish, she backed out and surfaced for another breath.

Jess continued to explore the depths of the shoreline for nearly an hour, joyfully swimming around the large rocks and negotiating the occasional patches of weeds that grew from the bottom in gnarly bunches. She explored these carefully, finding fishing lures, lead weights, and trash. She always explored plant growth carefully, because as a child she had once found a charm bracelet on the bottom of a small lake near her grandparents' home, tangled in a mat of cabomba grass. Now, in the shadow of the nearly vertical stone shoreline of the lake, she explored an expanse of weeds that were about four feet tall. Into one particularly thick tangle of the greenish-gray plant she intentionally sank herself deep to watch the antics of a large turtle, different from the one she had seen before. This one was common looking, a mud turtle of some kind, and it was digging into the bottom with its broad clawed feet, feeding. It paid no attention to her as she lay on her belly on the bottom of the lake, enjoying her window into the turtle's simple life. Finally, she realized that she had to breathe, so she reluctantly pushed off the bottom, extricated herself from the entangling plants and headed for the surface.

As she rose toward the mirrored underbelly of the lake's surface, she felt a tug on her waist, the last of the plants releasing her. She soon realized, however, that her rate of ascent was faster than normal. Looking down she saw that her weight belt was missing, snagged, no doubt, on a plant stem. Weight belts were designed with quick release buckles so that they could easily be ditched in the event of an out-of-air emergency, but sometimes the buckles worked against the diver. No big deal, she thought; she wasn't wearing enough neoprene to prevent her from diving without the belt; she'd just have to kick a little bit harder on the way down. Breaking the surface, she once again motioned to Dan, who was stretched out on the rocks, but he didn't respond. Asleep, no doubt. Oh well, she sighed; maybe he'll be wide-awake for a night on the town when we get back.

Jess rested for three or four minutes, snorkeling on the surface, watching the sunlight create dappled patterns in the water. The beams swung back and forth like tiny searchlights. Throughout, she kept a careful eye on the patch of weeds she had just left, knowing that her chances of finding the belt were iffy to begin with, and damn near impossible if she lost sight of them.

Finally, she felt rested and ready to go. After taking another series of three deep breaths, she raised her legs into the air and kicked powerfully down into the water. She felt the buoyant tug of the neoprene for the first fifteen feet or so, after which the water pressure compressed the tiny bubbles in the rubber enough that it lost much of its buoyancy. Heading for the bottom, she homed in on the patch of aquatic weeds. She found them easily enough, but the belt was nowhere to be found. Even the turtle was gone. Probably took the belt, she thought, and smiled, causing water to seep into her mask. She had lost other items while diving – a knife, several abalone irons, even a light. The only thing that she had found was the light, and only because it was on when she dropped it. The other items had become the property of whatever capricious force it was that controlled the relationship between divers, their belongings, and the bottom of the ocean. It was a very strange thing and a known, often joked-about phenomenon among divers. You could drop something (they all had), watch it go to the bottom, follow it down without taking your eyes off of it, and it would disappear as soon as you got within five feet of the bottom. Somewhere, they all surmised, there was a great collection of equipment for sale by Neptune in the belly of the Andrea Doria or some other wreck.

Jess crawled around the bottom for the better part of two minutes until her chest was heaving and she had to surface for air. She did, rested for a while, and dove again. This time, she swam a perimeter search around the plant bed, finding nothing. Just as she was about to give up, her eye detected movement to her left. Looking over, she saw the turtle, engaged in his feeding activity, and quickly realized that she had been searching the wrong patch of plants. Swimming over, shaking her head, she began to sweep her hands through the fibrous, knotty stems, looking for the belt.

She was on the verge of having to surface again when she finally found it, half buried in the silt at the base of the plants. Grabbing the blue nylon webbing she pulled it free of the bottom, causing a minor silt explosion in the process. By now her lungs were hammering in her chest for air, so she reluctantly dropped the belt and rocketed for the surface, breaching like an Alaskan whale and taking a great, deep, sweet breath as soon as her face cleared the water. Now she knew that she could find the belt again, so she floated on the surface, glancing at the shoreline. By now Dan was awake, stretched out on the rock, his head resting on his hand, watching her. He grinned and waved; she grinned back, touching the top of her head. Five minutes later, she ventilated and dove for the belt.

This time, she zeroed in on it immediately. Lifting it from its resting-place, she knelt on the bottom and swung it around behind her, catching the end and closing the buckle. As she rose, she swam toward the boulder-studded cliff face, meandering slowly upward as she poked her head into the myriad crevices and caves that pocked the underwater cliff. At about fifteen feet she came to a place where a large, oval-shaped boulder protruded several feet from the face, creating an overhang above a small, shallow cave. Poking her light into the depression, she noticed something odd in the deep silt that blanketed the floor of the hollow, a round shape that appeared unnatural, as if the silt disguised something that was not meant to be there. Reaching down, she fanned at the silt, creating a large opaque cloud that quickly filled the hollow.

Jess had now been down for nearly two minutes, and needed air badly, but was too curious to leave just yet. Besides, she knew that if she surfaced, chances were that she'd never find the cave again, so she forced herself to calm down and waited for the cloud to clear while she groped blindly. When her hand passed over a round object about the size and shape of a small melon, she paused, and using both hands, worried the object free of the silt. Pulling it out of the cave, she was amazed to find that she was holding what appeared to be a ceramic pot, almost completely filled with thick mud. Surfacing with her find, she cleared her snorkel on the way up and immediately rolled over onto her belly so that she could breathe through her snorkel and examine the pot below the surface, hidden from view. It was obviously quite old, and while intact, it did have a spider web of thin cracks in the brownish glaze that covered it. The pot was decorated with an intricate pattern of thin lines that formed fantastic shapes that danced around its perimeter.

Gently swishing the pot back and forth in the water, she created comet trails of mud as she washed it out. As soon as she felt that the mud was gone, she looked inside the mouth of the pot and was startled by what appeared to be a tiny face peering up at her. Looking more closely, she found that the face was in fact attached to a dull metallic figurine, about ten inches tall, still mired in a dune of mud in the bottom of the jar. Tugging on it carefully, she saw that the object was intricately formed and appeared to wear what looked like an apron around its waist and a fan-shaped headdress around its face. It was heavy, and as she gazed down into the face that bore no signs of tarnish, she realized that she was holding an idol of solid gold.

CHAPTER 45

Captain's Cabin, aboard the Carla V

Turning, Lee entered the final passageway, with Billy close behind. Between them, they carried air-powered chisels that could be quick-attached to the auxiliary hose on their tanks; sledge hammers; pry bars; lift bags; and goodie bags to transport whatever bounty they ultimately removed from the safe—if they chose to do so. They had toyed with the idea of bringing a cutting torch, but had decided against it. First, they didn't have enough hose to snake from the surface down to the ship for the gas. Second, Lee hated torches. He didn't like to use them, and when he did, he wasn't very good at it. He had a special dislike for arc welders. He hated the way they made the water inside his mask bubble, as electrolysis released hydrogen and oxygen. Great, he thought; an explosive mixture surrounding my face, with an arc hot enough to melt steel six inches away. Perfect. No, he thought, no torch for this job. They'd finesse the safe open, or rip it out and transport it to the surface where they could beat on it with a pile driver, if need be.

At the door to the captain's cabin, they halted. With a wide sweep of his arm, Billy motioned Lee to enter first. Nodding, Lee swam into the captain's quarters and turned right just beyond the door, in the direction of the safe.

In most vessels, the only things that aren't bolted down

are passengers. Furniture is securely attached to floor and walls, to prevent shifting in heavy seas. This was the case aboard the Carla V. The safe was bolted to the steel bulkhead, hidden in a now deteriorated oak cabinet above the captain's desk.

Lee positioned himself in front of the safe, and pulled from his BC pocket the slate upon which he had written the combination. Billy stood just behind, illuminating the area with light. Slowly, Lee reached for the large black knob, and tentatively twisted. It didn't budge. Twisting harder, it grated, releasing smoke-like seeps of rust from around the knob. Then, it released, and spun freely. Damn, thought Lee. Either I just twisted the knob off the mechanism inside, or they really did build this thing well. We'll see.

Looking up, he could see the mirror-like underside of the large air bubble that had collected at the top of the chamber, the result of exhalations from their many visits. They both knew that there was enough air collected up there for them to poke their heads through and talk or breathe, if necessary. Looking once again at the slate (he had had the numbers memorized for months, but he looked at them anyway), Lee carefully followed the instructions given to him by the French manufacturer.

The ever present sounds of diving were all around them as he completed the combination sequence: the rushes and squeaks of their regulators; the clicking, like marbles in a bag, of parrotfish chewing up the surrounding reefs; the groaning and rumbling of the metal hull as it shifted this way and that in the currents. Grasping the rust-mottled chrome handles of the safe door, Lee twisted. With a slow groan, they moved slightly, and then with a shriek of metal on metal, they turned 90 degrees to the full open position. The safe was unlocked.

Moving aside, Lee made room for Billy, who now swam up with two pry bars. The safe builders had assured him that while the body of the safe should be intact and relatively rust-free, the edges of the door and its frame would most likely be heavily rusted, since they were bare metal. Sure enough, when he tugged, the door didn't budge.

Handing one of the pry bars to Lee and giving him a thumbs-up sign, Billy inserted the end of his bar in the space between the top of the safe door and the doorframe. With a sledge, he tapped it in another quarter inch, until it was firmly wedged. At the bottom edge of the door, Lee did the same thing.

Now, the difficult part, thought Lee. This was the big question: would the door open with pressure, or was it so completely rusted together that it would have to be torched open? Only one way to find out. Nodding to Billy, Lee wedged himself between the wall and the desk, and grasped the end of the pry bar. Billy took up a similar position on the other side, and together, they applied even pressure to the two levers.

At first, nothing happened. Tiny rust flakes sifted down from the pry bars; the door was stuck tight. Releasing the pressure, Lee steeled himself, grabbed the bar once again, and pulled. Water leaked into his mask where his face was contorted with the strain. He ignored it. Looking up, he saw that Billy was pulling with his massive arms to the point that the bar he was holding was beginning to bend.

Suddenly, the door moved half an inch with an agonized screech. A brown snowstorm of rust drifted to the canted floor. Moving closer, they tried to peer into the darkness within. No good; they would have to open the door further.

Repositioning the bars on the now exposed inner lip of the door, they pulled and yanked until they could get their hands around the door. Lee reached down and removed his fins, and with his back firmly planted against the bulkhead, pushed with his legs while Billy pulled on the door from the other side. With an anticlimactic squeak, the door swung open.

Reaching for the light, Billy swung its beam into the

safe. There, neatly stacked and banded, lay thick bundles of bills, the half million or so of currency that was rumored to be there all along. The captain had told the truth.

As Lee floated there, gazing down at the stacks of currency, memories of the last six years came flooding back. Endless strings of letters and phone calls, all to collect snippets of information that eventually came together and fused into a possible fortune aboard the Carla V. Weeks of study to learn every square inch of the ship, preparing for every eventuality. Trips from Cartagena to London to Lyon, and back again. The endless frustration of dealing with Lloyd's, with the Rome shipping officials, and with the Italian bureaucracy in general.

He remembered the close calls associated with their exploration efforts. Somewhere down there, deep in the bowels of the Carla V, lay the diaphragm and front cover of his old regulator. As he swam close to the top of a massive hold, the retainer ring on the second stage had popped out without warning, allowing the diaphragm and its chrome cover to pop off. He had managed to make it back outside by covering the poppet with the palm of his left hand and simulating the action of the diaphragm. A dicey morning, but there had been others. The worst, of course, was the day his pressure gauge hose had failed. With 3000 pounds of pressure escaping from the pinhole in the hose, it damn near whipped him to death by the time Billy managed to grab the hose and shut off his air. Lee still cringed every time he turned on a tank valve.

But now, it was all worth it. Their efforts had born fruit, and he gazed down upon a fortune that was his and his alone. Holding his breath, Lee impulsively reached for a handful of happiness. Seeing what he was about to do, Billy yelled through his regulator. "No!" and reached for Lee's arm, but he wasn't fast enough.

Paper is funny stuff. In water, it loses its substance, changing quickly to a jelly-like material that, while extraordinarily delicate, still retains its original shape if left undisturbed. In salt water, the cellulose that form the fiber matrix of the paper quickly decomposes and scatters with the currents. In an enclosed space, however, where water currents don't intrude—such as in a submerged safe—the jelly-like paper retains its original form, albeit without substance. As Lee's hands closed greedily around the mass of bills, it dissolved into a greenish cloud of pulp that quickly filled the cabin.

Gazing at the settling cloud, shocked beyond words, Lee slowly reached back into the safe, and extracted a small silver medallion lying there. Palming it, he looked at Billy, retrieved his fins, and slowly swam out of the cabin. Billy watched purple wrasses strike at the bits of paper, as Lee's light slowly danced down the corridor and disappeared. Gathering the remaining equipment, laughing softly around his regulator, Billy followed Lee down the dark passageway.

CHAPTER 46

The first indication Lexie had that something was wrong was when she was struck in the back with a fin, thrown violently from the water behind the boat. Walking over, she narrowly missed being hit in the face by the second one.

"Hey!" she called out, irritated. "Watch where you're throwing those things!"

She backed away as a mask followed the fins, slamming into an equipment storage compartment beside her.

Drawn by the commotion, Carl appeared beside her.

"What the hell's going on back here?" he asked, annoyed.

"Beats me," Lexie responded, stretching to see over the gunwale. Carl walked over to the gate that led to the dive platform, arriving just as Graves' head appeared at the rail.

"What's up?" Carl asked, as the diver climbed onto the platform.

"Fuck off," responded Graves, pushing Carl aside.

"Hey!" said Lexie. "You almost hit me in the head with that stuff. You can't go throwing gear – "

At this point, Graves reached her, and without warning,

shoved her roughly against the port rail with a curt "Get the fuck out of my way."

The next thing Graves knew, he was in the water on the port side of the *Grunt*. It took Carl about a second to ascertain that Lexie was OK—the flash of anger in her eyes told him all he needed to know—and reach the irate diver. Grabbing him by the back of the neck, Carl unceremoniously picked Graves up and threw him overboard. When he surfaced, sputtering, he looked up at Carl with undisguised hatred, standing now at the rail above him. After several seconds of visual standoff, Graves swam over to the boarding ladder where Carl met him, dragged him roughly aboard by the front of his BC and pinned him to the wall of the deckhouse.

"Listen to me very carefully, shithead. You get within five feet of her again and I'll shove a shark dart up your ass. Your charter is over: we drop you at the nearest port." Carl's voice was steady, calm, and deadly. Graves had no doubt that he would do what he threatened. When Carl released him, he stalked away and disappeared below decks.

A very different commotion followed. From the fantail came the sound of hysterical laughter as Billy broke the surface and let the regulator fall from his mouth. "Oh, my God," he gasped, "that was the funniest thing I've ever seen." Piling his gear on the corner of the platform, he tried three times to climb out of the water, but his laughter prevented him from doing so. Finally he succeeded and plopped himself down, leaning his head against the rail.

"Jesus, Billy, what the hell happened down there?" queried Carl, leaning over the rail. "Your buddy just popped out of the water like a pissed-off porcupine, and gave me a shove before trying to knock Lexie overboard. What'd you do to that asshole?"

Billy shook his head, a huge grin on his face. "I'd steer clear of him for a while if I were you," he replied, proceeding to recount the story of the ill-fated contents of the captain's safe. When he finished, no one spoke for several seconds.

"It's gone? All of it? There were supposed to be half-a-million dollars down there!" exclaimed Carl, helping Billy climb aboard.

"Yep, it's gone; there's nothing left down there but a cloud of paper dust and a bunch of fish with stomach aches from eating it. I guess he deserves to be a little pissed off, but it's his own damn fault. How many times did we cover protocol with him? He knew that we had to flood the safe with methylcellulose or Bermocoll before we could even think about removing whatever was in there. What was he thinking? He should have known better."

By now Michael had arrived from below decks, drawn by Billy's laughter and what appeared to be a social gathering at the fantail. They explained to him what had happened, and after checking with Lexie to ensure that she was unhurt *(I'm just pissed off, dammit!)*, he sat down on the equipment storage cabinet.

"Let me make this easy for you, boss," Carl offered. "This guy's as fucked up as Hogan's goat, and I don't want him with us anymore. As soon as I cooled him off, I told him his charter was over. If it wouldn't pollute the place, I'd vote to leave him here on Serranilla. But since that probably isn't an option"—he turned to Michael and raised an eyebrow before continuing— "I say we drop him at our next port, and I suggest we make that port soon. It ain't gonna be comfortable with that asshole aboard, so the sooner we lose him, the better. That's just my opinion."

No one disagreed; they had to make port soon anyway to take on stores and do some minor repairs on the vessel, so they decided to meet in the galley for lunch, and afterward have a crew meeting to determine their next port of call.

First, however, there was the matter of their current charter customer. Michael was seething, but had the presence of mind to take Billy and Carl with him to confront Graves.

Knocking on his stateroom door, they asked to be let in. There was no response. Michael knocked louder, and called through the door. "Mr. Graves, we need to talk. Now." For a moment there was no response; then, a voice. "Get the fuck out of here. Just get the fuck out." Michael looked over at Carl, who had very little patience for this sort of thing.

"Man, I already threw you overboard once, and I'll do it again if you don't open this door. Only next time you'll go through the fucking porthole. Now open the door before I open it." They heard mutterings, the sound of someone getting up. Seconds later, the door swung wide. Graves didn't look at them; he turned and returned to the bed, where he'd been sitting.

"Look," Michael began. "I understand why you're pissed, but listen to me very carefully. The woman you shoved is my wife, and I have half a mind to kick the living shit out of you. But I'm not going to do that. What I *am* going to do, however, is end your charter. It's over. Now. You will pay us the second half of the agreed upon fee and you will pay us for six days of salvage. That's pretty generous, considering the actual terms of our agreement. We will drop you at the next port that has an airport, and from there you're on your own. As for the port, we'll let you know where it'll be after lunch. Beyond that, watch yourself aboard my boat. The law of the sea applies, and I will not hesitate to invoke it."

Graves said nothing.

Billy added, "I'd steer clear of the galley if I were you. Lexie keeps knives in there."

They left the man in his stateroom, but not before they heard him mutter, "Fuck you" under his breath.

CHAPTER 47

Lake Titicaca

Jess didn't know what to think about what she had found. She floated face down on the surface, completely immobile, breathing through her snorkel and gazing at the golden idol. She had no idea what she was looking at, nor did she have any idea how old it was. She did recognize the style from some of the Inca art that she had seen in class during her program in Peru, but was unwilling to allow herself to believe that this thing was – what – 450 years old? And made of gold? No way.

Suddenly, she became aware of someone calling her name. Looking up, she saw Dan standing at the shoreline, trying to undress without falling in the water and bellowing out her name repeatedly. It took a few seconds, but she finally realized that he was on his way to rescue her. She had been lying so still on the surface that he must have thought she was in trouble.

"Hey Dan, I'm OK!" she called out to him. Pausing in his clumsy attempt to remove his left leg from his jeans, he looked noticeably relieved when he saw her motioning to him and calling his name. Losing his balance, he sat down hard on the rock. She was now floating feet down on the surface as she carefully maneuvered the golden statuette into the white canvas goodie bag attached to her weight belt. Checking the buckle that had caused her to lose the belt in the first place, she verified that it was tight, but kept her left hand over it just the same.

"Sorry about that," she called. "I stayed down a little too long and was resting. I'll be in in just a few minutes."

He waved an acknowledgment to her before getting dressed again, a look of slight disappointment on his face.

How sweet, she thought; he was hoping to rescue me. I'll have to make it up to him later.

The impact of what she had found had not yet struck her. The pot alone was a wonderful find, but gold—was it really gold? This was too much for her to comprehend. A flood of thoughts collided inside her head: What was it worth? Could she keep it? Could she—should she—get it out of the country? Who should she tell about it, if anybody? These thoughts bounced and collided against each other as she considered the gravity of her find. Before she began to kick toward the shore, she took a few minutes to carefully note her exact location relative to the shore using crude triangulation. Looking around, she noted that she could draw a line between a rock on the shore that looked like a giant peach and a house on the far shore that was painted a brilliant blue. She then turned and drew a second imaginary line that intersected with the first at her exact position. This second line ran from a faraway television tower to a dead tree on the shore behind her. Mentally noting the four points, she swam for shore, intent on writing them down before she forgot them.

CHAPTER 48

Peruvian jungle south of Cuzco, November 1533

Their numbers exceeded 200, but the children and elderly had now begun to fall behind as a result of the brutal pace that the warriors had set. They all knew that they had to widen the distance between themselves and the Spaniards, and while they did have the better part of a day's advantage, the Spaniards had horses that could easily outrun a human. Their scouts had driven deep into the jungle through which they had already passed to check on the progress of their enemies, and while the reports indicated that they were still far behind, they would not be for long.

Moving down the long trail of his compatriots carrying their impossibly heavy burdens, Condori whispered words of encouragement to all that he encountered. Most of them, even the children, had baskets on their backs filled with gold, supported by woven headbands around their foreheads. They were strung out along the trail in a great winding line, and in the course of the last three days had walked more than 120 miles to the south in their attempt to distract the Spaniards who pursued them from the holy city of Cuzco. If they wanted the gold, they would have to follow, and the Inca would not make it easy for them. For the Inca knew the jungle, and like any culture acquainted with its surroundings, they had a considerable tactical advantage over their adversaries. The Spaniards would follow, and might even capture or kill some of them, but they would never find the gold, and would never leave the jungle alive. Of that, Condori was certain.

He also knew that the Inca had another advantage: the altitude. They were acclimated to the high mountains and sparse atmosphere of the Andes; the Spaniards were not. They would not be able to keep up the pace.

It was late in the day with the sun low on the horizon, and they had not eaten in two days. Nevertheless, no one complained, not even the children. The elderly members of the group who could not match the pace of the younger members simply disappeared into the green deeps of the jungle, accepting their fate stoically. Chances were that they would succumb to a jaguar attack or snakebite long before the Spaniards caught them, but it didn't matter. Their culture would not allow their own frailties to put the others in danger. Instead, they crawled into the jungle and accepted whatever befell them.

Behind the group, runners had been posted as a distraction. They carried nothing, other than an obsidian knife or other lightweight weapon. When the Spaniards reached their positions, they would distract them, running like the wind along a secondary path, giving those ahead a better opportunity to widen the gap. If they were lucky, they would be able to confuse the pursuers to the point that they would lose their bearings and begin to chase the Inca back in the direction from which they had come. The ruse would not last forever, of course; sooner or later they would realize the error they had made, and would resume the search with murderous vigor. With luck, the Inca would have enough time to disappear so deeply into the jungle that they would never be found, and the Spaniards would be left to their own devices to escape. They never would; Condori and his men would see to that.

When night came, they crawled into the jungle and ate what they could find, then slept deeply for a few hours, posting guards along the path. On the fourth day, they turned away from the south-running river valley that they had been following and climbed to the high steppes of the Andes, passing the tree line at 3,000 meters and continuing upward until they were at twice that altitude. This, they knew, would give them a powerful advantage over the Spaniards; the Inca had spent their entire life in these mountains and were accustomed to working hard here; the Spaniards were not. They would have no strength, and would soon bleed from their noses and mouths. That would not stop them: their greed for gold was only matched by their greed for blood, but in this case, Condori and his followers would see to it that it was Spanish blood that spilled.

They walked along the spine of the mountains for two days, paying close attention to the reports from their scouts who reported that the Spaniards had been confused, and had even backtracked, but had finally figured out the ruse and were back on the trail. Rifle fire had killed two of their scouts, but the others were either hiding in the jungle or known to be safe.

Eventually, they came to a place from which they could see a vast expanse of flat land far below them, surrounded by the peaks of the tallest mountains and bisected by a meandering river. At 12,000 feet the valley was quite high, and shimmering in its center was a huge lake, wide at the ends but narrowing in the middle, fed by the river that divided the valley. "There is our destination," said Condori, "The sacred shores of Titicaca. Beyond it lies the deepest jungle, a place where these murdering invaders will never find us. And there we will hide this" – he said, gesturing with a golden ingot – " so well that they will never find it, and will die of greed before they die of exposure. They want our gold—but we will have their blood."

With that, he turned, and led the Inca toward the valley floor, and to the very deep lake that covered it.

CHAPTER 49

Lunch aboard *The Grunt* that day was quiet, particularly since Graves did not respond to Michael's invitation via intercom to join them in the galley. No one minded; his presence would have been awkward under the circumstances, and besides, it was up to him whether he ate or not. He could always sneak down later and help himself to leftovers, particularly since Lexie's and Billy's leftovers tended to be tastier than most peoples' first efforts. They feasted on grouper tacos, one of Billy's specialties, dirty rice and black beans, and washed it all down with fresh-squeezed limeade. "Shame he's missing this," mused Billy.

"Not really," responded Carl. "More for me," he said, as he grabbed the last two tacos from the plate.

Lexie shook her head. "I've never seen anybody react like that before. He scared the hell out of me. I don't think I've ever seen a person so pissed."

Billy chuckled. "Yeah you have, and look what happened to him," said Billy, referring to the man who had kidnapped and beaten her years before. "But how often do you run into guys who have just turned half a mil into goo with their own hands? I'd be pissed too, although I think I'd refrain from shoving somebody as big as Carl, and sure as hell wouldn't rough up the boat's babe with somebody like Carl behind me. That's just plain stupid. The good news is that we'll rid ourselves of his ass in a few days, and then we can go do something fun—like nothing."

That sounded good to all of them. They had been working nonstop for more weeks than they could remember, and as much as they enjoyed each other's company, even a boat as spacious as the *Grunt* could get a little tight after multiple weeks at sea. Shore leave was definitely in order, so they cleaned up the galley and headed up to the bridge, where Michael and Billy had laid out a mosaic of charts on the table directly behind the pilothouse. Gathering around one end, coffee mugs in hand, they listened as Michael proposed their next move.

"OK, we're here," he began, pointing with a ruler, "just east of Serranilla. I'd say our work here is pretty much over (a snort from Carl), and we need to put in for a rest and do a little work on the bus, not to mention the fact that we need to shed some undesirable cargo."

He grabbed the corner of the chart and swung it around so that it faced them. "I have a harebrained idea that I think you'll like. How about if we sail east for the Leewards and surprise James? We haven't seen him since we did that salvage job off Barbuda, and since he's got the shop and a protected place to put in, we could relax in Saba for a few days, get the work on the boat done, put dickweed on a plane, and then head to Sint Maarten or wherever for R&R. Any objections?"

Lexie was the first to respond. "So after spending weeks with a bunch of smelly divers, you're going to drag me all the way across the Caribbean to a rock with no beaches? What am I supposed to do while you're out there scrubbing this thing's belly, or whatever it is you're going to be doing? I love Jimmy to death, and I'll visit for a day or two, but I need to smell something besides neoprene and diesel for a few days."

She thought for a moment before continuing. "Tell you what. I'll hang around for a bit, then I think I'll take *The Edge* over to Simpson Bay for shopping and sun. You can pick me up on your swing back toward Panama, or I can fly back over and meet you on Saba. That okay with everybody?"

It was clear that she expected no objections, and there were none.

"She who must be obeyed has spoken," Michael announced. "We'll meet you there after we make repairs, and spend a few days looking at naked women over in Marigot." Lexie rose to the challenge.

"That's OK," she replied. "By the time you guys get there I'll have all the studs scoped out anyway."

The banter between Michael and Lexie brought a chuckle from the group. After visiting for a while, they called it a night and headed for their cabins. Michael kissed Lexie lightly on the cheek and told her that he'd be along shortly. He and Billy had a bit of chart work to do before turning in.

"Wait up for me," he smiled at her, raising his eyebrows.

"Well, guess I'd better turn up the stereo tonight," Carl offered, putting his arm around Lexie. "You know, if Michael gets wrapped up with Billy and his charts, I keep a pretty warm bed, and you're always welcome. I even have the entire Barry White collection on CD."

Lexie put her arms around him and kissed him on the cheek. "How can a girl pass up such an offer? Are you listening, Michael? He has Barry White – the entire collection."

Michael just shook his head. "I give up—I can't compete with Barry White. Would Barry Manilow work?"

There was no answer from Carl and Lexie, other than a rather bad two-part harmony version of "I'm Gonna Love Ya Baby" as they disappeared down the passageway toward their staterooms, arm-in-arm, and a warning from Carl that they might want to turn up the stereo in the wheelhouse so as not to be disturbed.

CHAPTER 50

Jess reached the shore and slowly climbed out of the water, carrying the pot in one hand and the goodie bag in the other. As she emerged from the lake, Dan came over and offered to help her with her equipment, but she waved him off, handing him the pot instead.

"Check this out. I found it in a little cave down there at about fifteen feet. I think it's pretty old."

Dan sat down and examined the pot as she surreptitiously stashed the bag containing the idol in her equipment bag, burying it beneath her fins and snorkel, careful not to bang it with her weight belt.

"This is really something," said Dan, turning the pot over in his hands as he looked at it from all sides. "I think you need to show this to somebody, like a museum or something. This could be an important archaeological find."

She unzipped her wetsuit and peeled it off, revealing her bikini and causing Dan's speech about the pot to lose its momentum. As she carefully wrapped the wet neoprene around the goodie bag to cushion its contents, his discussion about the museum dwindled away.

"It's just – I mean, it's pretty old – I just think – " She squatted down next to him and kissed him on the cheek, which caused him to shut up entirely.

Don't worry, Dan; I plan to show the pot to somebody. Come on, I'm starving. Fix me something to eat."

Closing her dive bag, she hefted it onto her shoulder, and they walked back to the others, who had broken up into a group tossing a Frisbee and a few swimmers who were now sunbathing on the rocks. Sitting in the semi-shade of a large boulder, they fixed *bocadillos* of ham and cheese and ate them with fiery Peruvian pickles and fresh-made potato chips, purchased that morning from a local vendor at the boat launch. They washed it all down with bottles of Malta, the local non-alcoholic malt beverage that they had come to like.

"So what do you think this is?" asked Dan, turning the pot over to examine it more closely. "It looks like it has a design on it, but most of it has faded away. I can also see glaze. Look here along this crack – see where the glaze ends?"

She could barely discern a slightly different color where he was pointing, and as the pot dried, the difference became more obvious. "Do you think it hurts it to dry out like this?" Dan asked. "I mean, if it's as old as you think it is, it might fall apart or something. Maybe we should keep it in wet rags, or in a bucket with water."

Jess thought for a moment, then nodded. "I have an idea," she said, moving to the duffel bag that held their food. Extracting a large Ziploc bag containing two apples, she emptied them into the duffel and carefully slid the pot into the bag. "I'll fill this with water, and that'll keep it wet *and* protected."

That evening, while returning to the hotel on the bus, Jessica and Dan chatted quietly about the pot. "You should take it to the Museo Arqueológico," he suggested. "They'll know how to preserve it. And since you found it, they'll probably give you some kind of credit—hey, they might even pay you for it!"

Jessica humored him, responding that, yes, giving it to the museum was probably a good idea. She had not told him about the idol, nor did she intend to; she didn't plan to do anything with it or the pot until she had a better idea of what she had actually found.

What she *did* know was where she intended to start.

That night, after eating dinner with Dan and gently fighting off his amorous advances, she returned to her room, locked the door and pulled the curtains. When she knew she was alone and the room was secure, she pulled out her laptop and composed an e-mail message.

To: Michael@OceanAdventures.com
From: Jessica_Cutter@uccc.edu
Subject: Archaeology Find

Dear Mr. McCain,

My name is Jessica Cutter and I am a college student, currently studying Mesoamerican art on a semester abroad program with the University of Cuzco in Peru. We recently took a field trip to Lake Titicaca to study the local art and the construction of the reed boats that are common on the lake. During a free afternoon, we went swimming, and while snorkeling I found something that I think you might find interesting. The reason I'm sending this message to you is because I read your book, "Among the Ghosts of Spanish Sailors," and loved it. I'm thinking you might be able to tell me what to do with what I found.

I'm attaching two photographs; one thing was inside the other, compressed inside a ball of clay. It's six inches tall, and very heavy.

Thank you for reading my e-mail; I know you're very busy, so if you don't have time to help me, would you mind telling me whom I should call? Thank you very much.

Sincerely,

Jessica Cutter

P.S. Please tell your wife Lexie that I think she kicks ass.

* * *

Michael was sitting at the conference table when he heard his laptop beep, indicating an incoming e-mail message. Pulling it toward him, he looked in the inbox and saw the message from Jessica. Reading it, he smiled; he'd been deluged with reports of treasure finds since his and Billy's story had gone public, all of them wishful thinking. One guy actually mailed them the treasure he had found for their inspection: A weathered lead weight that some character had spray-painted gold. They had let him down gently; he decided he didn't want to pay to have them return it.

When he finished reading her message, however, he scrolled to the bottom and double-clicked on the photo attachment called, 'idol.' When it opened, he sat and stared at it, slack-jawed. Then he called up to the galley, where Lexie and Billy were beginning the afternoon's argument over what they would prepare for dinner.

"Lexie? Billy? Hey! Can you guys hear me up there? Billy? Anybody want to take a trip to Peru?"

FIN

ABOUT THE AUTHOR

Dr. Steven Shepard is the founder of the Shepard Communications Group in Williston, Vermont. A professional author, photographer, audio producer, and educator with more than 35 years in the technology industry, he has written more than 80 books and hundreds of articles on a wide range of (often unrelated) topics.

Steve received his undergraduate degree in Spanish and Romance Philology from the University of California at Berkeley (1976), his Masters Degree in International Business from St. Mary's College (1985), and his PhD at the Da Vinci Institute in Rivonia, South Africa (2009).

He is the creator and host of the Natural Curiosity Podcast, which is devoted to the discovery of the joy and wonder of the natural world and based on the idea that curiosity leads to discovery, discovery leads to knowledge, knowledge leads to insight, and insight leads to understanding. It's available on iTunes, or on SoundCloud.

Thanks to a childhood spent in Spain, Steve is native fluent in Spanish and routinely publishes and delivers presentations in that language.

He lives in Vermont with his wife Sabine, who has put up with him for more than 35 years.

52115145R00194

Made in the USA
Middletown, DE
07 July 2019